Kyle wanted to be a father.

So he'd tried to be a father to Sandy's children.

It was temporary. Perhaps even foolish. And now the thought of being without them made his bones ache.

For the first time Kyle began to see how much was at stake here. Other lives would be affected by his actions. Walking away from a woman was one thing; walking away from kids was…something much worse.

Was Sandy right? Had he been playing a game? Teasing her with the sparks they felt when they were together?

Kyle didn't want to hurt Sandy. Or her kids. He didn't want to get hurt himself. If it was just a game to him, he needed to walk away now.

Simple enough, he told himself. He would walk. Because it *was* just a game, right?

Dear Reader,

Special Edition's lineup for the month of July is sure to set off some fireworks in your heart! Romance always seems that much more wonderful and exciting in the hot days of summer, and our six books for July are sure to prove that! We begin with bestselling author Gina Ferris Wilkins and *A Match for Celia*. July's THAT SPECIAL WOMAN! goes looking for summertime romance and gets more than she bargained for in book two of Gina's series, THE FAMILY WAY.

Continuing the new trilogy MAN, WOMAN AND CHILD this month is Robin Elliott's *Mother at Heart*. Raising her sister's son as her own had been a joy for this single mother, but her little family seems threatened when the boy's real father surfaces... until she finds herself undeniably drawn to the man. Be sure to look for the third book in the series next month, *Nobody's Child*, by Pat Warren.

Father in Training by Susan Mallery brings you another irresistible hunk who can only be one of those HOMETOWN HEARTBREAKERS. Also continuing in July is Victoria Pade's A RANCHING FAMILY series. Meet Jackson Heller, of the ranching Heller clan, in *Cowboy's Kiss*. A man who's lost his memory needs tenderness and love to find his way in Kate Freiman's *Here To Stay*. And rounding out the month is a sexy and lighthearted story by Jane Gentry. In *No Kids or Dogs Allowed*, falling in love is easy for a single mom and divorced dad—until they find out their feuding daughters may just put a snag in their upcoming wedding plans!

A whole summer of love and romance has just begun from **Special Edition!** I hope you enjoy each and every story to come!

Sincerely,

Tara Gavin
Senior Editor

Please address questions and book requests to:
Silhouette Reader Service
U.S.: 3010 Walden Ave., P.O. Box 1325, Buffalo, NY 14269
Canadian: P.O. Box 609, Fort Erie, Ont. L2A 5X3

SUSAN MALLERY

FATHER IN TRAINING

Silhouette®

SPECIAL EDITION®

Published by Silhouette Books

America's Publisher of Contemporary Romance

To all the boys I had a crush on in high school. To Rob for that one perfect summer. And to Randy. I know this is coming a little late, but the sentiment is no less heartfelt for being tardy....
I'm sorry.

 SILHOUETTE BOOKS

ISBN 0-373-09969-X

FATHER IN TRAINING

Copyright © 1995 by Susan W. Macias

Books by Susan Mallery

Silhouette Special Edition

Tender Loving Care #717
More Than Friends #802
A Dad for Billie #834
Cowboy Daddy #898
The Best Bride #933
Marriage on Demand #939
Father in Training #969

*Hometown Heartbreakers

Silhouette Intimate Moments

Tempting Faith #554
The Only Way Out #646

SUSAN MALLERY

makes her home in the Lone Star state, where the people are charming and the weather is always interesting. She lives with her hero-material husband and her two attractive but not very bright cats. When she's not hard at work writing romances, she can be found exploring the wilds of Texas and shopping for the perfect pair of cowboy boots. Susan loves to hear from her readers. You may write her directly at P.O. Box 1828, Sugar Land, TX 77487.

KYLE'S FAMOUS YAMS

1 cup dried apricots
1 cup Marsala wine **
1 29 oz can cut yams in heavy syrup
½ bag miniature marshmallows

Cut the dried apricots in quarters and place in a small bowl. Pour in Marsala wine and let them soak overnight.

Heat oven to 350°F. Drain yams and put in a medium-size bowl. Mash yams. Drain apricots and add to yams. Stir until mixed together. Spray an 8-inch square pan with cooking spray. Put yam-and-apricot mixture in pan. Smooth down. Cook for ½ hour.

Put oven on broil. Top casserole with miniature marshmallows. Put under broiler until they brown. Watch carefully, as it only takes about a minute.

Enjoy steaming hot. However, cold leftovers make a wonderful snack!

**Nondiet orange soda may be substituted for the wine.

Chapter One

Sandy Walker had come to Glenwood for old-fashioned family values and a place to raise her children. She hadn't expected to find a tall, dark stranger riding a Harley up her driveway.

She stood alone in front of her newly purchased house, right next to the two-year-old station wagon that had brought her and her three kids safely to the small town. She wasn't nervous, exactly, she told herself as the man rode closer. She was...curious.

He stopped the motorcycle about ten feet from her car, killed the engine and expertly nudged the kickstand in place. Then he stood, straddling the bike. They grow 'em big in Glenwood, she thought dryly, wondering if she should be concerned. The man was a good head taller than her own five feet seven inches.

He reached up and removed his helmet. She'd half expected to see long hair spilling onto his shoulders, but instead he was clean-cut, with short, dark, wavy hair that would barely fall to the top of a dress-shirt collar. Aviator sunglasses hid his eyes. He had a square jaw and a slight smile teasing his lips.

"May I help you?" she asked formally, striving for her let's-be-pleasant-but-I'm-a-little-busy tone.

"That was my line, Sandy." The teasing smile broadened. He had a nice mouth and white teeth. He could be in one of those toothpaste ads. He could—

She took a step back. "You know my name?"

He reached for the zipper on his jacket, then pulled it down in one long smooth motion. "It hasn't been that long, Sandy. Have you forgotten that everyone here knows everyone's business? Word's been out since the day you bought the old Michaelson place. Welcome home."

The man spoke as if he knew her. She supposed he could have. She'd spent five years in Glenwood, from the time she was twelve until she left for college. She'd had lots of friends, although most of them had been female. Still, it wouldn't have been difficult for this man to find out her name. The shiver of apprehension that slipped up her spine was the result of living in Los Angeles. People did things differently in Glenwood, she reminded herself. Neighbors were friendly, they cared about each other. That was why she'd moved back in the first place.

He'd finished unzipping his jacket. Now he shrugged out of it and swung his right leg clear of the motorcycle. He folded the garment and laid it across the seat, then turned toward her.

Sandy swallowed. Hard. It was a perfect summer afternoon, with the temperature creeping toward eighty. Bright sunlight flooded the front yard of her house, tall oak trees and a couple of pines cast long shadows on the driveway. She could smell flowers and freshly mowed grass. She could hear the chirping of birds and faint snatches of conversation from around back where her kids were exploring the property. It was all very ordinary.

So there was no reason for her heart to start pounding in her chest, her palms to get sweaty or her mouth to drop open. She was a completely rational, thirty-two-year-old woman who had never made a fool of herself over a man. Not even when she'd been a teenager. She'd never swooned over rock stars or guys in the movies. She was far too sensible to dream for what she could never possibly have. She'd never once felt weak at the knees. Until this moment. Until a guy on a Harley took off his black leather jacket and exposed the most incredible body she'd ever seen.

His red tank shirt emphasized the muscles in his arms and chest. He was tanned and broad, with the kind of strength that comes more from hard work than hours in a gym. Worn jeans closely fit the lower half of his body, outlining long legs and powerful thighs. Sunlight glinted off the silver tips of his cowboy boots. He looked like a male model. Better than that, he looked like a female fantasy come to life.

Maybe there was a photo shoot somewhere in town and he'd gotten lost. But that didn't explain how he knew her name. Or what he was doing walking purposefully toward her.

She panicked and started backing up. "Who are you?" she demanded, clutching her car keys in her right hand and wondering if she should just make a run for it.

The man stopped less than two feet in front of her. He reached up and pulled off his sunglasses. "You don't remember?" he asked, obviously disappointed.

Remember? He wasn't the sort of man a woman would forget. Even one who didn't consider herself the least bit romantic or given to feminine fancies.

Her gaze focused on his. Thick lashes framed impossibly dark eyes. Lines fanned out toward his temples as if he spent a lot of time smiling. He was good-looking enough to melt butter in a snowstorm. And familiar.

She blinked. The sense of horror started low in her belly and spread, like a rash. She'd been a widow for almost two years and in that time she'd never been tempted to look at a man twice. In all her *life,* she'd never been tempted to look at a man twice. Appearances weren't that important to her. So why did she have to notice this particular man? Why now? Why him?

"I saw that," the man said. "You *do* remember me."

She blinked again. Lord have mercy. "Kyle Haynes," she said softly.

"Bingo." Then before she could move or stop him, he bent down and kissed her cheek. "Welcome back, Sandy Morgan. It's been, what, fifteen years? You look terrific."

The brush of his lips against her skin forced all her nerve endings to go on alert. She hated that, so she chose to ignore the sensation. His low, sexy voice made her shiver, as if someone had run a feather across her skin.

"It's Sandy Walker," she said firmly, holding out her hand.

What was supposed to be an impersonal handshake turned into something much more when he took her hand in his. His palm was warm, his fingers long. She didn't know whether to jerk her hand free or jump into his arms.

He grinned. "Sensible Sandy. Walker, did you say? Is there a Mr. Walker?" He glanced around at the front yard, then bent over and stared at the interior of her car. All the while still holding on to her hand.

Heat crept up her wrist to her forearm. Her skin began to tingle, while her heart continued its erratic dance inside her chest. She pulled free of his touch, then casually wiped her fingers against her white shorts. As if she could brush away the lingering sensation of warmth.

"Mr. Walker was killed in a climbing accident two years ago," she said abruptly. "I'm a widow."

Instantly, Kyle's smile faded and his eyes darkened with concern. "I'm sorry."

He sounded as if he really meant it. "Thank you." She paused, not sure what to say next. He was still standing close to her. Too close. She moved back a little more, until she bumped into the station wagon. "What are you doing here?"

"In Glenwood or on your property?"

He didn't smile, but there was no missing the teasing glint in his eyes. Some things might have changed, apparently the Haynes brothers weren't one of them. When she'd first arrived in town, all those years before, she'd been intrigued by the stories about the four brothers, their father and uncles. No female between the age of fourteen and seventy-five had been immune to the famous Haynes charm. Even Sandy had succumbed briefly, dating Jordan Haynes the summer she turned sixteen. It had been a short romance, not even lasting a month. In the end, she and Jordan had decided they made better friends than they did a couple. After that, she'd gotten to know each of the brothers, including Kyle, who was, if she remembered correctly, a couple of years younger than her.

He'd grown up, she thought, eyeing his chest. He probably broke three hearts a day before lunchtime, just to stay in practice.

"Why are you still in Glenwood?" she asked, going for the safer of his two questions. She wasn't worried about giving in to the famous Haynes charm. A playboy bachelor was the last thing she needed in her life. Still, keeping her guard up was wise. Her body's reaction to Kyle's closeness told her she wasn't quite as immune as she would like to be.

"I work here," he said. "I'm a deputy. My brother Travis is the sheriff."

"Like father, like son," she said, remembering Kyle's father had once been sheriff of the small town.

Kyle's dark eyes clouded, as if she'd brought up a painful memory. "Not exactly," he said, then smiled slightly. "What about you?"

"I'll be teaching at Glenwood Junior College. Business English and Business Communications."

"How come my teachers never looked like you?"

She wanted to put her hands on her hips and mutter, "You've got to be kidding," but she resisted. Instead, she offered him a tight smile and wondered how long she was going to have to stand there listening to her hormones sighing in appreciation of his perfect male form.

"Don't you want to know what I'm doing in your driveway?" he asked.

She would rather know what he was doing standing so close. It was getting difficult to breathe regularly. Damn it all, she thought crossly. She didn't need this aggravation. She'd come to Glenwood to get away from her problems, not to create new ones.

"You're part of the local welcoming committee," she said hopefully as a hideously awful thought occurred to her. It couldn't be true, she told herself firmly. She wouldn't let it be true. Fate wasn't that unkind.

She was wrong. Fate might not be unkind, but it had an interesting sense of humor. She knew it the moment Kyle turned and pointed back the way he'd come. She peeked around him. At the end of the long, tree-lined driveway was a small four-room gatehouse—a rental unit that she now owned. The real estate agent had told her the leasee was a police officer. She closed her eyes briefly and prayed he hadn't really meant a deputy.

"I'm your tenant," Kyle said.

Sandy swallowed a groan. It didn't matter, she told herself. It couldn't matter. "You live there with your wife?" she asked, daring to have one last flash of hope.

"Nope." His grin broadened. "I'm not married."

She noticed something in his eyes as he held her gaze a second longer than was comfortable. A brief flicker of interest. Sandy folded her arms over her chest. Even as her heart continued to flutter in her chest, and her palms grew damp, she firmly squashed any romantic thoughts her foolish hormones might want to generate.

Kyle wasn't interested in *her.* She was sensible enough to know the truth about herself. She didn't need to wear a paper bag over her head, but she'd never once stopped traffic. She was okay-looking, nothing more. Kyle was gorgeous. The kind of man who made a woman forget how to breathe. His not-so-subtle come-on was simply reflex. Not interest. She wasn't his type. More important, he wasn't hers.

She nodded at him, then smiled impersonally. "It was very nice of you to welcome me back to Glenwood, but I don't want to keep you from whatever you have planned." She waved toward the motorcycle. "I'm sure we'll run into each other from time to time."

He didn't take the hint. Instead, he moved closer. "When the real estate agent told me you'd be arriving today, I made sure I was available. I figured you'd need some help getting the old place ready."

"I have everything under control. The furniture doesn't arrive for several days. Between now and then, the children and I will be able to clean the house. I've made a list." She nodded toward the front seat where she'd left her clipboard.

Instead of glancing that way, Kyle stared at her intently. "Children?"

Finally, Sandy felt she was gaining control of the conversation. Most single men lived in fear of a woman with children. If she couldn't calm down her hormones, at least she could drive away the object of their desire. "Yes. Three of them. My daughter Lindsay is twelve, Blake is ten and little Nichole is eight."

"I love kids," Kyle said, and looked around the yard. "Where are they?"

Her heart sank. Actually, her spirits sank and her heart increased its lovesick pounding in her chest. She sighed. It was not turning out to be a great day. She should have guessed when Nichole started the morning by eating too many pancakes for breakfast, then throwing up in the car.

"I'd really like to meet them," he said. "That way, when they start to bug you, you can send them down to my place."

Sandy resisted the urge to snort with disbelief. No doubt Kyle had a revolving door at his house, and attractive young women circled through with the regularity of the tide. He wasn't the sort of man she wanted influencing her children.

"That's very kind," she said politely.

"I mean it. My brother Travis has two girls. I—"

He was interrupted by the clatter of running feet. Sandy turned toward the sound as her eldest came skittering around from the back of the house.

"Mo-om, this place is awful. Did you know there's a field behind our house?" The twelve-year-old's mouth twisted in disgust. "A field! Like we're pioneers, or something. I haven't even seen one store or movie theater. What are we supposed to *do*—" Lindsay stopped talking at the exact moment she stopped walking forward. She glanced from her mother to Kyle. Her mouth opened, then closed.

Sandy watched Lindsay and bit back a sigh. She recognized the look of wonder in her daughter's brown eyes. It had probably been shining in her own the first moment she'd seen the grown-up and improved version of Kyle Haynes. But she was a mature woman, able to control her instinctive reaction. Lindsay was caught between girlhood and a world she didn't understand. Her daughter flushed and clasped her hands in front of her. The awkward beauty of a coltish preteen became simply clumsy as she shuffled her feet and stared at the ground.

Sandy had known Lindsay was growing up fast, but she hadn't expected to get a demonstration of the fact. Yet here it was. Lindsay's first awareness of someone of the opposite sex.

"Lindsay, this is Mr. Haynes," Sandy said. "He's our neighbor."

"I live in the gatehouse," Kyle said as he approached her daughter. He held out his hand. Lindsay glanced at her, then the man. She stuck out her hand and giggled when he took it in his. "Nice to meet you, Lindsay. I knew your mom when she was just a couple of years older than you are right now."

"Really?" Lindsay stared at her as if she couldn't ever imagine her mother being young. "What was she like?"

"Pretty much the way she is now. We used to call her Sensible Sandy."

Lindsay rolled her eyes. "Figures. She still wants to organize the world. I guess she hasn't changed at all."

"You're right. She still looks—"

"There's Blake," Sandy interrupted, not wanting to let Kyle continue. She had no idea what he planned to say. Probably some unrealistic compliment about how great she'd looked in high school. "Blake, come and meet our new neighbor."

Her son came around the side of the house. As always, when she saw him, she bit back a sigh. Blake was physically the most like his father. He had dark red hair, freckles and wore glasses. But while Thomas's light brown eyes had gleamed with humor and a zest for life and adventure, Blake's expression was serious, as if the weight of the world rested on his slim shoulders. He preferred to read rather than play outside, and he didn't make friends easily. Sandy wondered if all parents worried about their children as much as she worried about hers. She was doing the best she could to make them feel safe and secure after losing their father, but she wasn't sure her efforts were enough.

"This is Mr. Haynes, Blake," she said, smiling at her son and nodding for him to shake hands with their neighbor.

"Call me Kyle."

Blake mumbled something that could have been a greeting, then dropped his arm to his side and stared at his shoes. Before Sandy could think of something to say that would include him in the conversation, Nichole came running toward her.

"Mommy, Mommy, there are flowers and birds in the backyard." Wide green eyes tilted up at the corners as the eight-year-old grinned. "I saw a bluebird."

Lindsay planted her hands on her hips. "That wasn't a bluebird."

"Was too." Nichole spotted the stranger. She ducked behind her mother, then stuck her head out shyly and smiled. Dimples appeared on both cheeks.

Kyle crouched down next to her. "Hi there. You must be Nichole."

"Uh-huh." Her youngest nodded.

"I'm Kyle. I live right there." He pointed to the gatehouse, then rose. "This one's going to be a heartbreaker when she gets older."

"I know. Killer dimples," Sandy said.

Kyle winked at the little girl. "I've always had a thing for green eyes."

Sandy fought the instinctive urge to point out *her* eyes were green, too. What was it about this man that got to her? Maybe it was spending the last two years living alone. Since Thomas had died, she hadn't been on a date. She wasn't interested in getting involved. So why was she so completely aware of Kyle?

Lindsay leaned against the station wagon and tossed her long brown hair over her shoulder. She gave them what Sandy called her "I'm so sophisticated" look.

"Is there anything fun to do in this hick town?" Lindsay asked.

Kyle glanced at her. "You don't like Glenwood?"

"I'm from L.A. It's like this is a different planet."

Kyle grinned. Lindsay swallowed. Sandy ruffled Nichole's red curls and knew exactly how her daughter felt.

"You'll like it here," he promised. "Life's going to seem a little slower, but there's lots of fun stuff for kids to do. There's softball and soccer." He glanced at Nichole. "There's a team for girls just your age. And my brother Travis has a daughter who's eight."

"That's fine for the children," Lindsay said, her tone pointing out how much more *mature* she was than the other two. "But what about me?"

"We'll find something," Kyle promised.

"It's really not your problem," Sandy said. "I appreciate the welcome and all that, but we've got work to do. Children, say goodbye to Mr. Haynes."

Blake muttered something under his breath, while Nichole just smiled winningly. Lindsay gave her mother the hate stare, then said, "Goodbye, Kyle. I'm sure we'll run into each other again."

"I'm sure."

He turned and started toward his motorcycle. Lindsay noticed the bike for the first time.

"Way cool," she said and started after him.

Sandy grabbed the girl's arm. "Another time."

"But Mom—"

"We've got to get the house ready."

Kyle picked up his jacket, then turned toward her. "Have you been in the place yet?"

She glanced at the house. "No. We've just arrived."

He hesitated. "Maybe I should take a look around first."

"Why?"

"The house has been closed up for a while. You don't know what could be inside."

If she hadn't been afraid he would think she was as immature as Lindsay, she would have rolled her eyes. Couldn't he come up with a better line than that? "The roof and plumbing have just been replaced. We're not afraid of a little dirt or a few spiderwebs."

"I hate spiders," Nichole said.

"I know, honey. I'll take care of any we find." She returned her attention to Kyle. "We'll be fine. I promise."

Sandy grabbed Nichole and Blake by the hand, then started toward the house. "Come on, Lindsay," she called as her daughter stood there staring foolishly at Kyle. Lindsay's attraction to the older man was understandable. He was incredibly good-looking. Handsome, tall, strong, with a smile that could— She forced herself away from the specifics. He had everything a girl could want in her first adolescent crush. But the idea that Lindsay had just discovered the opposite sex made Sandy feel old. Lindsay had just taken her first steps into womanhood. Sandy felt as if that part of her life was over. She was only thirty-two. According to women's magazines, she was entering her sexual peak. Unfortunately, she had no plans to find a man and take advantage of her condition.

"See you around," Kyle called.

"Bye."

As she reached into the pocket of her white shorts for the house key, she realized that Kyle hadn't been scared off by her children. If anything, he'd seemed genuinely interested in them. That was unusual. Most men couldn't run fast enough in the other direction.

So what, she thought as she fitted the key into the lock. Maybe he was pretending. Of course, it didn't matter if he wasn't. He wasn't going to be interested in a woman like her, and she sure didn't want to get involved with a man like him. Or any man. She was very happy being single and in control of her life.

"You guys ready?" she asked as she pushed open the door.

None of their responses were very enthusiastic. Sandy felt a twinge of guilt. She'd uprooted her kids from everything they'd ever known. It was the right decision, she reminded herself. They would adjust. Being raised in a small town like Glenwood was better for them than a big city like Los Angeles. Still, the guilt persisted. She knew it would be hard on them. The move was going to be hard on her, too. But doing the right thing usually was.

She stepped into the house. The foyer was huge, larger than their old living room had been. The house was dark. Dust covered the hardwood floors and cobwebs hung from the ten-foot ceiling. But the structure was stunningly beautiful.

Sunlight filtered through a crack in the drapes, highlighting the fancy molding and the curved staircase that led to the second story. The old place needed a good cleaning and a coat or two of paint. They could easily get that done before the movers arrived with their furniture.

"Mom?" Blake said, tugging on the sleeve of her red T-shirt. "What's that over there?" He was pointing to a far corner of the foyer where something small and dark moved.

"I'm not sure."

"I'm getting out of here," Lindsay said.

"Don't be ridiculous," Sandy said. "It's nothing." She started walking toward the small shadow. "It's just—"

The shadow moved toward the light. Sandy, Nichole, Blake and Lindsay screamed in unison.

Chapter Two

Kyle was halfway up the front-porch stairs before they finished screaming. He raced across the porch, flung open the door. Four people turned toward him—four pairs of eyes begged for help. As he hurried toward Sandy and her kids, he instinctively went for his pistol. There was nothing at his hip except for his jeans. Damn.

"What is it?" he asked. Everyone answered at once.

"That thing there," Sandy said, pointing behind her. She shivered.

"Totally gross," Lindsay agreed.

Nichole moved closer and clutched his leg.

"It's coming toward us," Blake cried.

The four of them shrieked and descended upon him. Sandy pressed against his left side. Lindsay huddled behind his back. Nichole kept a hold on his right leg, while Blake held on to Sandy.

Kyle almost didn't mind. Having Sandy plaster herself against him gave him a nice warm feeling in his belly...and a few inches farther south. She stared up at him with her big green eyes. Mascara darkened her lashes, but other than that, she didn't seem to be wearing any makeup. He liked the freckles scattered on her nose and the way her normally firm mouth quivered at the corners. She smelled nice, part floral fragrance, part something a little more sensual. He could feel her breasts, and one hipbone. Her legs brushed against his and he wished he were wearing shorts instead of jeans.

But there were children present, he reminded himself. So he turned his thoughts from the very enticing Sandy Walker to the large empty room in front of them. Aside from a few cobwebs and some dust, he couldn't see anything to get excited about.

"What are we hiding from?" he asked.

Sandy pointed toward the corner. "That...that thing!"

He squinted, trying to see into the shadows. One of the shadows moved. "It's a mouse."

"Oh, God, I know. The place could be infested with them. I hate rodents. Mice, rats. Yuck."

Yuck? Sensible Sandy had said yuck? He liked that.

Kyle tried to take a step, but they wouldn't let him. "I want to go check it out," he said, trying to free himself from Nichole. She just held on tighter. Her small hands clutched at his jeans as if she would never let go.

"Why?" Sandy asked. "I'll have to call an exterminator."

"You can't kill it, Mom," Lindsay said from behind him.

"Fine, then it can live in your room," Sandy snapped.

"Mo-om!"

Nichole glanced at her mother. "Mommy, don't hurt the mouse. Please."

"Honey, you don't understand. We can't live with it running around. Mice are dirty. They get in the food and they could make us all sick."

Nichole's eyes, so like her mother's, darkened with tears. "You can't kill it."

"Ladies," Kyle said. They ignored him.

"We'll talk about this later," Sandy said.

"That means the mouse is going to die for sure," Lindsay grumbled.

"Ladies," he repeated.

"You don't know everything," Sandy said, her voice strained. "There are humane ways to get rid of mice. I don't want to see it killed any more than you do, but it and its friends cannot live here with us."

"The mouse has friends?" Nichole asked.

Kyle raised his right hand to his face, stuck his thumb and index finger in his mouth, then blew hard. The piercing whistle silenced them instantly.

"Now that I have your attention," he said, "will everyone please take one step back and let go of me?"

Sandy stared up at him for a moment, blushed, then quickly moved away, brushing her hands against her shorts. "Sorry," she mumbled, obviously flustered. "I guess we overreacted to the mouse."

He wanted to tell her that she didn't need to apologize. He'd liked her pressing up against him. It did him good to know she wasn't as completely in charge as she wanted the world to think. It also evened the score a little. She'd been tying him up in knots since the first time his brother Jordan had brought her home sixteen years ago.

Something about her had set his adolescent heart on fire and he'd never forgotten her. Still, this wasn't the time or place to review old memories.

Kyle glanced around the empty foyer, then at the small mouse that had returned to its nest in the corner by the stairs. "I want to look over the rest of the house before you get to work," he said.

Sandy bristled. Her spine stiffened and her hands curled into fists. "I've already had the house inspected," she said, staring at him. "The man told me the building was in excellent condition and that the only problem I should expect would be cleaning up after a lengthy vacancy."

Kyle tried to remember if she'd always had this much trouble accepting help. He couldn't say for sure. Maybe it was something she'd learned while she was gone. "Did he say anything about mice?" he asked.

She hesitated. "Well, no. He probably thought they were normal for as long as the house has been vacant."

"You want to be by yourself when you find out what else this guy considered normal?"

"Oh. I hadn't thought of that."

He grinned. "So you don't mind if I check out the rest of the house?"

Her hands relaxed. "Um, no. Thanks. I appreciate the help."

"I'm not staying in here with that," Lindsay said, pointing at the mouse's nest.

"Why don't you kids wait outside while your mom and I check things out," Kyle said. The children didn't budge.

Sandy looked from him to her kids, then sighed. "Lindsay, take your brother and sister outside and keep an eye on them, please."

Lindsay walked to the door without looking back. Blake followed silently. Only Nichole hesitated.

"Go on, sweetie. I won't be long. It's warm outside. Why don't you go and see if you can find that bluebird again?"

"Okay." Nichole smiled.

She had dimples in each cheek and her mother's eyes. Kyle felt a slight twist in his gut. Sometimes he got the crazy notion that he should have risked settling down and having kids. He knew better. It was like wishing for the moon. Something to think about when he'd had too much to drink or got lonely, but completely irrational. He wasn't the type. Long-term relationships didn't work out.

When the children had left, Sandy turned to him and nodded purposefully. "Let's begin in the kitchen," she said, and turned to the right.

"It's this way." He motioned to their left.

"But they sent me a floor plan."

"Then your floor plan was reversed. The kitchen is through here."

"How do you know?"

"I used to know Kelsey Michaelson. I've been in this house before." He looked at the dust and cobwebs. "But not in a long time."

"I see." She started toward the kitchen.

"Hold on." He caught up with her and took her hand. Her fingers were warm against his. She looked startled when he touched her. Good. He would deal better with Sandy if he kept her off guard. "Why don't you let me lead the way."

Her gaze narrowed as she pulled her hand free of his. "Why?"

"In case we run into something creepy or slimy—or yucky."

"All right." She stepped back to allow him to pass.

He led her through the empty dining room. The hardwood floors were dirty, but otherwise in great shape. He stopped and bent down. "These will clean up and look terrific," he said, brushing his fingers against the wood.

She stopped next to him. Close, but not too close. He grinned. If his instincts were correct, he made Sandy nervous. The thought pleased him.

"The realtor told me all the floors are in excellent condition," she said. "I've been reading up on refinishing, in case some of them need a little work."

"You can't do that yourself."

She planted her hands on her hips. "Because I'm a woman?" She didn't wait for him to answer. "Give me a break. I don't need a man in my life to make things work. I can do it all by myself, thank you very much.''

He stood up slowly, moving closer as he did. "Not because you're a woman. Because there's probably a thousand square feet of hardwood flooring on the first floor alone. It would take you months if you did it yourself, and some of the materials you have to use can smell pretty nasty. You wouldn't want your children breathing in that stuff for so long, would you?"

She held his gaze, searching his face as if looking for deception. "That makes sense," she said grudgingly.

"And because you're a woman." He grinned, then held up his hands in a gesture of surrender. "Just kidding, I promise."

A slight smile pulled at the corners of her mouth. "You haven't changed at all."

"Not enough to matter," he agreed. "Come on, let's check out the house."

He led the way to the large bright kitchen. Big windows opened onto the side yard and driveway. The curtains looked as if they'd been lunch for a hungry swarm of moths, while an army of ants trooped across the white tile counters. Sandy checked out the pantry and utility porch behind the kitchen, and Kyle opened cupboard doors.

"I don't see any signs that your mouse has relatives living here," he said.

She paused in the doorway to the pantry. "I won't ask what you're looking for." She folded her arms over her chest. "At least there's a lot of storage space in the pantry."

Kyle walked over to where she was standing. He put his arm around her shoulder and tried to draw her close. She resisted. He settled on giving her a brotherly squeeze.

"You're discouraged," he said.

She shrugged.

"It's going to be a lot of work, but I'll help. By the time the furniture arrives, we'll have the place clean and painted."

Sandy made a great show of pulling free of his arm, then walking to the other side of the kitchen. "I appreciate your willingness to help," she said. "But no thanks. The kids and I want to do this by ourselves. We don't want, or need, a man in our lives. The children and I have everything under control."

"I could tell by how you all reacted to the mouse."

She looked away. "Yes, well, that was different. I wasn't expecting to find a mouse. Now that I know there might be more, I can handle it."

He glanced around at the dusty cupboards, the trail of ants and the limp, gnawed curtains. "You're not planning to sleep here tonight, are you?"

"We're staying at a motel in town." She took a step toward him, then paused. "Look, Kyle, you're being really nice and neighborly, but it isn't necessary. I'm not the sort of woman who needs rescuing. I knew the house hadn't been lived in when I bought it. It needs a little cleaning and some paint. We'll manage."

"The ceilings in most of the rooms are over ten feet high," he said. "Do you have the equipment to handle that?"

"I'll buy a ladder." She pointed back the way they'd come. "I don't want to keep you."

She was throwing him out. Okay, maybe putting his arm around her *had* been a little too much, but she'd looked as if she'd needed a good hug. If she was a widow, she probably hadn't had a hug in a long time. Unless she was seeing somebody. He frowned.

"What's wrong?" she asked.

He stared at her. She wore her wedding ring on her left hand. Was she still in love with her late husband, or did she use the ring to warn men off? From what he remembered

of Sandy, it could be either. And he was willing to bet there
was no other man in her life.

"Kyle?"

"Hmm? Nothing's wrong. I was just thinking. Okay,
Sandy. You win. You want to take care of this by yourself, you go ahead. If you need me, I'm just at the end of
the driveway."

"I'll remember."

She escorted him out the door and down the porch steps.
Her three children were waiting for them by the station
wagon.

"Any more mice?" Lindsay asked.

"None that we saw," Sandy answered briskly. "So
there's no reason to avoid the cleaning." She opened the
back of the car and started pulling out buckets and
brooms. Lindsay and Blake groaned. Nichole grabbed a
feather duster and smiled.

Kyle didn't want to leave them. The job was too big.
There was no way they would finish before the furniture
arrived. The downstairs had been bad enough. Who knows
what it was like upstairs. There could be carpet to tear up
and—

Let it alone, he told himself. Sandy had made it clear she
wasn't interested in him or his help.

"See ya," he said, and started toward the gatehouse.

"Wait," Sandy called.

He turned toward her.

"Would you mind calling an exterminator about the
mice?" she asked. "The phone here won't be hooked up
until tomorrow." She looked down at Nichole and smiled.
"We need one who doesn't kill the mice, but just traps
them and takes them away."

"No problem," he told her. "If you need anything
else—"

"I know. I'll let you know. And thanks for calling the
exterminator." She waved, then turned back to the sta-

tion wagon. The children gathered around her, Lindsay and Blake grumbling about their chores.

Kyle walked over to his motorcycle and slipped on his leather jacket. After pulling on his helmet, he settled onto the seat and started the engine, then slowly drove back to the gatehouse.

He parked the bike by the back door, next to the small garage where he kept his Camaro. Ever since he'd found out Sandy had bought the Michaelson place, he'd been eager for her to arrive. He could have walked the twenty or so yards between their two houses, but he'd taken the bike, because, dammit, he'd wanted to impress her.

Sandy had been so impressed she couldn't wait to get rid of him. He'd come on too strong. He shouldn't have teased her. Impatiently, Kyle grabbed his jacket and helmet and headed for the back door. When had he started second-guessing himself about his behavior with women?

He unlocked the gatehouse door, then stepped into its compact kitchen. His entire place would fit into about a third of Sandy's downstairs, but it suited him fine. The living room was large, as was the master bedroom. There was a small study alcove off the dining room, and the bathroom had an oversize shower. He lived alone, he didn't need any more room. He liked his house, even if it was a little quiet sometimes.

After dumping his jacket and helmet on the kitchen table, he crossed the floor to the refrigerator next to the window. He pulled out a soda and popped the top. Before he could turn away, a faint sound of laughter caught his attention. He looked out the window. Sandy and her three kids still stood by their station wagon. Blake was carrying a bucket full of cleaning supplies. Lindsay was loaded down with brooms and mops. Sandy wrestled with a ladder that was taller than she was but that would never reach the high ceilings. They were all looking at little Nichole, who held the feather duster behind her like a tail. She

pranced around the yard, scratching like a chicken looking for worms. Sandy said something and they all laughed
again. Then they started toward the house.

Nichole climbed the stairs and went inside last. The yard
was empty, the laughter gone. He was alone. He told himself he should be used to the silence. But he wasn't. He
glanced at the phone. There were any number of people he
could call. Any number of women. They would spend his
afternoon off with him, and the night, if he asked. He
didn't, as a rule, bring women to his place. He preferred
visiting them at theirs. That way, he could leave when he
wanted to. He preferred to be in control. A little like
Sandy.

Had it really been fifteen years since he'd last seen her?
He remembered her leaving as though it had just happened. She'd been going off to college. In his heart, he'd
known she wasn't coming back. She'd never suspected how
he felt about her. Even if she had, she wouldn't have cared.
She had been seventeen—almost eighteen and already
graduated from high school. No one had known how he'd
dreamed about her.

Kyle turned away from the window and walked into the
living room. He grabbed the book he'd been reading and
carried it over to the leather recliner in front of the small,
stone fireplace. But instead of reading, he closed his eyes
and pictured Sandy as she'd been all those years ago. What
was it about her that appealed to him? She wasn't all that
pretty, at least not in an obvious way.

Someone had once figured out that between the four of
them, the Haynes brothers had dated every cheerleader in
town for ten years straight. When Kyle had been old
enough, he'd carried on the family tradition. He'd dated
the prettiest girls, the most popular ones. But not always.
Once he'd dated the class brain, just because she always
tried to look superior whenever they spoke. He'd sensed
something else lurking behind her glasses and quick an-

swers. It had taken him the better part of a semester to get her to go out with him, but it had been worth it. In fact, next to his crush on Sandy, dating Melinda had been the highlight of his high school years. She'd gone off to MIT and was now working for NASA. They still kept in touch at the holidays.

But Sandy had eluded him. He'd just been a kid of fourteen. He hadn't known what to do with his feelings, how to tell her or what would happen if he did. And then she'd left. But he'd never forgotten. Now she was back.

He took a sip of his soda. All this time later, the two years difference in their ages didn't seem to matter so much. But she still wasn't for him. She'd chosen her life, had married and had three kids. She was a widow. No doubt the next man she picked would be just like her husband. Kyle had heard that Sandy's husband had been a professor at a prestigious Los Angeles university. Kyle knew he couldn't compete with that. He was just a deputy in some hick town. He loved his job and he didn't want to change it. Not that anyone was asking him to. Sandy hadn't given him a second look. He grinned. Maybe her eyes had widened a little when he'd taken off his jacket, but so what? He knew he was good-looking. All the Haynes boys were. That and fifty cents could buy a cup of coffee. A woman like Sandy wouldn't care about that. She would be more concerned about what was inside a man. About his character. She would want guarantees and that was one thing he'd never been able to give anyone.

Three days later, he stood outside washing his car. The white finish gleamed in the bright morning sunlight. He moved slowly, his brain and body not working well together after pulling a sixteen-hour shift. His replacement had gotten food poisoning, so Kyle had volunteered to stay through the night. He fought back a yawn. It didn't used to bother him, but since hitting thirty, he hadn't been able to pull all-nighters with the same ease. The worst part about the double shift was relaxing enough to sleep when he got home. Usually his mind was cranking along at fifty miles an hour, while his body was so tired he could sleep standing up. He'd learned that performing an undemanding physical chore allowed him to unwind so that he could get to sleep.

He tossed the soapy sponge back in the bucket, then reached for the hose. He turned the nozzle, adjusting the spray to a light mist, when he heard voices behind him. A quick glance told him Lindsay, Blake and Nichole were walking down the driveway. Kyle continued rinsing his car.

He hadn't seen his neighbors since they'd first arrived. He'd been working a lot and generally trying to stay away. Sandy had made her feelings clear. If she didn't want his help, far be it from him to impose. But he'd thought about her a great deal. And when she'd left after that first day of cleaning, he'd gone by the house to make sure the doors and windows were locked.

"Hi, Kyle," Lindsay said when the kids reached the split in the driveway that led to his garage. "That's a cool car."

He glanced at the Camaro. "Thanks. How's the house-cleaning coming?"

Lindsay wrinkled her nose. "Mom's driving us crazy."

"Mommy's blowing her mission," Nichole said and smiled at him. "She said a bad word, too."

"Her mission?"

"Children," Lindsay said, then patted Nichole on the head. "You'll have to forgive her. She's very young."

Kyle thought about pointing out that Lindsay wasn't that old herself, but he didn't want to hurt her feelings. "What does she mean?"

"The moving company left a message that they would be late delivering the furniture. The truck blew its transmission." She moved closer to him and lowered her voice. "Mom called them and said she was going to blow more

than a transmission if they didn't get our stuff up here."
She glanced at him and swept her lashes up and down several times. "So we're stuck."

"When do they think the truck's going to arrive?"

"In another three or four days. I don't think it matters that much. The house is still a mess. We're not getting a lot done."

"I am," Nichole said. "I've got three stars." She held up the right number of fingers. "When I get five stars, I get to buy a new book."

"Stars?" he asked, confused.

"One of Mom's attempts to keep us as organized as she is," Lindsay said. "She's got a chart up on the wall. Everyone has chores listed. When you complete a certain number of chores, you get a star. After so many stars, you get a reward."

"What's your reward?" he asked Blake.

The boy looked up, obviously startled that he'd been noticed. Light brown eyes peered at him through thick glasses. Except for the freckles across his nose and the shape of his mouth, Blake didn't look anything like his mother. His slight shoulders hunched forward. "I haven't picked one yet."

"Oh, he'll get another game for his silly computer. He sits in front of it all the time."

Blake glared at his older sister, but didn't defend himself.

"What about you?" he asked Lindsay, then wished he hadn't. She moved even closer and stared up at him intently.

"I want clothes. Something pretty."

"Uh-huh. That sounds, uh, nice." He cleared his throat.

If his brothers could see him now, they'd all roar with laughter. Any of them could handle a flirtatious woman with no problem. But a vamping preteen was out of his realm of expertise. He wished Sandy would show up.

"So you guys are having trouble with the house?" he asked.

Lindsay rolled her eyes. Nichole giggled, and even Blake nodded.

"It's too big," Nichole said. "I washed the kitchen cupboards forever and they're still not done."

"We haven't even started on the upstairs," Lindsay said. "Mom wants us to get the painting done, too. She's crazy. This isn't how I planned to spend my summer."

"I know it's hard," Kyle said. "But your mom really needs your help. This is hard for her, too. Moving to a strange town, and all."

"No one asked her to drag us to this dumpy place." Lindsay's brown eyes snapped with anger. Her posing was forgotten as she drew her eyebrows together and glared. "There's nothing to do. There are no kids around here, no beach, nothing. I hate it. I don't care if the house never gets finished."

"Glenwood isn't so bad," he said. "There's a mall on the other side of town."

"Wow," Lindsay said sarcastically. "A mall. Gee, now I love it here."

Nichole skipped over the hose and motioned for him to bend over. "Lindsay's being a brat," she whispered loudly. "Mommy says it's just a stage."

He crouched down and smiled at the child. She had curly red hair, but her mother's beautiful green eyes. "You're a pretty little girl."

Nichole dimpled. "I know. Mommy told me."

Kyle grinned.

"There you are," a voice said. "I'd wondered where you'd run off to. I told you not to bother Mr. Haynes." Sandy stood at the end of his driveway. Like her children she was wearing shorts and a T-shirt. Unlike his noncommittal response to their clothes, he found her outfit intriguing. Her red shorts exposed long tanned legs. Her round hips drew his eye toward her waist, then up to her breasts. She wasn't overly curvy, she was . . . just right.

He stood up slowly. "I'd rather they call me Kyle, and they weren't bothering me. I heard about the truck."

She wouldn't—or couldn't—meet his gaze. "Yes, well, I just got off the phone with the moving company. The truck will be here Monday for sure."

"But it's Friday," he said. "What will you do until then?"

"Stay at the motel where we've been staying. The kids don't mind. It has a pool."

"By the time we get back there, we're too tired to go swimming," Lindsay grumbled.

Her mother shot her a warning look. "The extra time will give us a chance to finish the house."

Lindsay groaned.

"How's that coming?"

She stared at his car, then at the ground, finally her gaze landed on his knees and settled there. Kyle wanted to believe she was having trouble looking at him because he was wearing cutoffs and nothing else. He wanted to believe the sight of his bare chest and legs left her speechless. He wanted to believe he would one day win the California lottery. Right now they seemed equally likely.

"Fine," Sandy said shortly. "Just fine. We're cleaning and soon we'll start painting."

"We're never going to finish," Lindsay said.

"Nonsense. I've come up with a new plan. It will allow us to work more efficiently."

"Mo-om." Lindsay planted her hands on her hips. At that moment, she looked exactly like her mother. "We're kids, not slaves."

"And just an hour ago, you were trying to convince me you're all grown up. You'll have to pick one, Lindsay, you can't have it both ways."

Kyle opened his mouth to offer his help, then thought better of it. He didn't want to give Sandy another chance to shoot him down.

Sandy glanced at his car, then at him. "We'd better let you get back to work. Have fun. Come along, children."

She took Nichole's hand and started down the driveway. Lindsay followed slowly. Only Blake hesitated. He stared at the car for a moment.

"Do you like Camaros?" Kyle asked, suddenly curious about the quietest member of the Walker family.

Blake nodded. "Does it go fast?"

"Pretty fast." He grinned. "I'm a deputy in town, so it's not right for me to break the law. I keep her at fifty-five."

"Blake, come on, honey," Sandy called.

"Maybe you and I could go for a drive someday," Kyle offered.

Blake stared up at him, nodded, then ran off to join his mother.

As Kyle picked up the chamois, he watched Sandy and her kids enter the big house. He remembered how dirty it had been. Yesterday, the exterminator had come by to drop off his traps, so the mouse problem was being handled. Still, there was the whole upstairs that Lindsay said they hadn't even started on. And painting. How would they get that done?

He wiped off the roof of the car. Maybe he shouldn't offer to help. Maybe he should just take care of it. She would hate that. Of course, if he didn't give her a chance to refuse, she would have to hate it silently.

He looked at the oversize home again, then tossed the chamois down and went inside his house. He knew exactly how to take care of Sandy's problem. He had brothers, and they all owed him.

Chapter Three

It was like being descended upon by locusts. Tall, handsome, *male* locusts. There were only three of them, but that was enough.

Sandy stood at her front door Friday afternoon and stared at the men in front of her.

"We're here to help," Kyle said.

"But I don't—"

He pushed past her into the house. "Sure you do. Be polite, say thank-you, then show us what needs to be done. We're not going away."

Lindsay came running down the stairs. When she reached the bottom, she stared at the three men. "Wow."

Yeah, *wow,* Sandy echoed silently. There was enough testosterone in the room to float a football team.

"She's speechless," the tallest of the men said. They all had dark hair, but this one had cool gray eyes and was wearing a gold earring.

"Sandy?" Kyle said, coming up and putting his arm around her. "Not her. She's just mentally organizing her next attack. Sandy always has a plan."

She usually had a plan, she admitted to herself. She just didn't have one right at this minute. Besides, how was she supposed to think when Kyle was standing so close? She told herself she should pull away, but her legs weren't listening. It had been bad enough when she'd walked over to his place that morning. He'd been wearing shorts and nothing else. Just the thought of his bare chest was enough to make her hyperventilate.

"Maybe you should introduce us," the third man said. He was obviously one of Kyle's brothers, but Sandy couldn't remember which one. He had the same dark hair and warm brown eyes. He was handsome as sin. They all were.

"Good idea," Kyle said. "This is Lindsay." He pointed to the preteen still standing on the bottom stair, gaping at them. "And this is Sandy."

Kyle's brother waved at her daughter, then nodded at her. "Hi, Sandy. I'm Travis. The second oldest of the Haynes brothers. You dated Jordan, right?"

She shook the hand he offered and grinned. "I'm amazed you could keep any of us straight," she said. "Girls came and went through your lives with the speed of light."

Travis chuckled. "Maybe, but a few were memorable."

Sandy felt herself blush at the compliment.

The man with the earring moved toward her. "I'm Austin Lucas." His gray gaze met hers. He was almost as handsome as Kyle, but there was something dark about him. Dangerous. She noticed a ring on his left hand and wondered who'd been brave enough to tame this man.

"Hey, enough of that," Kyle said, stepping between them. "You're married, she's not interested, let's get to work."

"I picked up the paint you ordered from the hardware store," Travis said, stepping out onto the porch.

"We've brought a decent ladder, too," Austin told her.

Sandy barely heard them. She couldn't seem to notice anything, not even when Blake and Nichole rushed into the room to see what was going on. All she could do was stare at Kyle, at his dark brown eyes and that lock of curly hair that fell over his forehead. He'd almost sounded . . .

She shook her head and told herself to quit being silly. He hadn't sounded anything. It wasn't possible. A man like Kyle wouldn't be interested in a woman like her. And even if *he* was, *she* wasn't. She wanted a mature, responsible man, not a handsome hunk who probably had women lined up for miles. None of which explained why Kyle had ended the conversation between herself and the other man. Or why he'd specifically told her that Austin was married. Kyle wasn't jealous. Was he?

It was a dangerous train of thought. Mostly because her heart hadn't recovered from its earlier aerobic workout when she'd gone to find her children and had also found Kyle practically naked.

His chest had been as big and broad as that tank shirt had promised three days ago when she and her kids had arrived. His tan went clear to the waistband of his shorts, and probably lower. The sprinkling of dark hair, the faint outline of impossibly firm muscles and the heat radiating from him had made her palms itch to press against him. She'd wanted to touch and taste and—

"Mom, how long are you going to stand there staring into space?"

Lindsay's question jerked her back to the present. She landed with an emotional thud, then blushed hotly as she wondered if everyone knew what she'd been thinking about. She glanced around frantically. No one seemed to have noticed. Austin and Travis trooped past her carrying ladders, paint cans and drop cloths. Kyle was standing next to her, studying the list she'd posted to the wall detailing the chores that had yet to be done. Only Lindsay stared at her, exasperated.

"Mom?"

"I was thinking," she said quickly, then cleared her throat. "Kyle, this is very nice of you and your brothers, but I really can't—"

He turned and smiled. Her heart rate increased. Thank God he was wearing a T-shirt so she didn't have to deal with his chest again. "Of course you can. Just say 'Gee, Kyle, you're a nice man. Thanks for your help.'"

"Kyle, you *are* a nice man, but—"

He turned and touched his finger to her lips. Electricity shot through her body, starting at her mouth and jolting clear down to her toes. Her blood heated as an unfamiliar longing stirred to life deep inside her belly.

"No buts," he ordered. "You can't do all this work by yourselves, Sandy. We both know that. You can give in gracefully, or you can fight me and look like a stubborn fool. The choice is yours."

His eyes were an impossible color. Not black, just a deep, dark shade of brown. Long lashes framed his eyes. He had a straight nose with a small bump on one side. She wondered if it had once been broken. From what she remembered, the Haynes brothers weren't afraid of a good fight.

She forced her thoughts away from the man and back to the task at hand. Her children stood around her, gazing up at her hopefully. They'd worked hard these last few days. Unfortunately, Kyle was right. They couldn't do it all themselves. They'd barely finished the downstairs. There was still the upstairs to clean out, not to mention the painting. Her body ached, her muscles screamed in protest every time she even thought about climbing the stairs. This was supposed to be their summer vacation, and they needed a break.

"Thank you," she said at last.

Lindsay and Nichole cheered.

"Just because we're accepting help doesn't mean we're not going to work," she said. "Girls, you know the routine. Start upstairs with the bedrooms. Blake, you come with me and we'll tackle the bathrooms." She looked at Kyle. "Travis and Austin are painting. What are you going to do?"

He winked. "Supervise."

By five that afternoon, the smell of paint drifted through the house and all of the upstairs had been cleaned. Kyle had done more than supervise. He'd taped off windows, painted the wooden window frames and all the downstairs baseboards. Travis and Austin had finished painting the kitchen and then had moved into the dining room.

Lindsay dumped the last of the dirty water and leaned against the bathroom counter. "Now what?" she asked, her voice tired, her face flushed.

Sandy gave her a weary smile. "Now we take a break. There are sodas in the ice chest. Take Blake and Nichole, and go outside and rest."

"Can you carry me down the stairs?"

"I think you can make it."

Lindsay started out of the bathroom, then paused. "What about dinner? I'm starved."

"I thought about ordering pizza."

"Really?" Lindsay's brown eyes widened with surprise. "But whenever we ask for it, you always say it's expensive and has no nutritional value. You never order pizza. I only get to eat it when I'm staying with a girlfriend."

"I'm ordering it tonight."

"Okay, cool." Lindsay walked down the hall. "Blake, Nichole, come on. Let's go get a soda. And guess what?"

Nichole came running out first. "What?" she demanded.

"We're having pizza for dinner."

Nichole clapped her hands together. "I want *three* slices."

"You can't eat that much."

"I can too."

Blake joined his sisters, but didn't speak. The three of them went downstairs and their voices faded.

Sandy stood in the doorway of the guest bathroom and stared after her children. Was pizza that big a deal? She tried to remember if she'd ever ordered it for them before. She shook her head. She'd always preferred to cook. It was more economical and nutritious. She'd known Thomas could be counted on to eat junk food when given a chance, and the children didn't always spend their lunch money wisely, so she'd felt it was her duty to provide a good, wholesome meal at dinnertime. But she didn't think she'd been so strict about food that ordering pizza was an event worth noting on the calendar.

Besides, she needed to pay back her helpers, and she was reasonably sure they would accept food while they would be insulted by an offer of money. Thinking of which, things had been quiet downstairs for some time.

She followed the children down to the first floor. All the windows were open and a sweet breeze blew through the house. Cans of paint had been neatly stacked in the foyer. The drop cloths were folded next to them, and a ladder lay on the floor of the dining room. The house was silent.

"Kyle?" she called.

"In the study," he answered.

She went down the long hallway beside the stairs. There was a small bathroom behind the living room, then a set of double doors that opened onto a study. She stepped into the room.

An old stone fireplace with bookshelves on either side filled one wall. Opposite were more bookshelves. Large windows let in sunlight. The room smelled of lemon-scented furniture polish. She and Blake had cleaned all the wooden shelves and paneling the previous day. Only the wall containing the windows was painted. Kyle was on his knees at the windows, finishing the baseboard.

"Where is everyone?" she asked.

"Austin and Travis left already."

"But they didn't say goodbye."

"They'll be back tomorrow."

"I was going to order pizza."

Kyle stood up. "Good, I'm starved."

She glared at him. "It's not just for you. I wanted to say thank-you."

"You can thank them tomorrow morning. They'll be here about eight. With all of us working together, we should be able to get all the painting finished."

"Why is everyone being so nice to me?" she asked, convinced Kyle was trying to pull something on her.

"Don't look a gift horse in the mouth." He frowned. "You know, I never understood what that meant. Who'd want to look in a horse's mouth, anyway?"

"Why am I sure you're purposely changing the subject?"

"Because you have a suspicious mind." He crouched down and put the top on the paint can. After tapping it back in place with a hammer, he grabbed the can and his brush and headed for the kitchen. She trailed after him.

"Travis and Austin left because they both have families who are expecting them for dinner," he said. "They're going to come back tomorrow because I asked them to. I've been helping Travis remodel his house for the last year. Before that, I spent hours working on Austin's loft. So stop thinking the worst of me."

"That's it?"

"That's it." He set the paint can on the counter and stuck the brush under the faucet. "If you're still ordering pizza, I prefer sausage to pepperoni, and I like mushrooms. Or have you changed your mind?"

She still felt there was something he wasn't telling her, but she couldn't be sure what. "I don't want to keep you if you have plans," she said. "It *is* Friday night."

"I'm available."

For what? she almost asked.

She stared at his broad shoulders, his narrow hips and long legs. He was the most tempting man she'd ever seen, and she was just staring at the back of him. If he was to turn around and smile at her... She sighed. She wasn't sure exactly what she would do, but she was pretty sure it would be embarrassing.

Sometime when she was alone, she would figure out why she was reacting to Kyle this way. He wasn't her type. She didn't have a type. She'd only dated a little in high school and college. Then she'd met Thomas and they'd gotten married right away. She'd been so positive when she'd met him, confident that she'd found her soul mate. Someone kind and responsible, willing to share life's burdens. How was she to have known that this tenured philosophy professor was just an adolescent in disguise? She'd learned one thing from her marriage—that she didn't want to be the only adult in a relationship. When she got involved again— if she got involved again—it was going to be with someone who understood life wasn't a game. It was going to be with someone who took things seriously and lived up to his commitments.

It was not going to be with an overgrown playboy who had a body that sent her stomach plummeting to her toes. And never with someone like Kyle.

"You're looking fierce about something," he said, turning to study her.

"What? Oh, I was just thinking. I'll order the pizza now." The phone had been installed the previous day. She walked over to the phone books that had been delivered and flipped to the right page. "Which place do you recommend?"

He set down the wet paintbrush, leaned over her shoulder and studied the list. The scent of him—male sweat, paint and something else, something subtle but compelling—drifted to her. She inhaled deeply, savoring the aroma. It made her think of tangled sheets on a Sunday morning. Of croissants and coffee after great sex.

The clear visual image startled her so much, she tried to back away. But Kyle was right behind her. She bumped into him, her head hitting his chest as her heel came down on the toe of his athletic shoes. At the moment of contact, she jerked forward and her hipbone rammed against the counter. She yelped.

"You okay?" he asked, putting his hands on her shoulders.

"Sorry," she mumbled. She could feel his fingers through her T-shirt. The heat surprised her. As well as the way her muscles turned to liquid. She cleared her throat. "Ah, which place?"

He slid one of his hands down her arm and onto the page of the phone book. "That one," he said, pointing. "Why don't you tell me what you want to order and I'll call? They'll have to deliver it to my house, anyway."

"Your house? Why?"

He stepped back. She didn't turn around. It didn't help. She could still hear the smile in his voice. "You don't have any plates here. Not to mention chairs. Don't worry, Sandy. There's nothing to be frightened of."

"I'm not afraid."

Sandy managed to get through dinner without embarrassing herself. She was thrilled. By the time all three kids had gotten cleaned up and they'd walked over to Kyle's gatehouse, it was almost time for the pizza to arrive. Between sorting out who wanted what to drink, picking off mushrooms for Blake and mopping up Nichole's spills, she'd even forgotten to be nervous. Until now.

Sandy grabbed the last of the plates from the table and carried them to the counter.

"I'll do that," Kyle said, but he didn't move from his chair in front of the window.

"I'll wash the dishes. I insist. It's the least I can do." She put the stopper in the sink and started running the water. From the living room came the musical introduction to a familiar cartoon video. "I'm a little surprised that you have videos for kids," she said without turning around.

"What did you think? That the house would be done in red velvet and paneling, with X-rated movies and mirrored ceilings? I live here, Sandy. It's my home."

Mirrored ceilings? She certainly hadn't thought that. But she had assumed there would be some signs of the seductions that must have taken place here. If the walls could talk.

She glanced around the small kitchen. Everything was clean and in its place. The floor looked swept, the only items on the counter were a pile of mail and the hat from his uniform.

"I didn't expect to find naked women in the closets, if that's what you're thinking," she said. "I would hate for us to cramp your style. It *is* Friday night."

"That's the second time you've said that. You're really hung up on which day it is, aren't you?"

"No. It's just that, well, you *are* a single man."

"And you're a single woman."

She swallowed. "No, I'm not. I'm a single mother. There's a big difference."

"Bull."

She risked glancing at him over her shoulder. He'd propped his legs up on the chair to the right of him and leaned back against the wall. His arms were raised, his hands tucked behind his head. A slow, lazy grin tugged at his mouth. He was six feet two inches of fed, satisfied, hunky male.

She forced her thoughts away from his body and back on the conversation. "If I've learned one thing in the two years Thomas has been gone, it's that most men don't want a woman with children."

"You mentioned that before, too. I happen to like kids."

"You're in the minority." She reached for the dirty plates and lowered them into the soapy water, then turned off the faucet. "It's been very enlightening to be single again. Things have changed since I was young."

"Because you're so old now?" he teased.

"I'm mature."

"You were born mature."

"Maybe." She rinsed the plates and slipped them into the dish rack. She hadn't been born mature, but she'd grown up fast in her house. She hadn't had a choice. Painful memories threatened, but she pushed them away.

"Do you miss him?" Kyle asked. His voice was quiet. "You don't have to answer that if you don't want to."

She picked up a glass and placed it in the soapy water. "Thomas, you mean? I do. Sometimes. I see him in the children. Blake looks a lot like his father. So does Nichole."

"But she has your eyes."

She almost dropped the glass. He'd noticed? Why? What did it mean? Nothing, she told herself firmly. After all, he was Kyle Haynes and she was just an ordinary person. Or she would be as soon as she got her body's reactions to him under control.

"I heard somebody mention he was a professor, right?"

"Uh-huh. Philosophy."

"You're kidding?"

She finished washing the last glass and pulled the plug. As the water swirled down the drain, she reached for a dishcloth and wiped her hands. "You sound horrified," she said, glancing at him.

"I am. Philosophy? Why would anyone do that on purpose?"

"Thomas was a very good professor."

"I bet he was. Is there a more boring subject?"

"Some people like intellectual pursuits."

Kyle didn't look convinced. "Did you guys, you know, talk about philosophy a lot? Is it something you discussed over pizza?"

"We didn't have pizza very much." Ever, she reminded herself. Maybe that's what had gone wrong in her marriage. There hadn't been enough pizza. Sandy shook her head. That was crazy. What had gone wrong in her marriage was that Thomas had refused to grow up. He'd left her in charge of everything while he'd run off to play. She'd spent most of her marriage being a single mother.

"I didn't mean to bring up unhappy memories," he said.

Sandy took the seat opposite him and rested her forearms on the table. "They're not unhappy in the way you think. It's been two years. I've gotten used to the fact that he's never coming back. The children and I have started a new life together. In many ways, it's better."

He shifted on his chair and leaned forward. Before she knew what he was going to do, he reached out his hand and touched her fingers. Sandy told herself to pull back. Except she couldn't. Sparks leapt between them. She was surprised when she didn't actually see them arcing across the table. A warm feeling of lethargy moved up her arm, heating her blood and making her yearn for something more. Something . . . dangerous.

The cartoon video played on in the background. She could hear her children talking. Beyond the house were the sounds of the night. A car driving by, crickets chirping. She felt caught in some powerful force. Slowly, she raised her gaze from the table to Kyle's chest, then higher to his face.

Stubble shaded his jaw. There was a dab of paint on one cheek. His eyes darkened to the color of a midnight sky. Her gaze dropped to his mouth and the shape of his lips. She wondered what it would be like to be kissed by that mouth. Kyle had probably kissed hundreds of women. She'd kissed about five men. No doubt she would be completely out of her league. Still, the thought had merit.

Tension crackled around them. She wanted to lean closer, but the table was too long. She thought about getting up and walking over to him. Would he pull her close and kiss her? Would he hold her in his arms and—

He yawned.

Sandy straightened, blinking frantically as if she'd just been doused with a bucket of cold water. "I hope I'm not keeping you up," she snapped.

"No." He covered his mouth with his hand and yawned again. "It's not you. I pulled a double shift last night. Normally it doesn't bother me, but I didn't get any sleep today. Sorry."

"You haven't had any sleep since the night before last?"

He shook his head. "It's catching up with me."

Now that she looked closer, she could see faint shadows under his eyes. There were lines of weariness around the mouth she'd been admiring.

"I should have realized," she said, rising to her feet. "I'll get the kids and we'll go."

"They can finish their movie."

"Nonsense. They've seen it before. You need to be in bed."

She hoped he couldn't tell what image had sprung to her head at the word *bed*. It was too embarrassing. She'd been sitting there having incredibly erotic thoughts, and he'd been struggling to stay awake. Figures.

"Okay," he said, standing. "I'm pretty tired. But I'll be back tomorrow to finish the painting."

"You don't have to."

"I want to."

"But, I—"

He grabbed her hand and pulled her close. Kyle did a whole lot of touching, she thought, wondering if she should step back or just plain give in. Her body was already humming. Jeez, she'd spent the last two years without a single sexual thought, but since arriving in Glenwood, she couldn't get sex off her brain.

"You talk too much," he said lazily. "In my experience, women who talk too much are generally hiding something."

"I'm not one of your women." She jerked her hand free, but didn't step back. "I don't have anything to hide and I don't want anything, so don't waste any of your smooth, practiced lines on me."

"I promise." He made an X over his chest, then stared down at her. "You have the most beautiful eyes."

"I thought you just promised you weren't going to try any of your lines on me."

"It's not a line, it's the truth. Green is one of my favorite colors."

She stared up at him, immobilized. She told herself to run. This wasn't happening, and if it was, it was happening too fast. She couldn't get involved with Kyle Haynes. He would use her and dump her. He was irresponsible, immature. She didn't need any more children in her life.

But the feelings he aroused in her were far from maternal. She felt trapped by the heat of his gaze. Or maybe it was her own stupidity that kept her standing so close to him, staring into his dark eyes and praying he would just kiss her and get it over with.

"Kyle, this is a mistake," she said desperately as his head lowered toward hers.

"Tell me about it. But I've been waiting sixteen damn years for this, so either run or pucker up."

Chapter Four

"Sixteen years?" Sandy asked, staring at him. He couldn't have meant what he'd said. Kyle had been waiting to kiss *her?* "What are you talking about?"

"It's not important."

Nothing in his expression gave away what he was thinking. His mouth was still impossibly tempting, his gaze steady. She must have misunderstood him. But for a brief moment, she desperately wished it had been true. That Kyle had thought of her and longed for her all this time.

Get a grip on reality, she told herself. Kyle had no more spent the last sixteen years missing her than pigs had suddenly sprouted wings and taken flight.

So why was he staring at her so intently? And why were they still standing close enough for their bodies to generate the heat required to start a bonfire?

She told herself she was a fool, but that wasn't new information. She'd suspected it for a long time. She continued to stare at his face, then lowered her gaze to his mouth.

With every bit of energy she could summon, she willed him to kiss her.

He bent forward, lowering his head until their lips nearly brushed. She could inhale the masculine scent of him, feel his sweet breath on her cheek. She could almost—

"Mommy, can we go get some ice cream?"

Nichole's voice cut through the silence in the kitchen. Sandy stepped back at the exact moment Kyle shook his head and straightened. She glanced over her shoulder, but the doorway to the living room was empty. Nichole hadn't seen anything.

"Ah, sure, honey," Sandy called.

She walked around Kyle and stepped into the other room. All three children were sitting on the floor facing the television. They didn't know what had almost happened. Relief swept through her, leaving her a little shaky. At least she told herself it was relief. The tremors in her legs couldn't possibly be the result of her having just been so close to Kyle.

"Let's go now," she said.

Lindsay glanced up at her. "The movie isn't over yet."

"I know, but you can finish it another time. It's getting late, and Kyle needs his rest. He was up working all last night."

Lindsay grumbled something under her breath, then stood up. Blake joined her without saying a word. Nichole turned off the video and the television, then bounced to her feet. "I want chocolate ice cream."

"No problem," Sandy said. She pushed the children through the kitchen, barely stopping long enough to thank Kyle for his help that day. Once outside, she took a deep breath and sent off a brief prayer of thanks that nothing had happened. If she was this nervous and shaky after *almost* kissing him, imagine what she would have been like after the real thing!

* * *

Sandy was avoiding him. Kyle dipped the brush into the can of paint, then wiped off the excess. There was no denying the truth. If he walked into a room, she walked out. Aside from mumbling a greeting to him that morning, she hadn't said a word to him. Not even to ask him how he liked his coffee. She must have asked Travis, because shortly after he'd started work, she'd silently handed him a cup, then disappeared before he could say anything. He'd taken a sip of the steaming liquid. Black, two sugars. Yup, she was avoiding him.

He glanced around the bedroom he was painting. He was about finished with the windows and the trim. Next, he would use a roller on the walls. Conversation and bits of laughter drifted up from downstairs. He knew Travis was still working down there, as were Sandy and her kids. Austin was up here with him, but in another bedroom. Kyle didn't mind the quiet, but it gave him too much time to think. About Sandy and about last night.

He shouldn't have tried to kiss her. He wouldn't have except she'd been looking at him the way a woman looks at a man she's attracted to. He was familiar with the look. He'd been getting it from women since he'd turned sixteen. It had never been anything but a convenience before. Yet last night he'd been glad Sandy was attracted to him. He'd wanted to kiss her, even knowing her kids were in the other room. Not his brightest idea. From what he remembered—and it didn't look as if she'd changed all that much—Sandy wasn't the type to fool around. Besides, she'd only been back a week. What did he really know about her?

Kyle pushed open the window, then painted over the smudge mark his fingers had made. A breeze blew into the room, chasing out the paint fumes. He set his brush on the newspaper that covered the floor and poured some paint into a tray. After screwing the extension into the roller, he started painting the ceiling.

The smooth back-and-forth movements relaxed him and freed his mind to wander. Last night, Sandy had filled his senses. Even after she'd left his house, he'd been able to inhale the scent of her body and feel her close to him. There was something about her that got to him. In sixteen years, that hadn't changed. He still remembered the first time he'd seen her. Jordan had brought her home one day after school. Kyle had been sitting at the kitchen table working on his algebra homework. The door had opened and the most beautiful girl he'd ever seen had walked into his life.

It had been spring, and warmer than usual. She'd been wearing a green dress, the exact color of her eyes. Even now, he could remember every detail about that moment. The way she'd hesitated before stepping into the kitchen, the brush of her light brown hair against her shoulders, the curiosity shining from her eyes, the way the neckline of her dress had dipped slightly, exposing nothing, but making him think about her body. He had reacted to his thoughts in a painful and embarrassing way. When he'd wanted to politely stand and greet her, he'd had to stay seated.

She'd carried her books in her arm. His brother had been holding her other hand. Kyle remembered staring at their joined hands and feeling as if he'd been punched in the stomach. The most beautiful girl in the world belonged to his brother. It was hopeless. Then she'd smiled at him. A warm, wide smile that had made him forget to breathe. After that, he hadn't cared about anything but her.

He was sure Jordan had introduced them, although he couldn't remember the conversation. He'd recognized her name. She was known as "a brain." Sensible Sandy. Travis had teased Jordan about dating her, asking if she organized his kisses the way she organized everything else. Kyle hadn't paid attention to the good-natured ribbing. He'd never understood his brother's interest in girls. Until that day.

He dipped the roller in the tray, then continued working on the ceiling. It had all happened a long time ago, yet that afternoon had been one of those significant moments that had changed his life. He'd never looked at girls the same. He'd started returning some of the teasing smiles sent his way. He'd stolen his first kiss, his first embrace, had wished for his first lover, although that hadn't happened for a few more years. But through it all, he'd dreamed of Sandy.

All this time later, he still wasn't sure what it was about her that got to him. To him, she was beautiful, but he knew most people didn't share his opinion. Her strength and intelligence had scared off lots of guys. He'd wanted to tell her it didn't scare him; he'd admired her. But she wouldn't have cared. He was two years younger than her. Now it didn't matter, but when she'd been sixteen and he'd been fourteen, those two years had seemed like an uncrossable barrier. When he'd finally gathered the courage to speak to her, she'd been friendly but not interested. He was just her boyfriend's kid brother.

He drew the roller across the flat ceiling toward the corner. He'd used the brush to paint along the edges and now he blended the paint to make a smooth coat. He grinned as he recalled how happy he'd been the day Jordan had announced he'd broken up with Sandy. The woman of his dreams was now available. He'd quickly realized not only was he too young to ask her out, but now she would stop coming to the house and he wouldn't get to see her at all. He'd spent the next few months standing outside the high school hoping for a glimpse of her.

It had been a year later that he'd walked into his kitchen and found Sandy talking with Jordan. His heart had thudded wildly in his chest, his face had flushed and his voice, which had changed two summers before, had started cracking again. For a horrible moment, he'd thought they were back together again. He quickly found out they were just friends. For reasons he could never understand, Sandy had preferred his house to her own. She'd spent much of her senior year hanging out with the Haynes brothers. By then, Kyle had been fifteen, and a high school student. By taking inconvenient routes to classes, he caught glimpses of Sandy during the day. She was nice to him, friendly but never encouraging. No matter what he did, she never really saw him as anything but Jordan's kid brother.

One night, when his mom had gone to a parent-teacher meeting, Sandy had volunteered to cook dinner. While she'd watched over a pot roast, he'd wrestled with an essay for English. Sandy had sat next to him and helped him. She'd leaned close, pointing out the awkward construction and mismatched sentences. He'd barely been able to write, with her right next to him. The scent of her body had driven him wild. He'd wanted to kiss her, to touch her, to do anything to let her know how he felt. He could still remember the freckles on her nose and the light in her eyes as she'd smiled at him.

Their arms had brushed together. Electricity had raced through him, from his head to his toes. When the paper was finished, he'd waited for her to move away, but she hadn't. He'd stretched his arms wide, yawning exaggeratedly, then he'd casually dropped his arm over her shoulders. He'd hugged several girls by then, but with Sandy he felt as if he were doing it for the first time. He couldn't think of anything to say. His mouth had gone dry, his tongue twisted up. She'd turned slightly toward him, her smile soft and knowing.

"I think you're a great guy, Kyle," she'd said. "You're going to make some girl very happy."

She should have just shot him and been done with it. Not even the brief kiss on his cheek was enough to make up for the humiliation of that moment. He'd tried and he'd failed. He didn't have a chance with her.

Kyle started on the walls of the bedroom. The hell of it was, after all this time, he still hated the way she'd dismissed him. Years later, he could still taste the defeat.

Was that what this was about? he wondered. Was he just trying to prove something to himself and maybe to Sandy? Or had those long-ago feelings simply been lying dormant, waiting for her to return?

He shook his head. That was crazy. He hadn't been waiting for her to return. But he sure wished he'd kissed her last night. The thought of holding her in his arms had kept him awake until after midnight. Maybe what he should do is—

"You're almost done in here."

He turned toward the voice and saw Lindsay walking into the bedroom. The preteen gave him a winning smile, then tossed her ponytail over her shoulder.

"It's going pretty fast," Kyle said, dipping the roller into the tray. "Whose room is this going to be?"

Lindsay moved close to him and fluttered her eyelashes. Obviously she hadn't gotten over her crush. "Mine."

He was sorry he'd asked. Still, he didn't say anything to her. He didn't want to hurt her feelings. He, of all people, knew what it was like to be dismissed by the object of his affection. Yet he didn't want to encourage her, either. The situation made him damn uncomfortable.

Lindsay crossed the room to the window. "We're going to put up a wallpaper border."

"That'll look real nice."

"You think so?"

She stared at him earnestly, as if his answer mattered more than anything. Kyle finished the wall opposite the window and nodded. "Yeah, sure it will. Did you come up to see how I was doing, or did you want something specific?''

"Oh, Mom's ordering sandwiches for lunch. What would you like?"

"Lean roast beef with everything."

She wrinkled her nose. At that moment, she looked just like her mother. Kyle grinned. "You don't approve?"

"I hate onions."

"Then I won't make you eat any."

Lindsay laughed. Kyle couldn't figure out if he was making it better or worse. Before he had a chance to decide, Travis poked his head into the room.

"Lindsay, your mom's looking for you," he said.

"Okay." She glanced at Kyle. "I've got to give her the orders. You can come downstairs if you'd like. Everyone is taking a break."

"Thanks. I'll do that." He waited until she left, then grimaced at his brother. "What am I going to do about her?"

Travis came into the room and laughed. "I can't help you, little brother. Lindsay is way out of my league."

"Thanks for nothing." Kyle slipped the roller into the tray, then turned toward the last unpainted wall. "When you were first dating Elizabeth, did you have any problems with her daughter, Mandy?"

"Mandy was six at the time. She only ever saw me as a substitute father. Can't you just tell Lindsay you're too old for her?"

"Sure. But then I'll hurt her feelings and humiliate her."

"I wish I had something better to tell you."

Kyle shrugged. "Me, too." He raised his arms and moved the roller up and down above the closet door. "I'll think of something."

Travis grinned. "I don't understand why there's a problem in the first place. You're usually so good with kids."

"It's different this time."

"Why?"

Because I think I care about Sandy. Except he didn't want to admit to that. Not yet. Just thinking about it was enough to make him break out in a cold sweat. He knew better than to care. It was dangerous. If his brothers, father and uncles had taught him one thing, it was that Haynes men didn't make good husbands and fathers. They'd been failing at it for several generations. He frowned. Except for Travis. His brother had been married for over two years. He and Elizabeth had had a daughter. They were happy. So Travis had escaped the Haynes family curse. That didn't mean Kyle was also going to get lucky.

"Maybe you should think about settling down," Travis told him.

"I'm not the type. My relationships don't last."

"That's because you leave the women before they can leave you."

"What am I supposed to do about it? Stay, and let them leave me?"

"How about trusting they might want to stay?"

Kyle put down the roller and stared at his brother. They were about the same height, with the same dark hair and eyes. Travis was four years older. His marriage had softened his hard edges and made him a happy man.

"What if they don't stay?" Kyle asked.

Travis's smile faded. "What if they do? It seems to me you're already changing things."

"What does that mean?"

"We're here." He moved his arm out to indicate the room, then the house beyond. "You've never involved your family with one of your women before."

"Sandy's not one of my women. She's—"

Travis waited, his eyebrows raised.

"Forget it," Kyle mumbled and turned back to the painting. He concentrated on moving the roller down the narrow strip of wall between the closet and the corner. "Don't you have work to do?" he asked.

"Not really. We're taking a break until the deli delivers the sandwiches. You could come down and join us. Or you could continue to hide up here."

Kyle grunted. "I'll be down when I'm done."

"Sure." Travis started out the door.

"And I'm not hiding," he called.

Travis laughed.

Kyle knew he hadn't been hiding, but Sandy was still sure avoiding him. All through lunch, she sat at the far end of the living room. Sunlight streamed through the bare windows. Someone had swept the hardwood floor, then mopped it until it gleamed. With no furniture in the large house, they'd each pulled up a piece of floor when the meal had arrived. Nichole had passed out sodas, then taken a seat near Austin. The gray-eyed pirate always had a way with the ladies, Kyle thought, watching Nichole charm the quiet man. Mercifully, Lindsay had stayed near her mother. Instead, it had been Blake who'd sat near Kyle. The boy hadn't said anything, despite Kyle's attempt to bring him into the conversation. In the end, Kyle had given up and instead, had watched Sandy not look at him.

He studied her, trying to figure out what it was exactly that got to him. In denim shorts and a red tank shirt, she was hardly dressing to be seductive. If he took her features apart, there wasn't anything special about her. Wide green eyes drew his gaze. He liked the way she wore mascara and no other makeup. Her nose was straight, her mouth turned up slightly at the corners, her chin was pointed, but not too pointed. Her body was well proportioned for her height, her breasts neither too large nor too small, her hips rounded, but not obvious. So why did she drive him crazy? Was it hormonal? Was it the result of too much reminiscing and not enough sleep?

Austin stood and stretched. "Back to work, everyone. We should be able to finish the painting today if we get going now."

Sandy scrambled to her feet. "I'll clean up," she said.

"I'll help." Kyle grabbed the wrapping from his sandwich, then picked up Blake's. The boy gave him a quick smile. The curve of the child's lips and flash of white teeth reminded him of Sandy. For a moment, he stared at the boy, wondering what it must be like to have a child of one's own. A fierce longing swept through him, shocking him with its intensity. He shook his head slightly, then continued to collect trash.

Everyone stood up and slowly left the room. At last, he and Sandy were alone.

"I can handle this," she said, not looking at him.

"I don't mind helping."

"I don't want to keep you from your painting."

"Are you afraid I'm not working hard enough?" he teased.

She'd bent over to pick up Nichole's half-eaten sandwich. Now she turned her head and looked at him. Her loose, shoulder-length hair shielded part of her face. "Not at all. I know everyone is doing a lot for me, and I really appreciate it." She tucked her hair behind her ear as she straightened. "We all do."

"I know." He walked toward her. "I was just kidding. I'll help you clean up here, then I'll go back upstairs and paint. Fair enough?"

She nodded. He wanted to think she was staring at his mouth, but he figured it was just wishful thinking on his part. No doubt about it, the lady turned him on. Unfortunately, he doubted his feelings were returned.

She continued to stare at him, then flushed slightly and looked away as if she'd just realized what she was doing. He watched the color climb up her cheeks to her hairline. The house was quiet, despite the number of people inside. He couldn't hear anything except his heart pounding in his chest and the faint whisper of Sandy's rapid breathing. At least he told himself it was rapid.

She twisted her fingers together. A paper napkin drifted from the trash she held and fluttered to the ground. He bent and grabbed it, then thrust it toward her. His fingers brushed her arm. She jumped.

"Kyle, I don't think—"

"Good," he said, cutting her off. "I know you're upset about last night."

She swallowed and stared at the center of his chest. "Last night should never have happened."

"Which part? The pizza? You and your kids eating at my house? Or what happened later?"

"What happened later."

Her voice was soft and low. He had to lean forward to hear her. She continued to stare at his chest. He wondered if she was afraid to look him in the eye because of what she would see or because of what she would reveal? He wanted it to be the latter.

"What exactly did happen?" he asked, deliberately taunting her.

She raised her gaze. He saw something hungry flash through her eyes, then she blinked and it was gone. "Nothing. Nothing at all. And I want to make sure nothing happens again."

Nothing except he'd almost kissed her and she'd almost let him. She wanted to make sure it happened again? Did she mean nothing or did she mean the kiss? "Are you sure?" he asked and moved closer.

"Yes." Her voice was a mere whisper. She trembled.

He touched her bare arm, just above the elbow. She pulled back. "I mean it, Kyle. I don't want there to be anything between us. I'm not interested."

He'd once played football with a sprained ankle and never let on until the game was over. He'd been cut pretty bad breaking up a fight and had finished his shift before going to the hospital. He'd been dumped once, a long time ago in college, and never told a soul. So it wasn't hard to continue to stare at her and not let her know what he was thinking. But inside, he reeled from the blow. As simple as that. She wasn't interested. Thanks but no thanks.

"No problem," he said, shoving his hands into his pockets.

She sighed. "I don't mean to be cruel or rude. I appreciate everything you've done for me. Bringing Travis and Austin to help, working around here, all of that. It's been great. But you and I have nothing in common. It would be best if we were just neighbors."

"Sandy, I understand. You don't have to give me a reason."

"But I want to. I want you to know it's not personal."

It felt pretty damn personal to him. She was calling the game on account of rain and he hadn't even got to bat.

She walked over to the trash bag by the entrance to the foyer and dumped the deli papers inside. "I'm not your type, and you're not mine," she told him.

What was her type? Someone like her late husband? Thomas, the philosophy professor. Someone intellectual. Someone who preferred opera to football, thick nonfiction books with footnotes to the latest spy thriller. Someone steady and dependable. Someone not like him.

"I hate for you to feel responsible for us. You don't have to keep coming over here and taking care of things. I'm really okay on my own."

In other words, get lost.

"I think you're right," he said.

"You do?" She looked doubtful.

"Sure. We'll be neighbors. Friends. We can look out for each other, but pretty much stay out of each other's lives. It's a good plan."

"Great." She smiled.

He thought his heart might start bleeding right then and there, but he didn't let on. Instead, he headed for the stairs. Friends. Neighbors. He'd sure lost his touch. He'd been thinking romance and she'd been putting him in the same class as the neighborhood golden retriever. Friends. What would Sandy say if she knew he'd been thinking, as well as friends they could also be lovers?

Chapter Five

He kept his word. Once the house was painted, Kyle disappeared from their lives as completely as if he'd never been there in the first place. He took his ready smiles, his quick wit and that way he had of looking at her that made her feel as if her bones were melting.

Sandy told herself she was pleased. It would be easier for both of them if they didn't risk getting involved. As she'd told him three days ago, he wasn't her type, she wasn't his. So what if she went up in flames every time she was near him? She would get over it. And she had. Which didn't explain why the house seemed so quiet without him and his brothers around helping.

Sandy stood at the bottom of the stairs and looked around. Her kids has been so good about helping—despite a few complaints—she'd given them a break and called in a service to clean the windows. Sunlight shone brightly through the freshly washed glass. All the rooms had been painted, the bathrooms scrubbed. Nichole and

Blake had even weeded the rose garden out back. All they needed now was for their furniture to arrive.

She walked into the kitchen, then through the utility room and out the back door. Her kids were sitting on the back porch drinking sodas. They were much too quiet.

"What's wrong?" she asked.

Lindsay studied the toe of her right athletic shoe. "Nothing. We finished papering the kitchen cupboards."

"Thanks."

Sandy took a seat next to her oldest. With Kyle no longer a daily fixture in their lives, Lindsay hadn't bothered to wear her nicest summer clothing. Today she'd pulled on a torn pair of shorts that had once been light blue but that had faded to a sort of institutional gray. Her T-shirt wasn't much better. There was a juice stain over the pocket, and one sleeve was coming off at the shoulder. Even her brown hair seemed limp, just lying on her back instead of bouncing with each step.

As usual, Blake sat off by himself, over in a corner of the porch with his back pressed against the house. Her son was playing with one of his hand-held video games for the first time since they'd moved. As she watched, his fingers moved nimbly over the buttons, destroying electronic bad guys and making his private world safe once again. His glasses slipped down his nose. Absently, he pushed them into place, then took a sip of his drink before returning his attention to his computer game.

Nichole scooted over to lean against her. "I'm hot, Mommy," her youngest told her. "Can we go swimming?"

Sandy shook her head. "We have to wait for the movers, honey. They called and said they would be here later today."

"If they don't break down again," Lindsay said.

"You're grumpy all of a sudden. What's going on?"

"I hate this place," Lindsay told her. "There's nothing to do. There are no kids my age, or anything. I can't believe you moved us here."

Mutinous brown eyes glared at her. Lindsay had Thomas's eyes. She had her father's sense of adventure. Unfortunately, she had her mother's temper. Sandy recognized a lot of the unfocused adolescent rage from her own youth in her daughter. Her little girl was growing up fast.

"You didn't seem to mind it too much a few days ago."

"A few days ago, something was going on around here."

Yeah, Kyle had been a part of their lives. Okay, so they all missed him. They would get over it. After all, they'd only known him a few days.

Sandy wished she could make her kids believe it was going to be all right. They would make friends and settle into a routine soon enough. She reminded herself change was never easy, but it was often for the best.

A loud rumbling broke the stillness of the afternoon. Lindsay straightened, even Blake looked up from his game.

"The truck's here!" Nichole crowed. She grinned at her mother.

Sandy reached out and ruffled the little girl's red curls. "I think you're right. Let's go see."

Nichole took Sandy's hand and skipped down the stairs next to her. Lindsay and Blake followed more slowly. As they rounded the house, Sandy saw a large moving van backing up down the long driveway. The driver checked his mirror, then glanced at someone waving him in from the porch. Sandy looked at the man who was standing there as if he owned the place.

Her heart told her who it was even before she recognized the tall, lean body and the short dark hair. Her knees quivered slightly and her breath caught in her throat. He hadn't gone away. She was a fool, from the top of her head down to her toes. A fool and glad he was there.

"Kyle!" Lindsay called as soon as she saw him. "What are you doing here?"

"Helping." He gave her a smile, but his gaze met Sandy's. "I saw the truck and figured you'd need some."

"Thanks," Sandy said, climbing up the side stairs to the wide, wooden porch. When she got close to him, she felt awkward. "You didn't have to."

"I wanted to," he said. "Just being neighborly."

The trunk jerked to a halt with the back end a few feet from the porch. Two men jumped out of the cab, then the driver, Al, climbed down. She recognized him from when he'd come to pick up her belongings in Los Angeles.

"Ms. Walker," the older man said, "we finally got here. Sorry about the delay."

Nichole rushed to the edge of the stairs. "Can we do my room first?"

Al grinned. "We sure can try, little lady. Come on, boys, let's get this stuff unloaded."

The back doors of the truck came off completely. The men stretched them across to the porch, eliminating the need to go up and down the stairs with the furniture. Al opened a side door to the truck. While his men were unstrapping the furniture, he walked toward her.

"If you could show me the layout of the house, we'll put everything where it's supposed to go. I didn't see any writing on your boxes. How are you going to know where they're going?"

Lindsay rolled her eyes. "Don't even ask. Mom has a system for everything. Wait until you see it."

"My room's pink," Nichole said.

"Pink?" Al asked.

"There are colored dots on all the boxes," Sandy said. "Come with me and I'll show you."

She'd tacked a big poster up in the foyer. Different colored dots lined the left side of the white cardboard. Next to each dot was the place those boxes went. "Red dots go in the kitchen, pink is for Nichole, dark blue for Blake and so on."

Al removed his Dodgers' baseball cap and grinned. "Well, I'll be."

"There's more," Nichole said. She pointed. "Look there."

Everyone looked up. A colored balloon floated from the doorway of each of the rooms. The color matched the dots on the chart.

"We should be able to unload your furniture in less than two hours," Al said.

"Great." Sandy was pleased. It had taken all day to load it. "Kids, you stay out of the men's way. I don't want you getting hurt. As soon as there are some boxes in your room, you can start unpacking."

"Swell," Lindsay grumbled.

"I'm here to help," Kyle said, falling into step with Al as the older man returned to the van. He paused by the door and turned back toward her. "I like the dots. I always said, given the chance, you could organize the world."

Sandy grinned. "I know I could!"

Two hours later, the van was gone, the furniture was in place and there were three hundred boxes to be unpacked. Sandy stood in the center of the foyer and wondered where on earth she was going to begin. She could hear the children in their rooms. Lindsay would get her things unpacked just fine, but Nichole and Blake would probably create bigger messes than they would fix. At least they were busy and not underfoot.

Her personal stuff could wait. She'd marked a couple of boxes with linens for the family, so those could be opened immediately. Next, she would start on the kitchen things.

Kyle came in the front door and walked over to stand in front of her. He had a couple of screwdrivers and a pair of pliers in his left hand. His white T-shirt advertised a local ice-cream store, his black shorts left far too much of his tanned legs bare to view. Telling herself he wasn't really *that* good-looking did nothing to calm her nerves. Usually, she could talk herself out of or into just about anything. It was how she'd stayed sane while Thomas was alive and acting like a child. She'd convinced herself that one day he would grow up. With the perfect vision of hindsight, she knew now that probably wouldn't have happened. But no matter how she tried, she couldn't seem to convince her hormones that Kyle wasn't worth getting excited about.

"I thought I'd hook up the cable," he said, pointing toward the family room.

"I appreciate the help, but I don't want you to think you have to be here. If it's your day off, you should be doing something you want to do."

He held her gaze for a long time. Part of the reason she wanted him gone was that she felt a little guilty for throwing him out the last time he'd been here. She could have been a little nicer about the whole thing. He'd been wonderful to her and her kids. But she couldn't risk getting involved. Even a one-sided crush, much like Lindsay's, would upset things too much.

He smiled slowly, exposing white teeth and making the skin by the outside corners of his eyes crinkle. Her heart fluttered foolishly. "I'm here because I want to be," he said. "Haven't you figured that out yet?"

"Oh."

Oh? Was that the best she could come up with? she asked herself. Why did he want to be here? Was he toying with her, lulling her into thinking he might, well, sort of find her slightly attractive, only to dump her at the first opportunity?

She almost asked the question, then realized that perhaps she needed to work on her self-esteem first. Kyle had been nothing but sweet and friendly since they'd arrived. She was the one acting skittish. But why wouldn't she? She was a single mom with three kids. She had a tendency to be bossy and mouthy. She was working on her flaws but she was still far from being perfect. Or glamorous. So why was he being so nice to her?

"Thanks," she said at last, then brushed her suddenly damp palms against her shorts. "The TV goes in the entertainment center. The VCR sits on the shelf above that."

His smile widened to a grin. "I think I can figure it out."

"Great."

But he didn't move. Instead, he stood there, looking sinfully handsome, staring at her. Self-consciously, she reached up and fingered her hair. It was loose this morning, held off her face by a headband. She wasn't wearing any makeup. She probably looked old and messy. Nothing that a man like him would—

A knock on the door interrupted her thoughts. She frowned. "I'm not expecting anyone," she said as she crossed the floor to the front door.

A pretty, dark-haired woman holding a sleeping toddler in one arm and a diaper bag in the other smiled. "Hi, I'm Elizabeth. This is my daughter Jessica, and Mandy is around here, somewhere. Honey, where are you?"

"We're coming, Mommy."

Sandy stared past the woman and saw a young girl racing up the porch stairs. She was holding a casserole dish in her hands. "We brung food," she said, then stopped slightly behind her mother, as if suddenly shy.

"Brought," Elizabeth said. "I swear, hanging out with your father's relatives is doing nothing for your education." She smiled fondly at her daughter, then glanced back at Sandy. "She knows more about the Forty-niners' starting lineup than she does about any of her subjects at school. Oh, you still look confused. I'm sorry. I'm Travis's wife. We've come to help you unpack."

"Elizabeth, come on in," Kyle said, coming to the door. "Mandy, how's my favorite munchkin?"

The little blond girl giggled. "I'm not a munchkin, Uncle Kyle."

"I keep forgetting. Maybe it's because all munchkins have blond hair just like you." He bent down and touched the two braids brushing against her shoulders.

"Do they?" she asked, her blue eyes wide and questioning.

"Kyle," Elizabeth said, the tone in her voice warning him to tread carefully. "Stop torturing my daughter."

Kyle chuckled, then took the casserole dish from Mandy. "No, honey, they don't."

Travis strolled up the stairs. He placed his hand on his wife's waist and guided her into the house. "Sandy, this is my wife, Elizabeth, and my daughters Mandy and little Jessica." He glanced fondly at the sleeping toddler. "We're here to help you unpack. Where would you like us to start?"

Sandy was speechless. She didn't know whether to be pleased or insulted. Kyle had arranged for people to help her without asking her first. She should hate that. Yet the gesture was so thoughtful. She liked Travis; there was every reason to believe she would like his wife, and she didn't have any friends in Glenwood yet.

Before she could think of what to say, Kyle took charge. He sent Mandy upstairs with instructions on how to find Nichole's room, thrust the casserole dish into Sandy's hands, then ushered Travis into the family room, where he promised they would take care of the "man" work.

Elizabeth stared after them, then laughed. "I guess that leaves all the women's work for us." She shifted the toddler in her arms. "It's Jessica's nap time," she explained. "She had a busy morning playing in the backyard. And driving in the car always puts her to sleep."

"You can put her on my bed," she said. "It would only take a minute to get the sheets unpacked."

"No, that's too much like work and we're going to have enough of that already." Elizabeth glanced into the living room. The floral-print sofa facing the wide windows had fluffy pillows. "Would you mind if she slept there?" she asked, nodding in the direction of the sofa.

"Of course not."

In a couple of minutes, Jessica was curled on the couch with her favorite stuffed toy, a lion missing an ear and the end of its tail. Elizabeth pulled a light blanket over the sleeping child. "She's our miracle baby," she said, straightening and following Sandy into the kitchen.

"Did you have trouble getting pregnant?"

Elizabeth laughed. "Not at all. But until Jessica, there hadn't been a girl born into the Haynes family in four generations."

Sandy set the casserole on the counter. "I didn't know that."

"That's a chicken-broccoli thing," Elizabeth said, motioning to the covered dish. "Just heat it in the oven at 350° for about a half hour and it will be fine."

"Thanks for bringing the food. I really appreciate your thoughtfulness. So will my kids when I'm too tired to cook. After a week of living in a motel, even they're getting tired of take-out for dinner every night."

Elizabeth stared at the piles of boxes. They filled the large space, with several pushed up against the wall and a few on the kitchen table. "Where should I start?"

"You don't have to help."

"That's why we're here, Sandy. Kyle put the word out. He's been there for us, so we're happy to help one of his friends."

Elizabeth didn't hesitate before saying the word *friend* but even so, Sandy wondered what Kyle had said about her. Or what he hadn't.

She looked at the boxes, then at the empty cupboards. How on earth was she going to get this house in some kind of order? "Feel free to open whatever box strikes your fancy," she said. "I've pretty much decided where everything should go."

"Sounds good to me." Elizabeth reached for the one closest to her and drew open the flaps. "Canned goods," she said, peering inside.

"The pantry cupboard is right there." Sandy pointed to the closed door on the other side of the double oven.

Elizabeth carried the box over to the counter closest to the pantry and started unpacking. "Kyle said you just moved to town. What made you decide on Glenwood, if you don't mind my asking?"

"My husband died a couple of years ago. After everything settled down, I decided I didn't want to raise my kids in Los Angeles. I'd lived in Glenwood for a few years when I was a teenager, so when a job teaching at the junior college opened up, I moved us here." She wrinkled her nose. "So far, it's not a popular decision with the family."

Elizabeth smiled. "It will get better. I moved here from L.A., too, although I wasn't a widow. So your husband passed away two years ago?"

"Yes."

"And you've recovered?"

Sandy paused. *Recovered* wasn't the word she would have chosen. That implied an emotional bereavement. She missed Thomas, but she hadn't mourned him as the lost love of her life. "I'm making a fresh start, if that's what you mean."

"It's good enough."

"How long have you lived here?" Sandy asked.

"Three years." Elizabeth placed the last can in the pantry and turned the empty box over. While she worked the bottom free so the box could lay flat, she stared off into the distance. Her brown eyes took on a dreamy expression. "I met Travis the second day I was here. He pulled me over for speeding."

Sandy stared at her. "That sounds really romantic."

"Oh, it was." She laughed. "I know it doesn't sound like much, but I had appendicitis, and he rushed me to the hospital. While I was there, he took care of Mandy, and when I was released, he insisted I stay with him while I recuperated. I didn't know a soul in town, I had a new job I wasn't going to be able to start and he was just there. My own personal knight in shining armor." She picked up another box and looked inside. "Glasses," she said, rustling the tissue they'd been wrapped in.

"Cupboard next to the sink," Sandy said, pointing.

Elizabeth carried the box around the piles in the center of the floor and set it down. "Jordan says the reason Jessica is the first girl born to the Haynes family in four generations is that we're the first couple to be in love and faithful to each other." She pulled out the first glass and set it on the shelf. "*I* think it's because my mother is one of four girls and her mother is one of six girls. All the relatives on her side of the family only ever have girls. Maybe our body chemistry only likes girl sperm. Of course, I would never tell Jordan that and ruin his theory."

Sandy cleared her throat. She emptied the box of plates and bowls and moved on to one filled with plastic food-storage containers. "How is Jordan? I mean, I knew him in high school. I'm curious as to how he—"

"Turned out?" Elizabeth grinned. She had a pretty, heart-shaped face with big eyes and a ready smile. "He's the quiet one of the bunch. He still keeps to himself. Travis calls him the black sheep because he became a fire fighter instead of a sheriff. He's still single,'' she added hopefully.

"No, thanks. Jordan and I were destined to be friends. We tried dating for a while, but it never worked out."

Elizabeth crossed the room. When she was standing next to Sandy, she spoke in a quiet voice. "What were they really like in high school? Were they as wild as everyone says?"

Sandy remembered her few dates with Jordan. He never tried to kiss her, so she couldn't speak to that reputation. She thought about the afternoons she'd spent in the Haynes family's kitchen, helping Kyle with his homework, listening to Craig, the oldest, brag about his exploits with the college girls or just talking with Jordan. "I think they were lonely. Their father was never here, their mother was angry all the time. I don't want to blame her, she lived in a difficult situation, but I think she could have done better for the boys. She should have taken them away, or not left so abruptly." She shook her head. "I shouldn't be second-guessing the poor woman. I can't imagine what it must have been like living with their father."

"Have they changed?" Elizabeth asked.

"No. They're still good-looking charmers with the ability to make a woman weak in the knees."

"Oh?" Elizabeth raised her eyebrows. "Is it all the Haynes men who make you react like that or is it just Kyle?"

"Just—" Sandy clamped her mouth shut. "I see Travis has been teaching you how to grill prisoners."

Elizabeth laughed. "Your secret is safe with me." She leaned closer. "Travis has this trick he does with his cowboy hat. It's silly, really. He takes it off and tosses it across the room. It always lands exactly where he wants it to." She rolled her eyes. "Drives me crazy. All he has to do is toss that damn hat and I'm putty in his hands. The worst part is he knows it and uses it against me. I can't stay mad at the man for more than two minutes at a time."

Elizabeth walked back over to the box on the counter and continued putting away glasses. Sandy bent over and thrust a handful of plastic covers onto a bottom shelf. She would organize them later. But instead of thinking about tidy stacks of food containers, she remembered how Travis had placed his hand on the small of Elizabeth's back as he'd escorted her into the house. She could see the look on his face as he'd stared down at his sleeping daughter. Thomas had never been one to bother with polite gestures and he'd never sat still long enough to watch the children sleep. If he wanted to play with them and they were napping, he just woke them up.

"Travis says Kyle was hurt the worst by his mother leaving," Elizabeth said.

Sandy flattened the empty box and reached for another. "He was. I'd forgotten about that, but I do remember when it happened. It was summer, right after Kyle turned fifteen. Jordan called and asked me to come over. All four boys were sitting there, around the kitchen table." She frowned at the memory. "They looked lost. Even Craig who was already on his own. I cooked dinner, I don't remember what, then sat up with Jordan and Kyle. Travis left to do something." Sandy remembered a pretty redhead who'd come by to offer comfort, but she didn't think Elizabeth would want to hear about that.

"I'm sure he was with a woman," Elizabeth said evenly. "Don't look so surprised that I guessed. Travis has been very honest with me about his past. I know why his first marriage failed, and the names of all the girlfriends he can remember. He spent a lot of time believing he didn't have what it takes to be a decent husband or father. I don't mind about what happened before he met me. As long as he doesn't try what his father did."

"Yeah, that was pretty awful." At least Thomas had been faithful to her. It hadn't been enough, but she consoled herself that things between them could have been worse. She fingered her ring.

"Kyle believes—" Elizabeth stopped and stared at her. Her brown eyes widened. "Oh, no. I'm so sorry. I didn't realize. When Kyle asked me over to help you and wanted us to meet, I sort of assumed... I'm sorry."

"What?" Sandy asked, baffled.

Elizabeth pointed to the ring Sandy still wore. "You must have loved your husband very much. I shouldn't be going on about Kyle when you're still in mourning. I'm sorry."

"Please don't apologize. I'm not still in mourning. I do wear the ring to remind me of Thomas, but not for the reasons you might think." She used this symbol of their marriage as a talisman against making the same mistake twice. She didn't want to get involved with someone who refused to grow up. Someone who wouldn't take his responsibilities seriously, and who would rather have a good time than do what was right.

"He must have been a special man," Elizabeth said.

Sandy was saved from answering when Kyle came in the room. He was carrying another casserole dish. He set it on the counter. "Nichole and Mandy have become fast friends," he said. "The TV and VCR are working great. Travis is assembling Blake's bunk beds and Lindsay is unpacking her clothes. The kid has a lot of them, huh?"

Sandy blinked. She didn't know which question to address first. "What's that?" she asked instead, pointing to the foil-covered dish.

Elizabeth started to chuckle. She put her hand over her mouth to muffle the sound, but even so, Kyle glared at her. "It's a casserole," he said, then turned to Elizabeth. "What's so funny? I'm just being neighborly."

Sandy wondered how long those words would come back to haunt her. "It's very nice, Kyle," she said.

"It's a yam casserole," he told her.

"Yams?"

"Don't you like them?"

"Sure, it's just... Thanks, really."

Elizabeth burst out laughing. "I knew it. Oh, Kyle, come over one afternoon and I'll teach you to make something else."

He frowned at his sister-in-law. Sandy didn't know what was going on, but it was pretty obvious his male pride had been bruised. "I'm happy with the yams, Elizabeth. Everyone else seems to like them."

"They're delicious, but maybe you could try branching out. Maybe a different vegetable, or something with meat."

"I'll go help Travis," he said, addressing no one in particular. He stalked out of the room.

Elizabeth continued to laugh, then finally quieted and wiped her eyes. "I shouldn't be so hard on him."

"What's the problem? Is the casserole awful?"

"No, it's wonderful. You're going to love it. It's just that it's all he knows how to make. It doesn't matter if it's a barbecue, the holidays or something like this. If he's expected to bring food, Kyle shows up with his yam casserole." She leaned over and lifted the foil, then plucked out one of the miniature marshmallows and stuck it into her mouth.

Elizabeth eyed her speculatively. "You should be honored. Now that I think about it, Kyle has only made his yams for family. He must think you're very special."

Sandy felt a blush climbing up her cheeks. She turned back to the box she'd been unpacking and started working. She didn't want to think about that. She didn't want to know why Kyle was being so nice to her. She was afraid if she allowed herself to hope, she would do something foolish, like maybe start to care. And she couldn't. Not about him. She knew exactly what she wanted in a man. This time she wasn't going to make a mistake. Kyle Haynes couldn't be more wrong for her.

Chapter Six

Kyle stood on Sandy's porch and shifted his weight from one foot to the other. He stared at the door.

Leave, he told himself. She didn't want him around, and he wasn't the sort of guy who showed up where he wasn't welcome. She'd made her feelings clear. Friends. Neighbors. Nothing more. So why was he standing here about to make a fool of himself? Why couldn't he resist her?

Maybe it went back to high school. Maybe deep inside him, some fourteen-year-old kid wanted his second chance. The years they'd been apart had done nothing to change his attraction to her. He only had to think about her, to see her smile, or watch her touch one of her kids, and he started wishing he was the kind of man who believed in love, marriage and forever. But he didn't. He believed that people he cared about left him. Sooner or later, whether they'd intended to or not, they disappeared.

So he left first. Because it was easier and safer. So what the hell was he doing standing on Sandy's porch? She wasn't the short-term affair type. She was a responsible woman, a widow with three kids. They had nothing in common. He should be grateful she was pushing him away. But he wasn't. He couldn't stop thinking about her, wanting her, wanting to be with her. He would either have to get over it, or get used to making a fool of himself.

He knocked on the door, then stepped back a couple of steps. He heard conversation inside, then Sandy called, "Fine, *I'll* get it." Seconds later, the door jerked open and she barked, "Yes? What do you want?" Then her gaze focused on him.

"Hi." He gave her his best smile, the one all the Haynes brothers had mastered. The one that brought women to their knees and made dogs roll over to have their bellies scratched. Sandy blinked. A flush stole up from the collar of her faded green cotton shirt. Her mouth parted slightly as if she was having trouble breathing. Her eyes widened and she self-consciously touched her hand to her cheek. Of course, that was *his* interpretation of her actions. For all he knew, she was wondering what it was going to take to get rid of her annoying neighbor. He preferred his version.

She wasn't wearing any makeup. He could see the tiny lines beside her eyes and the faint scattering of freckles across the bridge of her nose. There was a smudge of dirt on her chin. His gaze traveled lower, to the equally faded green shorts hugging her hips, to her long tanned legs and bare feet. She'd painted her toenails bright pink.

He widened his grin. She leaned against the doorframe and sighed.

"I've spent the last three days up to my neck in boxes," she said. "Blake and Lindsay are fighting, Nichole is clinging to me, making it hard to get anything done. I haven't had time to a shower in the last forty-eight hours, there's no milk or bread in the house. This is a really bad time for me, Kyle. I have no power to resist you. So please, just be a gentleman and leave me to fall apart in private."

He wanted to believe she meant what she said, that he really got her to. But he wasn't that lucky.

"I want to take the kids to an early movie and dinner," he said. "We'll pick up milk and bread on the way back and be home by eight. Say yes and I'll get them out of your way."

She stared at him as if he were speaking in a foreign language. "What?"

"I want to take your three children—" he held up the appropriate number of fingers "—to a movie. You know, at a theater. Then dinner." He mimicked eating. "Tonight. In about fifteen minutes. Can they be ready?"

"Why are you doing this?"

"To give you a break. You can unpack in peace, or just relax. Maybe take a long bubble bath." He folded his arms over his chest and tried not to think about his last suggestion. He was going to be in the company of children in a few minutes.

Her gaze narrowed. "What do you want with my children?"

"You make it sound like I want to kidnap them. Trust me." Her skeptical gaze told him trusting wasn't going to come easily to her. "You're the one who said we were friends," he reminded her. "I'm just helping you out."

He watched as she made up her mind. Emotions chased across her face. Finally, she sighed and nodded. "You win. I could use a break. They'll be ready in fifteen minutes." She shut the door, then opened it quickly. "Thanks." The suspicion was gone from her green eyes, leaving them wide and bright. "I appreciate this."

"My pleasure."

A half hour later, he parked the car behind the movie theater. Nichole and Blake scrambled out from the back seat. Lindsay sat in the passenger seat. Waiting. For him to come open her door, like this was some date. He closed and locked his door, then slowly walked around the car. He didn't want to encourage her, but he didn't want their evening to get off to a bad start by letting her sit there until she was forced to get out herself. All three kids had been pleased with the thought of getting out of the house and away from the unpacking.

He opened the passenger door. Lindsay gave him what she no doubt thought was her most grown-up smile, then stepped out.

Nichole and Blake were in shorts and clean T-shirts, but Lindsay had put on a white cotton dress. Her hair was pulled back in a French braid and lipstick darkened her mouth. He suspected Sandy didn't know about the lipstick, because Lindsay had put it on in the car. He'd tried not to notice and wished he knew what he was going to do about her crush. He didn't want to hurt her feelings, but she was starting to make him nervous. He had to watch what he said or did around her so she wouldn't misinterpret his words or actions. It was a pain. If only he could tell Lindsay that he liked her just fine the way she was. Like all of Sandy's children, she was a good kid. He suspected Lindsay wouldn't appreciate the comment, so he kept it to himself. Eventually, she would get the message. He hoped it wasn't too painful. He knew what it was like to be rejected by the object of his affection.

As they walked toward the theater, he grabbed Nichole's hand and placed his free arm around Blake's neck, leaving Lindsay to trail behind him. Subtle, Haynes, he told himself. Very subtle.

"You guys know what you want to see?" he asked as they approached the ticket window. There was a cartoon adventure movie starting in a few minutes.

Both Nichole and Blake pointed to that movie poster. Lindsay patted her little sister's head. "They're still such children. We could dump them at the cartoon and go see that one together," she said, pointing at another poster.

He looked at the second poster. It advertised a romantic comedy and showed a couple kissing. Kyle swallowed hard. Even if it hadn't been rated R he still would have refused. The movie wasn't really his kind, so if he had to sit through it, he would want it to be with Sandy.

"I want to see the cartoon, too," he said, heading toward the ticket booth. "Three against one. Sorry, Lindsay."

He let go of Blake long enough to pay for the tickets, then led them into the theater. There was a long line at the concession stand. They decided to find seats first. Once that was done, with Lindsay maneuvering to sit next to him, and him maneuvering to avoid that, he sent the girls off to buy the popcorn and sodas.

The theater filled up with parents and their kids. Kyle hadn't been to a children's movie since the holidays, when he'd taken Craig's brood. Sitting there in the noisy theater, he suddenly realized he'd missed the high-pitched conversation and laughter. Kids seemed to enjoy everything more. He watched a little girl carefully walk down the slanted aisle carrying a full bag of popcorn. When she made it to the row her mother had pointed to, she looked up and smiled in triumph.

Several boys chased one another up and down the aisle, but Blake didn't show any interest in the activity around him. He sat silently, staring at his lap. Kyle was surprised that the boy was always so quiet. He and his brothers had been loud enough for a dozen kids, or so their mother had told him. He couldn't remember ever sitting quietly, unless he was sick. Craig's three boys were the same.

"What do you think of the house?" Kyle asked. "It must seem more like home with all your stuff there."

"It's okay."

Blake pushed up his glasses, then glanced at Kyle. He wondered if the kid missed his father.

"There are lots of boys in the neighborhood. Have you met any of them yet?"

Blake shook his head and lowered his gaze back to his lap.

"Maybe I could introduce you to them," he offered.

Blake shrugged.

Kyle searched his memory for something he'd liked when he was Blake's age. There had to be a way to get the boy to open up. Being this well behaved wasn't natural.

Finally, he settled on the one thing they had in common. "I know it's hard to settle into a new place where everything's different. It probably makes you miss your dad more."

Blake shrugged again and continued to stare at his lap.

"My mom left when I was fifteen," Kyle said. "I had a hell, ah, a difficult time after she was gone. I missed her a lot."

"I've heard that word before. Mom says it's bad, but grown-ups say it all the time."

"Gee, thanks."

Blake gave him a quick smile, then the corners of his mouth turned down. "Did your mom die?"

"No. She just walked out."

"Oh. Sometimes people talk about my dad leaving, but I know he's dead. He's not coming back. Ever."

"I'm sorry."

"He didn't like me much." Blake hunched forward as soon as he spoke, as if he regretted the confession.

"Blake, your father loved you." He was sure of it. Sandy wouldn't have stood for anything less.

"He was gone a lot."

"Traveling on business?" He wouldn't have thought a professor would need to go away on business too often. Maybe there were big conferences on philosophy. Kyle grimaced. He'd rather be flogged and left out for ant bait than attend a convention where stuffy professors spent days discussing the lofty thoughts of some dead guy.

Blake shook his head. "He'd go surfing or climb a mountain. Sometimes he took Lindsay. She liked to do that stuff with him. Dad got mad when I read too much, or played on the computer. He wanted me to be on a Little League team, but I didn't want to. He took me climbing with him once, but he made fun of me when I got scared."

It was the longest speech he'd heard from Blake. His heart went out to the boy. But none of what he said made sense. Why would Thomas have been so mean to his son? So what if Blake wasn't the outdoor type? That didn't mean he wasn't a good kid. Maybe the boy had misunderstood his father.

He leaned back in his chair and knew he was kidding himself. If Blake thought his father was a selfish jerk, then the man had probably been one to the boy. Kyle knew he and his brothers had figured out what was going on with his parents long before anyone else suspected they knew. Children heard things and sensed the changes in a situation. So why had Thomas acted that way around Blake? Where was Sandy in all of this? He couldn't imagine her letting anyone hurt her son.

Kyle leaned close to Blake. "You know, I've never been very good at video games. Is there a trick to it?"

"Yeah." Blake grinned. "You have to practice, and stuff, but there are some secrets. I could show you."

"I'd like that."

The boy stared at him for several seconds, then smiled. Kyle ruffled his hair and grinned back.

"Tomorrow?" Blake asked. "I could bring the game by."

"Check with your mom first. If she agrees, that would be great." He glanced over his shoulder and saw the girls heading back, their arms filled with bags of popcorn. "We better give them a hand before they spill everything," he said, standing.

Blake giggled. It was, Kyle thought, a very happy sound.

Kyle eased his car to a stop in front of Sandy's house. A quick glance at the clock told him it was 8:05, exactly. Before he figured out how he was going to handle Lindsay getting out of the car, Nichole was pushing against the front seat and ordering her sister to move. Lindsay got out grudgingly. She hadn't been that happy with him since he'd had Blake sit on one side of him and Nichole on the other at the theater. She'd claimed the movie had been juvenile and hadn't spoken in the restaurant afterward or on the way home.

Sandy stood on the porch. Kyle couldn't read her expression. He got out slowly and grabbed the plastic bag containing the milk and bread they'd picked up, then slammed the door shut and headed toward the stairs. The children crowded ahead of him.

Nichole reached her mother first. "Mommy, Mommy, we had popcorn, then Kyle took us to dinner and I had spaghetti. I didn't spill very much and there was ice cream for dessert, but I was too full." Her red curls danced as she told Sandy what had happened. Her small body quivered with excitement. She flung her arms around her mother's waist. "I had the best time, and Lindsay was a brat only part of the time."

"You better watch it," Lindsay warned, glaring at her younger sister.

"I'm glad you had a good time, Nichole. Go on inside," Sandy said, giving her daughter a little push. "Did you have fun, Blake?" she asked as the boy approached.

Blake glanced back at Kyle and grinned. "Yeah." Then he ducked indoors.

Lindsay paused by her mother. "It was a cartoon. Can you believe it? The children there were so immature. Nichole and Blake hardly know how to act in a restaurant. You really need to do something about them, Mother."

"Maybe I'll do something about you, young lady," Sandy said.

Lindsay sniffed, then turned to Kyle. "Thank you for a lovely evening."

He paused on the top stair, confused. "It was..." Damn, he didn't know what to say. "I'm glad you three kids could join me."

Lindsay visibly flinched. "I'm not a child, Kyle."

Sandy saved him by taking the grocery bag from him and handing it to her daughter. "Honey, put this away for me. I need to have a little talk with Kyle."

Lindsay paused by the door as if she had something else to say, then she swept inside and let the screen bang shut behind her.

Kyle sat on the top stair and patted the wood. Sandy crossed the porch and perched next to him. She wasn't sitting very close. He could fit a whole other person between them, but it was probably as good as it was going to get. She folded her arms over her chest. Was she protecting herself from him or holding something inside? Did he really want to know?

He stared at the sky. It was still only midsummer. The sun didn't set until close to nine. It had dipped below the trees. The temperature was lower, though the evening air was still warm and pleasant. He could smell the jasmine by the house. He had a bush blooming by his back door. He liked the sultry scent, although not as much as the fragrance of Sandy's shampoo. She was too tense to have soaked in a bath, so he figured she'd taken time for a quick shower and nothing else.

"Why are you mad?" he asked. "We were on time. No one got hurt, or food poisoning, at least not yet."

"How do you know I'm mad?" she asked.

"If your spine was any stiffer, we could use it for a flagpole."

She surprised him by smiling. "A flagpole?"

"Well, maybe not a flagpole, but something."

Her smile faded. "You were five minutes late."

He glanced at her. "You're kidding, right? You can't be mad about that."

"I'm not." She glanced at her folded arms and shrugged. "Okay, I'm a little mad. But you're right, five minutes isn't very late."

"Were you worried?"

"Maybe. No. Yes."

"Why?" he asked. "Were you seriously concerned that I'd let something bad happen to them?"

"Not exactly. I wasn't being that rational. You asked if you could take them to a movie and dinner, and I was so grateful to be without them for a few hours that I said yes. Then when you were gone, I got scared. I realized I don't know you. What if you have some secret past no one knows about? What if—" She glanced up at him. Her green eyes were dark and troubled. "I overreacted, I guess. Probably because I'm so tired."

"Aw, honey, everything was fine."

"I see that now. It looks like everyone had a great time."

She hunched over slightly, resting her forearms on her bare thighs. She'd changed clothes while he'd been gone. She wore a sleeveless shirt tucked into red shorts. He wanted to slide next to her and give her a big hug. Or maybe just hold her close. Sandy looked as if she needed a little holding. But he didn't move. For one thing, she would probably get all huffy and push him away. For another, he was assuming an awful lot.

Maybe she didn't want to be comforted by him. After all, she'd been the one so set on keeping them "just friends." Kyle grimaced. How many times had he said that exact line to a woman he was dumping? They must have hated it as much. He swore he was never going to say it to anyone again.

"I'm not surprised you're feeling overwhelmed," he said. "This is a lot of responsibility for one person."

"Because I'm a woman, right?"

He turned until he was facing Sandy. His back pressed against the railing. He bent one leg at the knee and put that foot on the porch. His other foot rested on the bottom step. "You have a real problem with this woman thing, don't you? Have I ever said anything about your being a woman? Have I ever hinted that you couldn't do something because you're a woman?" He raised his eyebrows and waited.

She cleared her throat. "Well, not in so many words."

"Ah-ha! So you're *assuming* that's what I'm thinking. Why?"

"I know men like you, Kyle."

"Men like me?" He had a feeling he knew what she was getting at, but he wanted to hear the words. And he wanted to see her squirm, just a little, for being so quick to judge him.

"Men who have an easy time with, you know, women." She glanced at him out of the corner of her eye. "Stop looking at me like that... You want me to say it, don't you?"

He grinned. "Oh, yes. More than anything."

"Good-looking men. Okay? Are you happy? Most good-looking men assume all women are stupid. I guess because women have been doing stupid things to get their attention. Maybe I should stop jumping to conclusions about you, but it's difficult."

He wanted to strut around the yard like a rooster. Sandy thought he was good-looking. It didn't make a damn bit of difference, but he was pleased as hell. It meant she'd been thinking about him, and not just as her neighbor. At least he hoped it did.

"I'll accept that you think I'm handsome and incredibly charming—"

"I didn't say anything about being charming," she interrupted.

He ignored her. "*And* incredibly charming, if you'll accept the fact that I don't assume you're incapable of doing things simply because you're female. I have great respect for women."

She snorted. "I'll just bet you do. You must respect them all the way through that revolving door in your bedroom."

"Is that what you think?" he asked, his voice low and controlled. His smile faded along with his good humor. "Is that why you were upset when I took the kids? Do you think I was meeting with some woman and dragging them along?" His flash of anger surprised him. "I would never do anything like that. Despite my reputation, I don't have a revolving door in my bedroom, I don't bring women to my house and I sure as hell wouldn't act inappropriately in front of your children."

He started to stand up. Sandy leaned toward him and placed her hand on his forearm. Her gaze met his. "I'm sorry," she said. "Really. I didn't really think that about you, and I shouldn't have implied it. You were teasing me, and I couldn't think of anything funny to say, so I just lashed back. It was wrong of me. I'm sorry."

"Apology accepted," he said. He settled back down.

She squeezed his arm briefly, then withdrew her hand to her lap. "Getting back to your original statement, yes, this has been a lot of responsibility for just one person. Even for a woman." She gave him a slight smile. He returned it. The tension between them eased.

But his anger continued to lurk below the surface. Later, when he was alone, he decided, he would think about what she'd said and what it meant. He was annoyed that she'd heard enough about him to think he was irresponsible where women were concerned. Of course, she might just be assuming the worst based on what she remembered about his brothers.

"I worry about the kids," she said. "What if they hate it here?"

"We both liked it when we were their ages."

"That was a long time ago. Kids have changed."

"Not that much," he said. "Times have changed. It's tough now. There are more ways for a child to screw up his life than there used to be, but your children know right from wrong. I don't think you have to worry."

"Lindsay still hasn't forgiven me for moving her here." Sandy leaned her head against the railing. "She's so confused."

"She's not the only one," he muttered.

Sandy chuckled. "Did she give you any trouble tonight?"

"Not exactly. It wasn't what she said, it was more her expectations." He shuddered. "I didn't dare let her sit next to me at the movie."

Her chuckle turned into a laugh. "Poor Kyle, afraid of a twelve-year-old girl."

"It's easy for you to think this is funny. I'm the one trying to tap-dance around her feelings. I don't want to encourage her, and I don't want to hurt her. It's not easy."

Sandy sobered. "I appreciate your effort. I'll have a talk with her."

"With my luck, she won't listen."

"Children rarely do."

"Great." He leaned back and studied her profile. The sun had slipped below the horizon and the sky grew darker. Light from the house spilled out onto the porch. He could see the straight line of her small nose, the outline of her full mouth, the slight point of her stubborn chin. He'd always thought she was beautiful. That hadn't changed.

"The problem is," he said conversationally, never taking his gaze from her. "You work too hard and you've forgotten how to have fun."

Instantly she stiffened. "Excuse me?"

"You heard me. You expect too much of the kids. It's summer. They should be outside playing, not washing walls and painting."

She glared at him. "So I should do all the work?"

"That's not what I said. But you must admit you don't get out much."

"I want to know where you get off telling me what I should and shouldn't do with my children. You've known them for less than three weeks, Mr. Haynes, so I'll thank you to keep your opinions to yourself."

"Blake thinks his father didn't like him."

Her mouth opened, but no sound came out. She stared at him mutely, then rested her elbows on her knees and her head in her hands. "Damn."

"I shouldn't have said it like that."

"No, it's okay. I'd rather know. I've been afraid of that. Thomas wasn't very subtle when he was annoyed. I know he loved his children, but he wasn't always the greatest father." She raised her head and pushed her hair out of her face. "Thanks for telling me. I'll talk to him. Did he say anything else?"

Kyle shook his head. "That was about it. I had a good time with them tonight, except for Lindsay's problem, but I'm hoping she'll outgrow it. I wouldn't mind taking them out again."

"Why?"

"I like kids. I always have."

"So have a couple dozen of your own."

He shook his head. "It's not going to happen. I'm not the type." He couldn't risk it. He couldn't risk giving his heart to someone who was going to leave.

Sandy straightened. "I don't want them confused. You're not their father or stepfather."

"Can't I just be some guy they like?"

"I suppose." She didn't sound very enthusiastic about the idea.

"Is it because you don't trust me?"

"No, it's . . . I can't explain it."

"They haven't had a man in their lives since Thomas died. For that matter, neither have you."

"That's none of your business."

"I never said it was, I was just pointing out a fact."

She turned toward him. Her mouth pulled straight. "Are you so sure of your facts?" she asked, obviously irritated.

He stared at her for a long time, first studying her face, then glancing at her body. She tilted up her chin slightly, but otherwise didn't move. "I'm pretty sure, but I wouldn't mind being the one to change things."

"You have a lot of nerve, mister."

He grinned. "You're not the first one to accuse me of that. Come on, Sandy, would it be so bad to take your first steps with me? I won't let you fall."

She glared at him as if he'd asked her to dance naked in church. "I'm not interested in a relationship."

At least she hadn't said she wasn't interested in one with him. He thought about backing off and simply saying good-night, but he'd always had more curiosity than sense. Right now, he was noticing how fast Sandy was breathing and the way her nipples had hardened and were pressing against her shirt. According to the signals her body was sending, she wasn't as immune to him as she would like him to think. It was kind of like standing in front of a growling, tail-wagging dog. Which end did you believe?

Which Sandy was telling the truth?

"If you're not interested in a relationship, how do you feel about passion?" he asked, rising to his feet.

"What?"

He grabbed her hand and pulled her up next to him. "You heard me."

Wide eyes stared at him. Her mouth trembled. That mouth. Damn it all to hell, he remembered being fourteen and thinking he would die if he didn't know what her lips would feel like touching his. Those old longings overwhelmed him. Or maybe they were new longings. Or maybe he was just an old man playing a kid's game. He told himself to step away. He would have, too, if Sandy hadn't placed her hand on his chest. If she hadn't leaned forward slightly, inviting him.

It was stupid. It was inevitable. He bent down and kissed her.

Chapter Seven

Sandy wasn't prepared to be swept away. She wasn't prepared for the need that crashed through her. Like a wave from the sea, it broke over her body and tugged at her feet until she was sure she would fall and go under. She already couldn't breathe; what difference would it make if she found herself drowning in sensation?

Kyle's mouth pressed against hers. She told herself to pull back, but after the first moment of contact, she was lost. Lost in the passion, the heat and the need. Lost to feelings she'd long thought dormant. Lost to the excitement of being joyfully alive.

At the first brush of his lips, her body surged toward him. She wanted to be next to him, around him, feeling everything, touching everywhere. His mouth was firm, yet yielding, his breath sweet and warm. He didn't invade her or conquer her, he simply touched her. He didn't try to hold her still, or in any way keep her from turning away. He didn't have to. Perhaps he already knew how her heart thundered in her chest and her palms grew damp. Perhaps he was used to consummation by fire, but for her, it was the first time.

He stood one step down from her, so they were closer in height. If she had the strength to open her eyes, she would be able to stare into his. But she had no will, no power, nothing but need and passion. From the faintest of kisses, from the barest whisper of his mouth on hers, the tide lapped at her feet, tugging, pulling, until her self-control slipped away and was lost.

Lips on lips, chest to chest, thighs brushing thighs. Her hands clutched at his upper arms, as much to hold him in place as to keep her balance. His hands rested on her waist, comfortably, easily, as if he'd held them there a thousand times before. As if he knew she would not—could not—withdraw from him.

Her eyelids fluttered as she became lost in a world of sensual intensity. She told herself it was just a kiss. Nothing more. But she hadn't been kissed in so long, she could have wept from the wonder filling her. She could have perished from the hunger. His mouth pressed against hers, promising more, leaving her quivering. She clung to him as her world disappeared, leaving only the darkness and the feel of him next to her.

He moved back and forth, reminding her of the familiar movements of love, of the dance between a man and a woman. He was broader than Thomas had been, taller and more muscled. But his touch was softer, slower and more controlled. The contrasts and similarities filled her senses. She wanted him to kiss her forever. She wanted to forget all but this moment.

His mouth parted slightly and his tongue swept across her lower lip. She gasped as fire or electricity or lightning leapt between them, burning her skin. Her breasts tightened and her knees began to shake.

When he tilted his head, she prepared herself for the sensual assault. He didn't disappoint her. He brushed once more against her lips, then moved lower, trailing damp, openmouthed kisses along her jaw, then her neck. She arched her head back, groaning softly as he found the pulse point by her collarbone. He circled the throbbing vein with his tongue, then blew on the damp skin.

She slipped her hands up his arms, to his shoulders, then around to his back. The muscles there were thick cords, flexing and releasing under her touch. Sweeping her fingers up to his short hair, she let the silky strands tease her sensitized palms. Then, as she pressed her body more fully against his, she reveled in his strength and male hardness.

He slid his hands down her hips to her rear, where he cupped the full curves and drew her tightly against him. Instantly, her woman's place began to ache. She could feel herself swelling, dampening, readying for him. She wanted him to lift her up against him, moving her back and forth until they'd both found their release. Instead, he taunted her with a mimicry of the pleasure they could find.

His mouth returned to hers. She parted her lips without being asked, needing to know him, to take all of him inside. He tasted hot and sweet, as if his flavor had been fashioned for her alone. His tongue thrust against hers, strong and sure. She danced around his assault, teasing him, tempting him, wanting him. His hands moved up her back, then around to touch her breasts.

He cupped her curves, taking the weight in his palms. Through her shirt and bra she could feel the imprint of each of his fingers. Her breasts swelled. She arched toward him, silently asking for more. He squeezed gently and whispered her name. She clung to him as her legs buckled.

He brushed his thumbs against her hard nipples. Fire shot through her, down to her feet, then up to center in her woman's place. As he teased her nipples, he brought his mouth back to hers. This time, she was the aggressor, thrusting her tongue past his lips. She explored him and tasted him. Every cell of her body was aflame, humming with desire.

She wanted more. She wanted to be naked with him, to touch him and have him touch her. The passion shocked her. She didn't remember it being like this before. Certainly not in the last few years of her marriage. She hadn't been attracted to anyone since Thomas had passed away. Why now? Why with Kyle? And why, for heaven's sake, on her front porch where any of her children could walk out and see them?

Still, she didn't pull back. She couldn't. She wanted all of him, this minute. On the porch, on the grass, it didn't matter. She needed him.

His hands moved from her breasts to her shoulders. His hips angled away from hers. His mouth moved from her lips to her cheek, then he firmly set her away from him. She blinked, as if awakening from a long sleep. The intensity of the passion left her stunned, as if she'd experienced something life-changing and couldn't yet make sense of it. She was surprised by her reaction, but not frightened. It was good to know she could still feel something.

Dark brown eyes stared into her face. She wasn't sure what he was seeing there, but she refused to be ashamed. Despite the flush she felt on her cheeks, she pushed her hair back and met his gaze.

"I'm not sorry," she said defiantly.

"Thank God," he breathed.

"What?"

"I thought you'd get angry at me or something. That was a hell of a kiss." He sounded as if he'd been running for miles. The thought pleased her. She would hate to have been the only one affected by what they'd just done.

Kyle drew in a deep breath and settled his hands on his hips. "It's a good thing your kids are only a few feet away, or I would have been tempted to make love to you right here on the porch and risk entertaining the neighbors."

"Really?"

He laughed. An unexpected spurt of embarrassment caused her to duck her head. She stared at the proof of his maleness straining against the button-fly of his jeans and felt a fierce longing. She wanted to touch him there, to feel him surge against her hand.

He pressed his forefinger under her chin and forced her to look at him. "What are you thinking about?" he asked, lowering his hand to his side.

Embarrassment deepened to mortification. "Nothing," she said, her voice coming out in a squeak. She searched her brain for a safe topic. "Just that, ah, we can't do this again."

He looked as surprised as she felt. Where had that thought come from? But as soon as she said the words, she knew they were true. She couldn't risk it, not with him. He was completely wrong for her. She wanted a different kind of man, although she wouldn't mind if he kissed just like Kyle.

But instead of getting angry, he simply nodded. "Okay, what can't we do anymore?"

"You know." She waved vaguely, motioning to the space between them. He was still on the step below hers, so they were almost at eye level.

"No, I don't know. What?"

"Kissing. We can't kiss anymore."

"Sure we can. But what you really mean is you don't want us to make love."

Somehow it would have been better if he'd said "sex" instead of "make love." Sex was more impersonal. "Whatever. We can't."

"Why?"

It was a perfectly reasonable question. Unfortunately, she didn't have a reasonable answer. Why couldn't they have sex? Kyle was probably an expert at it, not to mention the fact that he wouldn't expect much from her—emotionally. They could have a fling. She'd never had one before. She wasn't sure how one went about arranging it. Did she ask specifically? "Gee, Kyle, how about some cheap meaningless sex for a few weeks. Just until I'm back on my feet?" No, she couldn't say anything like that. Could she? Maybe she was supposed to simply hint broadly.

She searched his face. By reputation, the Haynes brothers were interested in a good time and nothing else. She could take advantage of that, then get back to her regularly scheduled life. She could be just one of countless women.

Sandy drew in a deep breath, then let it go slowly. Who was she kidding? She wasn't the fling type. She was far too responsible. She had her life planned out and Kyle Haynes wasn't part of her program.

"If you're trying to think of a good reason we shouldn't become lovers, you're taking an awful long time," he said.

She couldn't risk telling him the truth. "The list is so long, I don't know where to start."

"I wouldn't be surprised."

But he wasn't smiling as he spoke the words, and there was something in his eyes, something dark and undefined that made her feel unsettled. As if he had a secret he was close to revealing. Sandy wasn't sure if she wanted to know what it was, or if she should pretend she couldn't see it. Before she could decide, he blinked and the secret was gone.

"Your problem," he said, leaning close enough to make her want to kiss him, "is that you've forgotten how to have fun."

"You said that before. It's still not true."

He had the audacity to laugh. "You've got your life so well planned, you wouldn't know a spontaneous thought if it bit you on the butt. Maybe if you stopped organizing the world for everyone else, you would have a little time to find some happiness."

He was right. She hated that. With a flash of insight that made her uncomfortable, she realized she could graciously agree with what he was saying and try to change, or she could get angry. It was easier to get angry. Easier because acknowledging how empty her life was would force her to face the truth.

She'd learned early she couldn't depend on anyone but herself. Trusting others left her open for heartbreak and loneliness. But Kyle didn't know that about her. He only saw Sensible Sandy who refused to have fun. He didn't see the way she worried about her children, her job and holding it all together. He didn't see how she hated always being the bad guy. He didn't see the fear.

"Who do you think you are?" she asked, stepping up onto the porch and backing away from him. "I don't need you or any man telling me what to do. I've been on my own for the last two years. The children and I have survived very nicely without your interference."

"Surviving isn't the same as living. You've shut yourself off from the best parts of life."

"That's just your opinion. In *my* opinion, I'm doing just fine. I've been fine and I plan on continuing to be fine. Now I think it's time for you to leave."

She held her breath and waited. A part of her wanted him to turn and go, but a voice inside cried out for him to force her into admitting the truth. She was desperate for some happiness, but she couldn't give up control to anyone. It wasn't safe. Thomas had taught her that, and before him, her mother. She had to be responsible for herself and her children. There wasn't anyone else she could depend upon.

Kyle stared at her, then he reached forward and grabbed her left hand. He tugged until she stumbled closer. Behind them, she could hear the sound of a TV show blaring through the open window.

He continued to hold on to her hand, then he glanced down and rubbed his thumb over her wedding ring. "You ever get lonely? You ever get tired of being the only one? Don't you ever want someone to help you, to care about you?"

She snatched her hand back. Yes, her heart cried. But she was too afraid to speak the words. Kyle tempted her with what she could never have. "Wanting it isn't the same as having it happen."

"Maybe it's right here in front of you, but you're too stubborn or too scared to see what's being offered. 'Night."

He turned and walked down the stairs, then disappeared into the darkness. Sandy stared after him, watching until she saw the light click on in the gatehouse. She stood there, abandoned, feeling the brush of his fingers against her wedding band and fighting the loneliness that threatened to consume her soul.

Grilled-cheese sandwiches and a tossed salad hadn't sounded so bad when she'd first suggested the children make lunch, but now, surrounded by the mess, she realized she'd made a mistake. Sandy stared at the cooked bits of cheese and the burnt spill next to the right front burner. She had no idea what it could be because they weren't supposed to have cooked a liquid. There were dishes piled in the sink and open containers of salad dressing and cheese on the counter. Her feet crunched on the crumbs underfoot. Exchanging cooking for cleanup had not been one of her better ideas.

It was Kyle's fault. The kids had been bugging her all morning and she'd just wanted them to go outside and leave her in peace. If he hadn't spoiled them by entertaining them, they wouldn't have been so bored with their usual activities in the afternoon and they wouldn't have gotten on her nerves, so she wouldn't have suggested they cook lunch and she clean up. It was also his fault because she wasn't as patient as she usually tried to be because she couldn't stop thinking about the kiss.

Sandy crossed to the window and moved the new crisp blue-and-white curtains aside. If she tilted her head slightly to see around the big oak tree in her front yard, she had a view of her entire driveway and the back of Kyle's house. Even now, he was outside with her kids, washing his car as he did every week. A warm afternoon breeze fluttered through the open window, bringing with it the faint sound of laughter. They were having a good time with him. Only a really horrible mother would begrudge her children that.

Sandy sat down at the dirty table and sighed. Okay, she was a bad mother. There was a part of her that resented her kids' easy relationship with Kyle. For her, nothing about him was simple. It didn't seem fair. Not only did they get to spend time with him, but he really seemed to like it. She half suspected he'd changed his work schedule just to be with them. Since the kiss—which in her mind often appeared in capital letters as "THE KISS"—he'd been working nights, coming home shortly after dawn, sleeping until about one in the afternoon, then hanging out with her children. As if he were their father.

She'd tried to ignore the situation. However, that was difficult when every other sentence Nichole spoke started with "Kyle says..." followed by whatever bit of wisdom he'd imparted. Lindsay was still pursuing him with the fervor of an old maid watching her last, best hope slip away. At least that was amusing and almost made up for her concern. But it was Blake who kept her from approaching Kyle and telling him to back off. Her quiet, uncommunicative, withdrawn son had started laughing.

Not a lot, not all the time, but enough for her to know that he was coming out of his shell. And she would do anything to see Blake return to the bright, outgoing boy he'd been before his father had rejected him. She would even admit Kyle Haynes into her life and accept the pain and suffering that would surely follow.

Sandy rose from the table and collected the last of the dishes. After setting them on the counter, she opened the dishwasher and started loading. A half-guilty smile tugged at her mouth. She hadn't rinsed the plates first. She who yelled that command every night as the children cleaned the kitchen. Unrinsed glasses followed, along with the silverware. When the dishwasher was full, she poured in the soap and started the cycle. Then she straightened and stared at the machine. If the most wicked thing she'd done in her life was to put plates in the dishwasher without rinsing them first, Kyle was right: she wouldn't recognize a spontaneous thought if it came up and bit her, and she desperately needed a little fun in her life.

But how? And with whom? Those two questions brought her mind back to the kiss. And Kyle. Why had he done it? Why had she responded? Where were they going to go now?

She capped the salad-dressing bottles and stuck them in the refrigerator. Next, she put away the bread. Finally, she reached for a dishcloth to wipe off the counters. But instead of tackling the task, she leaned against the tile. The second question was easiest to answer. She'd responded because Kyle's embrace had sparked some incredible passion buried deep inside of her. She'd never felt anything quite like it before. With Thomas, making love had often been spontaneous and usually fulfilling, but she'd never felt swept away or compelled beyond reason. She would never have considered doing it outside on the porch where practically anyone could have seen them. Maybe Thomas would have liked her better if she'd been more like that.

Was her response unique to Kyle or had she reacted so passionately simply because she hadn't been with a man in so long? Sandy turned and began wiping off the counter. She collected the crumbs, then tossed them in the trash. Next, she tackled the kitchen table. When everything was gleaming, she rinsed the dishcloth and wrung it out.

She walked back to the window and moved the curtain aside. Her three children were still helping Kyle with his car. She watched them and wondered when she'd gotten left out of the loop. Was it when she'd asked him to leave and implied he should never come back? Or was it before that? Was being out of the loop the price she paid for being in control?

The back door opened and Nichole ran in. "What time is it, Mommy?"

She glanced at the clock next to the oven. "Nearly two-thirty. Why?"

"I'm 'posed to be at Mandy's by three. We're going swimming. Don't you remember?"

Sandy reached out and touched her youngest's red curls. "Of course I do. Go get your bathing suit and a towel, and I'll take you right over."

Nichole grinned, then started up the stairs. Sandy followed more slowly. Nichole and Mandy had quickly become friends. Elizabeth had been wonderful, as had Travis. In fact, all of Kyle's family had gone out of their way to make her and her children feel welcome. Without her noticing it, he'd drawn her into a world where people cared about one another. She smiled wistfully as she remembered the last time she'd taken Nichole over to Mandy's. She'd walked Nichole to the front door. Before she knocked, she'd glanced in the window and seen Elizabeth and Travis kissing on the living room sofa. Travis had held his wife tenderly in his arms.

Sandy hadn't known what to do. Before she could decide, Nichole, who hadn't seen the adults, pressed the bell. Elizabeth and Travis had separated, then Elizabeth had smiled as her husband had whispered something in her ear.

Sandy suspected it had been a promise to continue what had been interrupted.

Sandy walked into her bedroom. The furniture was in place and most of the boxes had been unpacked. Except for the stack of pictures still waiting to be hung on the wall, no one could tell she'd only moved in a month ago. She changed her T-shirt for one that hadn't been stained by coffee, then pulled off her headband and reached for her brush. A shaft of sunlight spilling through the open window caught the diamond in her wedding band and made it sparkle. She put the brush down and stared at her ring. She still remembered the day Thomas had slipped the simple gold-and-diamond band on her finger. She'd had so many hopes for their future.

What had gone wrong? Where had she made the first mistake? She'd been so sure he was the right one for her. If only she'd known he was more interested in having fun than in being a husband or father. If only she'd known how lonely she would feel years before he'd actually died.

She touched the ring and remembered the feel of Kyle's hand holding hers. He'd rubbed the ring as he'd asked if she ever felt the loneliness. Maybe, instead of reacting with fear and anger, she should have told him the truth.

Sandy walked to the window. From the second story, she could see into Kyle's backyard. They'd finished with the car and were now digging in the garden and laughing. Who was this man who stole her children's hearts and made her forget her promises to herself?

Slowly, she drew the ring from her finger. It came off easily. The thin band of paler skin was the only proof it had been there. She'd thought she would feel naked, but she didn't feel anything at all. The circle of gold rested in the palm of her right hand. Thomas had already been gone two years. Was it time to let go? She didn't know.

She walked to the jewelry box resting on her cherry-wood dresser. She pulled open the top drawer and placed the ring inside. She would keep it there for today and see how she felt about not wearing her ring. If it bothered her too much, she could always put it back on.

Chapter Eight

Sandy backed the car out of the garage and turned it in the wide driveway.

"We gotta stop by Kyle's," Nichole said. "I left one of my dolls there, and I promised Mandy I'd bring her by."

Sandy stared at the gatehouse up ahead. She wasn't sure where her other two children were, but Kyle was standing in the afternoon sunlight, trimming a hedge. It wouldn't have been so bad if he'd been wearing slightly more than a pair of shorts. What was it with that man? Didn't the sheriff's department pay the deputies enough to provide for food *and* clothing? Or was it just her luck that every time she turned around, he was practically naked?

She let the car roll forward until it was even with the bend that led to Kyle's driveway, then put the vehicle in Park. "I'll wait here," she said. "Hurry, please, or you're going to be late."

Nichole flashed her a smile. "I'll be right back."

Sandy grinned as her youngest raced out of the car and called a greeting to Kyle. "I gotta find my doll."

"I think you left it in the garage," he told her.

He put down the clippers and glanced at the car. Sandy clenched her teeth. Please, God, let him stay where he was. She didn't need to be staring at his bare chest right now. Not when she was still in a weakened condition.

God was busy, or He had a different plan for her life because Kyle started toward her and he didn't show any signs of stopping. She drew in a deep breath and reminded herself she was a mature woman. She could handle this situation. It wasn't going to be a problem. She would remember to keep breathing deeply and focus on something neutral. Like the steering wheel.

He came around the back of the car. She followed his progress in the mirrors, mentally noting he had the audacity to look great even as a two-inch-high reflection. When he reached the driver's side, he waited until she rolled down the window, then he leaned forward and braced his forearms on the car. His forehead rested against the top of the car, his right elbow bumped against the door lock. She could see his face, the slight sheen of perspiration coating his shoulders and bare chest. She could see the tanned skin, the dark hair curling down to his waistband, the muscles. He overwhelmed her. If she was the fainting kind, she would have been a goner for sure.

"Hi," he said.

"Hi, yourself." The words caught in her throat, but she forced them out past stiff vocal cords.

Kyle grinned at her. White teeth flashed against his tanned face. His dark eyes stared at hers, as if he were reading her secrets. As if he knew she was having trouble remembering to breathe. Damn the man for being such a temptation and damn herself for being so weak.

It had been nine days since the kiss. She'd waved at him from across the driveway. She'd watched her children laugh and play in his backyard. She'd heard the rumbling engine of his motorcycle as he took off for she wasn't sure where. But she hadn't seen him up close. She hadn't gazed into his face and inhaled the masculine scent of him. She hadn't felt her thighs go up in flames, as they were doing now. At least she was sitting down.

She looked away from him before she could say or do something stupid. "I'm taking Nichole over to play with Mandy. Do you know where Lindsay and Blake are? I don't want to saddle you with them."

"No problem," he said. "I was just coming to tell you Blake is down the street playing ball. There's a half dozen boys about his age around here. I know most of them and suggested they stop by. They invited him to come play. I hope you don't mind."

Sandy stared at Kyle. "Did he want to go?" Her son usually resisted her efforts to get him to join in with other kids.

"Sure. Why not? Anyway, they'll be a while. Why don't you leave him at the game? I'll be here if anything happens."

"Thank you." Blake was playing with other boys his age. She was thrilled. More than thrilled, she was relieved. Maybe her son was finally returning to normal. She'd been worried about him for a while. She'd even taken Blake to a counselor before they'd left Los Angeles. The woman had told her it would simply take time for Blake to regain his self-esteem and want to play with other children. For weeks, Sandy had wondered if the woman had been wrong, but now it seemed he was on the road to recovery.

"I was thinking of a barbecue tonight," Kyle said.

"Oh?" Was that a statement of fact or an invitation? She wasn't sure she wanted to know.

"I've got steaks and corn on the cob. Lindsay said she'd make a salad. Is six-thirty okay with you?"

An invitation. That was simple. She would just say no. N-O. It wasn't a difficult word. "Sure, we'd love to." She groaned silently. Apparently, she was having more trouble saying no than she'd realized. Now she had to eat dinner with him. What were they going to talk about? How would she stand it, knowing she'd pushed him away? Not that she wanted to be with him. It was just—

"You okay?" he asked.

She needed to have her head examined. "I'm fine. When Lindsay volunteered to make the salad, did she mention who was providing the ingredients?"

"No. I don't have anything here, but I can go to the store."

She shook her head. "I'll go. It's only fair. I'll pick up some salad fixings after I drop off Mandy."

"Great. Ah, Sandy." Kyle shifted. He looked at her, then out the front windshield. "I think I've got a problem."

"What?"

"It's Lindsay. Her crush isn't going away."

Sandy laughed. "Twelve-year-old hormones can be pretty scary. Don't worry, she'll outgrow it."

He swallowed. "I don't know if I can wait that long. She makes me nervous. I don't know what to say to her."

"Why do you have to say anything?"

"I don't mean about the crush. Just in general. Like I told you the night I took the kids to the movies, I don't want to encourage her, and I don't want to hurt her feelings." He closed his eyes briefly. "She's always trying to be next to me. I'm hiding behind a ten- and eight-year-old." He glared at her. "Don't you even think about laughing at me."

"I wouldn't dream of it." She bit on her lower lip to keep from grinning. "But I do have one question. Why is this such a big deal? Aren't you used to women throwing themselves at you?"

His dark eyes met her own. "You're trying to set me up. If I say yes, then you're going to call me an egotistical jerk."

"I promise I'm not." She gripped the steering wheel and stared straight ahead. "I'm stating a fact. Why is dealing with Lindsay's crush such a problem for you?"

"She's just a kid. She's sensitive, vulnerable. I would find it easier to confront a woman. Besides, despite what you think, I don't have women lined up for miles."

She made a show of glancing around the outside of his house. "I can see that."

"You're not helping."

"I know. I'm sorry. Let's be logical. You're very good with children. Why don't you treat Lindsay like one of the kids?"

"I've tried that. She makes it a point to tell me how grown-up she is." He shuddered. "She offered to do my laundry."

Sandy chuckled. For the first time, she realized being around Kyle made her feel good. As if the world had been set right. "I can't get her to do her own laundry. Why don't you let her do yours, then you can do hers and we'll call it even?"

He growled her name.

She held up her hands in a gesture of surrender. "Okay, no more teasing. If you don't want to treat her like a child, then treat her like a teenager. You were one once. What do you remember?"

"That having a crush on someone could hurt like hell."

"Really?" She glanced at him. "You had a crush? On whom?"

He shrugged. "It's not important. The point is, I don't want her to be rejected like I was."

"You were rejected? By whom?"

He touched the tip of her nose. "You're suddenly interested in my past."

"Why not? It's fascinating. I never knew a Haynes had been rejected in love." She tried to remember back to high school. "Do I know her? Oh, probably not. You were a couple of grades back, weren't you?"

"Yeah, you're older than me."

She grimaced. "Thanks for the reminder. Was it one of the cheerleaders? That foreign-exchange student from Sweden? What was her name? I can't remember. Didn't she date Jordan?"

"Enough with my past. You're not helping here. What am I going to do with Lindsay?"

"Wait it out. Maybe something will happen to convince her you're just some guy who's not very interesting at all."

"Gee, thanks. I can't wait for that to happen."

She smiled. Their gazes locked and she felt her heart begin beating faster. Tension crackled between them. She hadn't realized how close they were, with him leaning in the car window. They were close enough that she could see the individual whiskers on his cheeks and chin, and the shape of his mouth. That same mouth that had tempted and teased her nine days ago. Suddenly, her lips felt dry and she was compelled to touch them with the tip of her tongue. She could see him follow the movement and he seemed to catch his breath. For a moment, she thought he might lean forward those last few inches and kiss her again. She wanted him to. She willed him to. Instead, he stretched his arm inside the car and grabbed her left hand.

"You took off your ring."

She pulled her fingers free of his touch and clasped them together on her lap. "So?"

"Why did you do it?"

"I'm not sure. Maybe it was time. I've decided to see how it feels. If it bothers me too much, I'll put the ring back on."

She wanted to tell him not to read anything into her actions, but that statement seemed like too much of a confession of what she was thinking. He wasn't that interested in her. If anything, he was probably intrigued by a woman who didn't willingly fall into his arms at every moment. Then she remembered the kiss and how she *had* fallen into his arms, so there went that theory.

"I found her, Mommy," Nichole called as she raced back toward the car.

"Good. We need to get going." Sandy didn't care if it looked as if she was running away. "See you later," she told Kyle.

He straightened. "Don't forget about the barbecue. And the salad."

"I won't." She waited until Nichole had buckled her seat belt, then hit the gas. The quicker she got away from Kyle, the quicker she would stop making a fool of herself. She was worse than Lindsay, mooning over a man she shouldn't want. If only she could stop thinking about his kisses.

Kyle stared after the station wagon until it turned onto the main road and disappeared. Then he glanced at the hedge he'd been trimming. The poor plant was about as neat as it was going to get. He should leave it alone. But if he did, that would mean his chores outside were finished and he wouldn't have an excuse to avoid the house. Lindsay was inside, making lemonade. Maybe he was a coward, but he didn't want to be alone with her. She terrified him.

He put the clippers in the garage, then hesitated by the back door. He was the adult, he reminded himself. He was the one in control of the situation.

"You're scared," a boy called.

Kyle whipped around toward the sound.

"Am not" came the answer.

He recognized the second voice. It was Blake. A thick hedge and several trees separated Sandy's property from a narrow private road. Kyle pushed through the bushes, ignoring the scratches from the branches, and came out at the top of a slight rise. The grassy slope rolled into the private dirt road. Two boys stood directly in front of him. Three feet away, facing them, was Blake.

Kyle could see he was scared. His eyes were wide behind his glasses, his body stiff. The taller of the other two boys moved closer.

"You're scared, and I'm gonna make you more scared. You can't tell me what to do."

Kyle recognized the neighborhood bully. "Gary Warner, stop that right now."

Blake looked up at him. Gary took advantage of the boy's distraction and hit him right in the mouth.

"Damn little brat," Kyle muttered. He started toward the trio. The third boy took off running. Gary hesitated, then darted for home. Blake stood there looking stunned. He touched his hand to his mouth. When he drew it away, he saw the blood. Instantly, tears rolled down his cheeks.

Kyle reached his side. The other two boys had disappeared, so he put his arm around Blake. "He popped you good. Let me see."

Blake sniffed and raised his chin. He continued to cry. Tears dripped from his eyes, but he didn't make any sound. The silence tore at Kyle's gut. He wanted to catch that little punk and teach him what it felt like to be bullied by someone. Instead, he stared at Blake's mouth. Carefully, he turned down Blake's lower lip.

"You've got a cut here," he said. "How do your teeth feel? Are any of them loose?"

Blake closed his mouth and used his tongue to check. He turned away and spat out blood. "They're okay."

"Good. Let's get you home and we'll put some ice on your mouth. You're going to swell up like a chipmunk."

Blake tried to smile, but the movement made him wince. He sniffed. "It hurts," he mumbled.

"I know, kid. It happened to me a bunch of times. I never seemed to remember the pain before I got in a fight. It'll get better." Kyle bent over and picked him up. Blake wrapped his legs around Kyle's waist and buried his head in his shoulder.

Kyle could feel the dampness on his skin. He wasn't sure if it was from the tears or the blood. He didn't much care. Instead, he started back the long way, going to the end of the private road, then turning left and walking until he reached Sandy's driveway. An occasional sob shook Blake's skinny body. He held the boy close, patting his back and murmuring soothingly. Poor kid. If this was his first fight—and from the way he'd reacted, it had been— he was scared, sore and defeated. Hell of a way to spend a summer afternoon.

As he turned down the fork in the driveway toward his house, he saw Lindsay waiting by the back door.

"Where were you?" she asked. "I finished the lemonade." She glanced at her brother. "What happened to him?"

"He got into a fight."

"Really?" Her eyes widened. "Mom's gonna kill you, Blake."

Kyle glared at her. "He doesn't need to hear that right now. Why don't you go home while I take care of your brother? When your mom gets back, would you please ask her to come see me?"

Lindsay glanced at the boy in his arms and shrugged. "Sure. I'll be by later to help you with the cooking, Kyle." She gave him her best smile, then sashayed up the walkway.

Kyle groaned softly.

Inside the house, he set Blake on the counter and examined his mouth more thoroughly. There was only one cut and it had almost stopped bleeding. But his cheek was swelling fast. Kyle grabbed a frozen bag of peas from the freezer and had the kid press it against his face.

Blake touched the bag to his skin, then jumped. "It's cold."

"It's supposed to be. It'll help take the pain away and make you look a little more normal so your mom might not kill me along with you."

Blake held the bag with his left hand and pushed up his glasses with his right. "It wasn't your fault. Gary is the one who hit me."

Kyle leaned against the counter at right angles to where Blake was sitting. He folded his arms over his chest. "I saw that. You want to tell me why?"

The boy lowered his head slightly. "We were playing ball. I even hit a double." He looked up and tried to smile. "That hurts. Anyway, the next guy to hit was Robby. He's nice. He said I could come swimming at his house."

"So Gary punched you?"

"No." Blake sighed. "Robby hit his ball out. Gary was pitching, and he got mad. The next time Robby came up to bat, Gary hit him with the ball. We all knew it was on purpose. But no one would stand up to Gary except for Robby and me. A lot of the boys went home. I guess they were scared."

Blake looked scared, too, as he told the story. Kyle knew he'd had nothing to do with cultivating the strength of character Blake showed, but he couldn't stop the feeling of pride swelling inside of him. The kid had guts. Standing up to a bully to protect a new friend. Sandy had done a hell of a job with her kids.

"Then what happened?"

"Gary started chasing Robby. I tried to protect him. Gary hit Robby, then he turned on me." He shrugged. "You saw that part." He sighed. "Lindsay's right. Mom's gonna kill me. She hates fighting."

Kyle knew it was wrong, but at this moment in time he wanted to get his hands on Gary and shake him until the kid's teeth rattled. He wouldn't, of course, but he would do the next best thing. When he went on duty, he would pay a visit to Gary's parents and have a talk with them. He knew the Warners and suspected they would be as angry as he was at their son's behavior.

"You weren't fighting," Kyle told him. "You didn't even raise your hands to defend yourself. Someone hit you. It's not the same thing."

Blake looked a little brighter. "Yeah?"

Kyle grinned. "Yeah." He moved closer to the boy. "How's that cheek?"

Blake lowered the bag of frozen peas. "It doesn't hurt so bad."

It might not hurt, but it sure looked ugly. A large bruise had formed on the left side of his mouth. The skin was puffy and discolored. At least the bleeding had stopped. Kyle touched the tender area.

"You'll live," he said, then stared at Blake. "Did your dad ever teach you how to defend yourself?"

Blake shook his head.

Figures, Kyle thought. He was probably too busy with his own life to notice how he was ignoring his son.

"Do you know why Gary hit you?" he asked.

"'Cause I said he'd thrown the ball at Robby."

"That's only part of the reason. Gary hit you because he thought he could get away with it. Bullies pick on people who let them. If you stand up to a bully, he usually backs off. At heart, they're cowards."

Blake frowned. "Gary didn't act like he was scared."

"He was. Trust me. Did you see how fast he ran off when I showed up? Also, he hit you when you turned toward me. It was a cheap shot, when he knew you couldn't fight back. What you need to do is learn how to defend yourself. I'm not saying you should start a fight, but if one finds you, you have to be able to keep from being taken advantage of. Do you understand?''

"I guess." Blake looked doubtful.

"It's not that hard. I'll show you." He took the bag of peas and set them on the counter, then he grabbed Blake under his arms and lowered him to the floor. He heard the sound of a car going past. Sandy was home. Lindsay would tell her what had happened and she would come right over. He couldn't wait to tell her how well her son had behaved. She was going to be proud of the kid for defending another boy.

"Stand like this." Kyle demonstrated the stance, with his feet apart and his weight balanced. "You need to be able to move quickly in either direction. There's no shame in ducking a punch."

Blake mimicked the action. "I wanna duck for sure, because it hurts to get hit."

"You're telling me." Kyle grinned. "So you want to make sure the other guy doesn't get a clear shot. Next, keep your arms up. You want to protect your face and body. Hunch over a little, giving him a smaller target." Blake bent in half. "Not so much. Like this."

Kyle hunched down, drawing his chest in. "Keep your head low, but watch what he's doing. Try to anticipate the move."

Blake lowered his arms to his side. "I can't remember all this."

"It's hard at first. We'll practice. In a couple of weeks, you'll be able to stand up to Gary and feel confident that he won't get in another sucker punch."

The back door jerked open. Sandy tore into the room. From the look on her face, Kyle knew she'd spoken to Lindsay. She didn't even glance at him. She rushed to her son's side and dropped to her knees.

"What happened?" she asked frantically. "Are you okay? Lindsay said you were bleeding. Oh my God, look at your face." She clutched his chin and stared at the darkening bruise. "You've been fighting."

Blake tried to smile, then he winced. "Kyle's been teaching me to do better, so next time Gary won't get in a cheap shot."

"A what? Never mind. Are you hurt anywhere else?" She ran her hands along his chest and sides, then down his legs. Blake giggled when her fingers tickled him. "Nothing's broken?"

"He's fine," Kyle said. "The other kid got off one good hit. That's all. I saw it happen."

The back door opened again. Lindsay came in. She wouldn't look at him. Sandy stood up and pushed her hair out of her face. "Lindsay, take your brother back to the house and put some ice on his face. I'll be right there. After I speak with Kyle."

He didn't like the sound of that. "Look, Sandy, it's not what you think."

She ignored him. "Now, Lindsay." Her daughter grabbed Blake by the hand and led him out the door. Sandy followed them and stood by the screen, watching until they were out of earshot. Then she turned on him.

"What the hell were you thinking? I leave my child in your care for a half hour and he gets in a fight. He's bruised and bleeding and I walk in on you trying to teach him how to do it again. Are you crazy? Where was your brain in all this? Your common sense? I don't want Blake starting fights."

He held up his hand to stop her. "Sandy, it wasn't like that."

"Sure it wasn't. Let me guess. You weren't thinking at all. You were too busy playing daddy."

"I was trying to teach him to defend himself."

"Against whom? You let him go play with children who are dangerous? I trusted you, Kyle. You said it was okay, and I believed you. You have to be more responsible than that. This isn't a game. The well-being of my children is at stake here."

She paced across the kitchen and back toward the door. "I can't believe this."

He couldn't believe it, either. She wasn't giving him a chance. "If you would let me explain."

She stopped in front of the door and spun to face him. Her chest heaved with each breath, anger darkened her eyes. "Explain what? That you were too busy with your car or your tan to supervise Blake? My ten-year-old son is bleeding and bruised from a fight. You're the one who let him go off with those other boys. You even admitted you saw what happened. Did you try to stop it?"

"Of course I did."

"Not hard enough."

"Dammit, Sandy, if you would shut up and listen to me, I can tell you what happened. You're jumping to conclusions."

"No, I don't want to hear it." She approached him and raised her arm until she was pointing at the center of his chest. She stopped when she was less than a foot away. "Your problem is you won't take responsibility for your actions."

He couldn't believe she was being this unreasonable. Maybe it was a parental thing he couldn't understand. He tried to hold on to his temper, although she was making it damn hard. "Your problem is you spend so much time being responsible, you've forgotten what it's like to live."

She glared at him. "Maybe I have. So what? I've learned the hard way that I can only depend on myself. My dad walked out before I was born. My mother was an alcoholic. I spent the first twelve years of my life looking after her. When she died, I moved here to be with my aunt. It was the first time I got to be a child. Maybe it wasn't enough. Maybe I couldn't stop acting like a grown-up, but I'm glad. Because I'm going to make it work. Despite you, and despite Thomas, who instead of being a husband was worse than any kid I could have had. Do you know how he died? Do you?'' Her voice was shrill.

He shook his head. He didn't know anything anymore. He'd never had a clue about Sandy's mother.

"He fell off a mountain. He'd gone away, like he did every summer. He usually disappeared for two months at a time. He'd wanted to take Lindsay, but I wouldn't let him. Thank God. He was careless, or unlucky, and he fell to his death. Now there's only me. I've got a mortgage and three kids. They're depending on me. So don't you tell me that I've forgotten how to live. Just getting through the day is a victory for me. My children are happy, healthy and warm every single night. The bills are paid and I'm keeping it all together."

He reached toward her and touched her face. "I'm sorry."

She jerked away from his hand. "Sorry doesn't cut it. You're used to getting what you want without having to work for it. Nice for you, but not realistic for the rest of the world. I don't know what kind of game you've been playing with me, but it has to stop. I don't want to get involved with you. I can't afford to be one of your conquests."

He felt as if she'd stabbed him in the gut. "It's not like that. I haven't been playing a game with you. Just because I'm not like you doesn't mean I'm a jerk like Thomas. You're judging me on my reputation and what you remember about my brothers. I've been here for you, Sandy. From the moment you arrived in Glenwood, I've made it easier."

Emotions chased across her face. He watched as she wrestled with the truth of that statement. Her mouth straightened and he knew he'd been judged and found guilty.

"So you've been neighborly. I appreciate that. But it doesn't mean I want you in my life. You're not Thomas, but you're just as dangerous."

"How?"

"Have you ever once had a long-term relationship?"

She had him there. "Define long-term."

She sighed. Her shoulders slumped. "That's the whole point, Kyle. I shouldn't have to. I don't want to have to deal with any more adult children, Peter Pan types or charming flirts. I'm tired of being in charge. I want someone to take care of me for a change. We both know you're not that person. I want you out of my life." She walked to the door. "I hope you understand, and even if you don't, I hope you'll respect my wishes."

Chapter Nine

Sandy left without giving him a chance. Kyle walked to the window and watched as she strode purposefully to her house. Once there, she climbed the three stairs, crossed the porch and went inside, all without once looking back at him.

She'd told him to stay away from her. Just like that. No explanations, no second chances. She'd made her decision and there wasn't a damn thing he could do about it.

He crossed over to the refrigerator and pulled out a beer. Several steaks sat on the second shelf. The vegetable crisper was filled with corn. So much for the barbecue. He told himself he didn't care. Sandy and her family had been taking up too much of his time, anyway. Now he would be able to do what he wanted, instead of hanging around with them. The words sounded great, but he knew he didn't mean them. He liked her, he liked her kids. With them, he was able to pretend it was real—that he had a chance at a family of his own.

After twisting off the cap of his beer, he took a long swallow. Was she right? He didn't want to consider that, but he had to. Was he irresponsible and immature?

"Hell, no," he said aloud, then wondered if he was just whistling in the dark.

Sandy was right about one thing. He didn't have a record of long-term relationships. He'd never been willing to risk committing before. In the back of his mind had been the fear that the woman he gave his heart to would walk out the door. People he cared about left. It was a fact of life.

But he wasn't a charming flirt who got by on his looks. At least he tried not to be. As a teenager, it had been convenient to take the easy way out. Most things in life had come to him without a lot of work. But that didn't mean he was irresponsible. He usually didn't care about the things that came easily. What he remembered the most was what he'd had to work for. Or what he'd never gotten. Like Sandy. Sixteen years ago, she'd trampled all over his male pride, and here she was, doing it again.

He walked into the living room and sat in the large chair in front of the fireplace. The leather was cool against his bare back. He closed his eyes. He knew for a fact he didn't act like a kid. He had a responsible job. He'd worked hard at the police academy, graduating third in a class of a hundred. He'd taken a job in San Francisco for a year, and he'd been the top rookie. But he'd missed life in Glenwood, and when Travis had offered him a job in the county sheriff's department, he'd been glad to come home. He knew deep inside that he could have made it in San Francisco, or in any other big city, if he'd wanted to.

He shifted on the chair and tried to look at it from Sandy's point of view. She'd been gone less than an hour and had come home to a bleeding kid. That would be enough to send anyone into a tailspin. She'd overreacted. He was pretty sure she would see that she'd been unreasonable and apologize. He'd been trying to help Blake by teaching him how to protect himself. Could a woman understand that? He smiled. He doubted Sandy would appreciate that particular question. Walking in on him teaching Blake to defend himself had only made it worse for her. In time, she would see that lesson was important to the boy.

He took another swallow of beer and settled the bottle on the floor. He was rationalizing because he didn't want to face the truth. Sandy could be right about everything. After all, he was a Haynes. Four generations of failed marriages and broken families were hard to argue with. So far, the only brother that was making his relationship work was Travis. He wondered how he'd gotten so lucky.

Kyle didn't know what a happy marriage looked like. His old man had been gone more than he'd been home. His father's idea of good parenting was to smack the boys up the side of the head every now and then, whether or not they needed it. He always said, if they hadn't gotten into trouble, they would. To consider it punishment in advance.

His mother had been physically in the house, but emotionally just as distant. Now that Kyle was an adult, he couldn't blame her for her bitterness. Being married to Earl Haynes had to have been a living death. Her husband hadn't believed in fidelity, or seen the wisdom in being discreet. He'd flaunted his affairs, excusing them by pointing out he always woke up in his own bed. Kyle grimaced. Yeah, like the old man had been a saint.

His mother had finally left the summer he, Kyle, had turned fifteen. He wondered if she'd waited until he was old enough to be on his own, or if her patience and sanity had finally cracked. Whatever the reason, she'd disappeared. There hadn't even been a note.

For Kyle, life had gotten worse. Jordan had been his only brother still at home, but he'd been a senior and had arranged his schedule to be gone a lot. Craig and Travis already had their lives. He couldn't count on them. It was just him and the old man. He'd had three stepmothers in three years, each one younger than the previous one. The last one had walked into his bedroom one evening and hit on him. He'd been too shocked to do anything but duck out the window and spend the night in the tree house. He'd moved in with a friend for the rest of the summer, then had left for college in the fall.

He opened his eyes and stared at his living room. He'd tried to be different from his father. They all had. No one wanted to mess things up that badly. For Kyle, that meant leaving before getting left. He wondered if that was just another description of running away.

A hand-drawn picture pinned to the wall fluttered in the breeze from the open window. Nichole had made it for him. It showed a group of butterflies in a field of flowers. At least he thought they were butterflies. They could have been birds. One of Lindsay's books sat on the coffee table next to a baseball puzzle he'd been working on with Blake. In a few short weeks, Sandy's children had become a part of his days. He wanted to be a father, so he'd tried to be a father to them. It was temporary, perhaps even foolish. Now the thought of being without them made his bones ache.

He knew they would miss him, too. So where did that leave him? Was this a blessing in disguise? If they broke things off now, if he stepped out of their lives, they would recover quickly and get on with things. If he continued to be there for them, they would start to depend upon him. Was he willing to risk that? For the first time, Kyle began to see there was more at stake here than himself. Three other lives would be affected by his actions. Walking away from a woman was one thing, walking away from kids was something much worse.

Up until today, he'd been playing a game. Sandy was right. With her, he'd been toying with the past, teasing them both with sparks they felt when they were together. He didn't want to hurt her or the kids. He didn't want to get hurt himself. If it was just a game to him, he needed to walk away now. Before it got ugly.

Simple enough, he told himself. He would walk. Because it *was* just a game, right? Sure he liked her. How could he not? She would do anything to protect those she cared about. She had a giving heart. He'd seen it years before when his mother had walked out and Sandy had come by to pick up the pieces. She wasn't afraid of doing the right thing, even if it made her unpopular.

Okay, he could handle liking and respecting her. So what? His feelings weren't serious. He didn't want to risk it all and get involved. Because Sandy would leave. Everyone left eventually. The price of being wrong was too high. He didn't need her or the kids.

He finished the beer and picked up a book he'd been reading. But the silence filling the room made it impossible to concentrate. He missed the laughter. He missed them. It wasn't that they'd been gone so long, it was knowing he might not see them again. Or Sandy.

Since she'd come back, she was all he thought about. For a while, he'd thought it was an adult manifestation of his adolescent crush. But what if it was something more? What if she was the one and he let her get away? What if she wasn't the one and she left him broken and bleeding? He'd thought her marriage to Thomas had been perfect. According to her, it hadn't been. She'd made a mistake. What if he was making a worse one?

Sandy adjusted the sheets around her son's shoulders. There was a light blanket folded at the foot of the bed. It was warm during the day, but always cooled off at night. She glanced at the open window, then back at Blake.

"Are you going to be all right?" she asked.

"Mo-om," he said. "I told you, it doesn't even hurt."

Her gaze moved to the bruise next to his mouth. It was about the diameter of a baseball. The swelling had gone down some, but it still looked ugly. By morning, the red would darken to purple.

"I saw you wincing at dinner."

"The soup was too hot."

"Sure it was." She brushed his hair off his forehead. The rest of the family had had tacos for dinner, but she'd fixed something easier for Blake to eat.

She still couldn't believe her son had gotten in a fight. Just thinking about it made her furious. The problem was, she didn't know if she was angry with Kyle or herself. She wanted to blame him for not taking better care of Blake, but ultimately the responsibility was hers. When she was around him, she didn't think—she just reacted.

"Don't be mad," Blake said.

She forced herself to smile at him. "I'm not."

"Uh-huh. Your eyes are getting all scrunchy. You're still mad at Kyle, aren't you?"

She leaned forward and kissed his cheek. "That's between us adults."

"Lindsay said we won't get to see him anymore. Is that true?" He sounded lost at the thought.

During the day, when her children were moving around, she thought of them as growing, determined people. But at night, in their beds, they seemed smaller and defenseless. Easily hurt by the pitfalls of life.

"It's my fault," she said, and touched his uninjured cheek. "I shouldn't have let you kids get so involved with Kyle so quickly. I haven't decided yet, but maybe it would be for the best if we didn't—"

"No!" He raised himself up onto his elbows. "No, Mom. Don't say we can't see him. The fight was my fault. Really. Gary threw a ball at Robby on purpose. When Robby started to stand up to Gary, I said he'd done it, too. So after he hit Robby, he started coming after me." He sagged back to the bed. "Kyle said if I'd tried to defend myself, Gary wouldn't have hit me. He said he's a bully and bullies only go after people who don't know how to defend themselves."

Sandy blinked in confusion. "Who are Gary and Robby, and what does this have to do with your getting hit?"

Blake took a deep breath. "I went over to Robby's to play baseball with the guys..."

Her son gave her a more detailed explanation of what had happened. She listened carefully. When he got to the part about defending Robby against the neighborhood bully, she took his hand and squeezed it. "That was very brave of you," she said.

Blake squirmed. "I didn't know he was gonna hit me."

"Still, standing up for someone you just met isn't something most boys would do. I'm glad you did the right thing. What happened next?"

"Gary and his friends chased me out of the yard and onto that dirt road. Gary said he was gonna beat me up. I didn't know what to do, but I didn't want to run. Then Kyle came through the bushes and yelled at Gary to let me alone." He grimaced. "When I heard Kyle, I looked at him. That's when Gary punched me. Kyle chased 'em off. He said the best way to deal with a bully is to know how to defend myself. He started to show me how." The un-bruised side of his mouth turned down. "That's when you came in and got real upset."

"I see." Sandy rose and walked to the window. She closed it halfway, then stared out at the night. From what Blake told her, Kyle had done what he could to stop the fight. Kyle had tried to tell her that, but she had been too busy assigning blame. Why? she wondered. Why did she always want him to be the bad guy?

"Mom, can I play with Robby again?"

She turned to look at her son. He hadn't had a friend in a long time. "Sure, honey. You can go over there, or have him come here. You two will probably want to avoid Gary, though.''

"Yeah. I don't like him."

She needed to talk with Gary's parents. Then she realized she didn't know the boy's last name. She would have to ask Kyle. If he was still speaking to her.

"Are you mad at Kyle?" Blake asked.

"Not in the way you think. Grown-ups have different kinds of mad."

"But we didn't go to his house for the barbecue."

No surprise there. She'd told Kyle she wanted him to stay away from her. She flinched. She'd overreacted. She saw that now. Once again she'd reacted to the fear of not being in control. "You wouldn't have been able to eat anything," she said.

"I know, but I could have, you know, been there." Blake looked at her. "I like Kyle, Mom. He's gonna teach me how to defend myself so Gary can't hurt me again."

Sandy wasn't sure how she felt about that, but she didn't want to get into it tonight. "We'll talk in the morning. Right now, why don't you get some sleep?"

"Okay." He turned onto his side.

She moved next to the bed, then bent down and kissed his cheek, being careful to stay away from the bruise. Then she turned off the light and left the room. Nichole was already in bed, but Lindsay was waiting downstairs. Sandy wasn't ready to face her oldest yet.

She paused by the top of the stairs and tried to remember everything she'd said to Kyle. It was all a blur. She remembered parking the car and starting to get out. Lindsay had come running outside and told her Blake had been in a fight and was bleeding. Her next clear memory was standing in Kyle's kitchen and telling him she wanted him out of her life. He'd tried to explain, but she hadn't let him. It was so much easier to make everything his fault. If it wasn't, she would have to look to herself. She would have to question why she did things. She couldn't afford to let her carefully constructed world crumble. It was all she had.

She sat on the top stair and buried her face in her hands. It was all too confusing. Her body was screaming at her, yelling, "He's the one, he's the one," while her head kept calling her a fool. Kyle had the potential to break her heart and that had her running scared. She'd made such a huge mistake with Thomas. She'd taken a look at the exterior package and had assumed he was what he appeared to be. Who ever heard of a philosophy professor who went rock climbing and cut class to surf? She didn't want to be stupid again.

So where did that leave her? If only Kyle hadn't asked her if she was ever lonely. By bringing the question to the light of day, she'd been forced to face reality. The truth was she'd spent her life being lonely. As a child, her days had been filled with secrets. Caring for an alcoholic mother hadn't been easy. After her mother had died, she'd expected to only feel relief. Instead, she'd mourned her parent. The move to Glenwood had allowed her to heal some, but she realized now it had come too late. She'd never been able to let go enough to be a child again. She'd crossed the line to adulthood and there wasn't any going back.

With Thomas, she'd hoped to finally find a place to belong, a relationship between equals, where she could be both care giver and care receiver. She'd wanted to let someone else carry the burden for a while. It wasn't to be. She'd found that out the first week of classes, when he'd skipped lectures to surf. She still remembered how shocked she'd been. He was the professor. He'd shrugged off her concern by pointing out there were only a certain number of good surfing days in the fall, and he intended to take advantage of all of them.

She'd tried to make the marriage work, but it was destined to fail. Thomas had been content to let her take care of everything and she hadn't been willing to let some things go undone in an effort to force him to help. So the loneliness had gotten bigger until it filled her life and left her numb.

Sandy rose slowly and walked down the stairs. She stepped into the family room. Their blue floral-print sectional sofa blended with the soft ivory walls. She'd found an old rug in the attic and had aired it for a couple of days. The blue and rust tones brought out the colors from the couch and the hardwood floors, making the room look homey. Lindsay sat in the far corner of the sectional. She had the TV on, but the sound turned low.

Sandy sat in the oak rocker she'd bought when she first found out she was pregnant. It felt like yesterday, but it was over thirteen years ago. She'd sat in the chair night after night with her hand on her belly, willing her baby to be happy and healthy. Lindsay sure wasn't happy today.

"I've about had it with your sulking," Sandy said, throwing down the gauntlet. If she didn't jump start her daughter into talking about what she was feeling, Lindsay would spend the next week moving from room to room and sighing loudly whenever anyone was in earshot.

"I'm *not* sulking," Lindsay said, glaring at her. "I'm simply wondering why you enjoy ruining my life."

"How is your life ruined?"

Her daughter rolled her eyes. "You *know*."

"Because I don't want you to see Kyle so much? Honey, it's not good for you to spend too much time over there. He's an older man. You have these . . ." She paused, not wanting to make the situation worse. "You have these ideas about him, but they aren't realistic. You're still a child."

Lindsay jumped to her feet. Her long brown hair spilled over her face. She brushed it back impatiently. Sandy recognized the movement as one she made frequently herself. They were more alike than they looked on the surface. Maybe that's why they were often at each other's throats.

"I'm not a child. I'm practically a teenager. I'm growing up, even if you don't want to admit it. Maybe because I'm young and beautiful and it makes you feel old."

Sandy forced herself to remain calm. "Talking and thinking ugly is going to make you ugly inside and out, young lady. I'm trying to treat you like the mature person you claim to be, but if you act like a child, I'll send you to your room just like I would with Nichole."

"Please." She put her hands on her hips. "I don't think it's fair for you to tell me who I can and can't see."

"I don't want you at Kyle's house by yourself." She met her daughter's mutinous stare. "I'm going to talk to him in a couple of days. If we get everything straightened out, then yes, we'll have contact with him. As neighbors. It's not right for you to be there all the time. He's got a personal life, and he doesn't need a young girl getting in the way of that."

"It's not like that," Lindsay said loudly. "It's not. He likes me. You're being mean because Daddy loved me more than you. You're afraid Kyle likes me more, too. You're punishing me for that."

She started to run out of the room. Sandy jumped up and grabbed Lindsay's arm. Tears filled her daughter's brown eyes. Sandy pulled her close and held her. Lindsay resisted, then sagged against her.

"Hush," Sandy murmured. "We're all a little on edge since we moved. It's been a big change for all of us."

Lindsay continued to cry.

Sandy smoothed the girl's hair and wondered where the first mistake had been made. Had it been letting Lindsay go off with her father? Who knows what Thomas had told the child. Lindsay had made this accusation before. Sandy wasn't sure what it meant. She suspected her daughter was afraid her father had loved her more, and she felt guilty about that. Or maybe Lindsay knew how Sandy had been hurt. Sandy hated to admit the weakness, but sometimes she had felt left out of Thomas and Lindsay's special world.

"I never resented the time you spent with your father," she said. At least that was true. She'd done her best to understand.

"Really?" Lindsay raised her head and looked at her. "But I heard you guys fighting about it. You didn't want me to go."

"That wasn't about you. I was afraid he wouldn't take good care of you. He was forgetful."

"I know." Lindsay gave her a shaky grin. "He left me at a rest stop a couple of times, but he always came back for me."

Sandy hugged her close. She didn't know whether to be furious or to laugh. It's a good thing she hadn't known that while Lindsay and Thomas were gone, or she would have worried herself to death. The important point was that Lindsay was fine now, and they were together.

"I love you," Sandy said. "No matter what, I'll always love you. I know you don't always agree with what I say or the rules I insist you follow, but I hope you know I set them because I think they're the best thing for you. I don't make rules just to be mean."

Lindsay sniffed. "I know, Mom. I'm sorry I said that. I didn't mean it. I was just upset about, you know."

Kyle. Sandy was afraid there wasn't anything she could do about her daughter's crush except let it run its course. Eventually, Lindsay would discover Kyle was just a guy. Or maybe she would notice a boy her own age.

Sandy stepped back. "Are we okay?"

Lindsay nodded. "I'm going up to my room and read. 'Night."

"'Night." Sandy walked into the family room and sat in the rocking chair. The TV continued to play silently. She ignored the images and instead wondered if she would ever learn how to be a parent. It felt as if every time she got one mothering skill mastered, her kids grew a little and needed something else. Maybe she should spend some time with Lindsay alone. They could do the female bonding thing.

Or she could just curl up under a rock until all these problems went away. She sighed. One thing was sure. She was going to have to talk to Kyle. She needed to apologize for some of the awful things she'd said to him.

He had every right to be furious with her. She couldn't remember all the names she'd called him, but she was confident she'd hurt him. She shook her head. Since she'd come back to Glenwood, she barely recognized herself. Her nerves were shot, her hormones in a constant state of arousal. Her body hummed at the thought of seeing him. It didn't make sense. She was dealing with a part of herself she'd long thought dead. She wasn't prepared for this; it wasn't fair. Her entire world was unraveling and she didn't know how to make the process stop.

Tomorrow, she would talk to Kyle, she promised herself. She would apologize and ask him about that Gary kid, and find out where the boy lived so she could speak with his parents. Next, she would discuss whether or not Blake really needed to know how to defend himself. She hated to think of her son getting in fights, but she also didn't want him beat up. This had to be some kind of guy thing she would never understand.

The list made, she was able to relax. It wouldn't be that difficult. Kyle was fair-minded. He would forgive her and things would go back the way they had been. He would be charming and far too good-looking, and she would resist temptation with all her might.

She ignored the little voice in the back of her mind that whispered the question asking what wonderful thing might happen if, just once, she forgot she was supposed to resist.

Chapter Ten

Kyle folded the blank piece of paper one last time, then laid it flat to smooth the edges. He grasped the bottom and aimed toward the open glass door that led into the hallway, then he let the paper airplane go. It soared toward the ceiling, looped around once, took a nosedive for the floor and crash-landed about a yard from the trash can.

Travis came in the from his office and stared at the crumpled plane. He glanced at the paper, then his brother and grinned. "Woman trouble. Who is she?"

Kyle didn't bother answering. He wasn't in the mood to be harassed with well-meaning advice. He rubbed his hand over his chin and tried to stay awake. He told himself his sleeplessness the night before had more to do with switching from graveyard to days than it did with Sandy, but he knew he was lying.

"Your silence means you don't want to talk about her." Travis sat on the corner of Kyle's desk. "Excuse me for mentioning it, little brother, but you look awful."

"Good. I feel awful."

"Is it Sandy?"

Kyle glanced up into eyes that were the same dark brown as his own. All four Haynes brothers had dark hair and eyes. He was the tallest; Travis was an inch shorter. They were most alike in looks. He, Travis and Craig were most alike in temperament, with Jordan being the moody one in the group. But they all had one thing in common—a history of failed relationships. At least Travis had managed to make his second marriage work.

"Maybe," he admitted.

"That's a yes." Travis leaned toward him. "What's the problem?"

"She hates me."

"Is that all?"

"Thanks for the sympathy." He wondered if he should just ignore the whole damn thing. That's what Sandy wanted. She thought everything that had happened with Blake was his fault. She'd been quick to judge and had refused to listen to his explanations. He shouldn't try to change her opinion. Only it wasn't that easy. He didn't want her to be mad at him.

"So what did you do?" he asked Travis.

"About?"

"Elizabeth." Kyle leaned back in his chair and rested his heels on the corner of the desk. "How did you know she was the right one? How did you know it would be different from Julie?"

Travis's first marriage had ended in divorce. He'd moped around for a year or so, then had started dating again. It had seemed that the Haynes curse was hard at work, until Travis had met Elizabeth.

Travis studied him for a long time. "It's that serious?" he asked.

"I don't know." He picked up a pen and studied it, then set it down. "Maybe. She got mad at me yesterday. Her son, Blake, got in a fight. She thinks I wasn't being responsible. She said a few things that forced me to take a look at myself."

His brother nodded. "When I first met Elizabeth, I knew I was attracted to her, but I didn't know she was going to be the one for me. When I finally figured it out, I was scared as hell."

"I remember."

Travis grimaced. "The Haynes curse. Four generations of men who managed to screw up perfectly good relationships. I'd been faithful to Julie, and our marriage still hadn't worked, so I knew it was more than that. But I didn't know what. I was afraid we'd been born with a gene missing or something." He grinned.

Kyle didn't smile back. Maybe his brother was right. Maybe there was something fundamentally wrong with all of them. It would explain a lot of things.

"Then I found out it was a lot simpler than that. I just had to decide."

"Decide what?" Kyle asked.

"Decide to make it work. I'd always thought I couldn't be a good husband or father. Look at what we were raised with. Then I figured out our father chose to be with those other women. He chose to be gone and ignore us and Mom. He chose to be a first-class bastard and I could choose to be something else."

"As easy as that?" It couldn't be that simple.

"It wasn't easy. I had a lot to learn. But Elizabeth has been patient with me and I'm getting better."

Kyle lowered his feet to the floor and leaned forward. He rested his forearms on the desk. "But how did you know she was the one?"

"I couldn't imagine life without her."

Kyle had spent most of the previous night trying to imagine what his world would be like now that Sandy had taken herself from him. He hadn't wanted to picture the long days, the silence. Even consoling himself with the thought that there were any number of women he could call hadn't made him feel better.

"What if she can imagine life without me?" he asked glumly.

"You mean you haven't seduced her with the famous Haynes charm?"

He shook his head. "I think she's immune. She accused me of skating by on my looks. Form over substance." He looked up at his boss. "Do I have any character?"

Travis laughed. "Hell, Kyle, you're my little brother. I'm not supposed to make you feel better, I'm supposed to make you suffer."

"That was when we were kids."

Travis sobered. "Yes, you've got a lot of character. You work hard here. Why do you think I offered you the job in the first place?"

"I never could figure that out."

"You graduated at the top of your academy class, and you were ranked highest of all the rookies on the SFPD. Why wouldn't I want to hire you? I spent the first year waiting for you to tell me you were going back to the city. That being a deputy in this little town was too boring."

"So how about a raise?"

"Talk to me after the county commissioners present the budget."

Kyle leaned back in his chair. Once he'd returned to Glenwood, he hadn't wanted to live anywhere else. This was home to him. He liked the pace of life, and the roots he had here. Everything in his life worked. Except for Sandy.

"I should probably just forget about her," he mumbled. She'd made her feelings pretty clear last night. He'd assumed she would realize her mistake and want to apologize, but what if he was wrong about that? What if she was still mad at him? Then, worrying about being a part of her life wasn't going to matter. She would chase him off with a shotgun if she saw him coming.

But the thought of not seeing her again, of not being near her and touching her, made his chest ache. He wanted to call her up and ask her to hear him out. He wanted to have her kids over, even Lindsay, and take them to a movie. He wanted to hear the laughter and feel as if he was a part of a family. Funny, growing up with both parents and three brothers, he'd never felt as if he'd belonged. With Sandy and her kids, he felt whole.

Normally, this was the point in a relationship where he thought about running away. This time, he didn't want to leave. At least not yet. He was willing to risk a little more. The thought scared him though. She could leave him trampled and bleeding. But he had to take a chance.

"I think you should wait for a sign," Travis said.

"That's the stupidest thing I ever heard."

"I'm serious. If something happens in the next five minutes that tells you it's meant to be, then go for it. If nothing happens, then forget about her."

Kyle glanced at his older brother. "You've been working out in the garden without a hat, haven't you?"

Travis shrugged. "It's just a suggestion. I'm a great believer in signs."

Before Kyle could respond to that, the station door opened and Sandy walked in. He felt his jaw drop. "Holy—" Talk about a sign.

Travis slid off the corner of his desk and stood up. "I told you."

Kyle rose and glared at him. "You're not so smart."

Travis chuckled. "I know. I saw her car pull up." He glanced at the clock. "Look, it's time for your break." Still laughing, he went back into his office.

Kyle opened the wood-and-glass door that led to the waiting area. Except for Sandy, it was mercifully empty.

She was standing by one of the wooden benches that lined the wall. It was quiet in the middle of the afternoon. They were alone.

She glanced at him. Her green eyes were dark with emotions he couldn't read. Or maybe he didn't want to know what she was thinking. He stuck his hands into his pockets and waited.

Sandy wore a peach sundress. He was used to seeing her in shorts, but he liked how the thin fabric molded itself to her breasts, then flared out at the waist. Skinny straps held the bodice in place. Her slight tan made her hair look lighter.

She twisted the shoulder strap of her purse several times, stared at the floor, then looked back at him.

"Hi," she said at last.

"Hi, yourself."

"I went by your house but you weren't there, so I figured you might be working."

"Here I am." He motioned to the benches. "You want to sit down?"

"Sure." She lowered herself to one end of the seat.

He didn't know how close to get, so he took the bench next to hers. There was about two feet between them. "What's going on? Are the kids okay?"

"What? Oh, they're, um, outside eating ice cream. We went to that place across the street. Blake's doing really well. Most of the swelling is gone, although the bruise is turning some pretty interesting colors."

"I'll bet."

He wondered if the conversation could have been more awkward. He wanted to ask why she'd come, but a part of him didn't care why. It was enough that she was here. He studied her face, the wide eyes, the slightly pointed chin, the trace of lipstick on her mouth. He wanted to kiss her. More than that, he wanted to hold her and have her tell him it was going to be okay between them.

She drew in a deep breath. "I've come to eat crow. I can eat it cold, if you insist, although it might go down a little easier if I can heat it in the microwave."

A fierce feeling of gladness swept over him. He forced himself to stay still. "I don't mind if it's warm."

She smiled slightly. "Thanks." Her smile faded. "Look, Kyle, I was wrong. I came home after dropping Nichole off and Lindsay told me Blake had been in a fight and he was bleeding. I just lost it. When I came into your place and saw you teaching him how to fight more—well, I reacted without thinking." She stared at the purse on her lap. "I don't remember everything I said. I just sort of went into protective mother rage. I was scared and I lashed out at you. Blake told me what happened. I know he wasn't really fighting. Gary hit him when he wasn't looking." She raised her gaze to him. "I also know you tried to stop it. I'm sorry about all the things I said. I hope you can forgive me."

At fourteen, he'd thought she was the most beautiful girl in the world. At thirty, he thought she was the most beautiful woman. There was something about her combination of features, or her eyes, or her smile that made him crazy when he was near her. She could turn him on with a glance. She could reduce him to a whimpering mass with just a word. He had it bad, and it scared him. But for once, he wasn't going to run away.

"Before I accept your apology, there's something I have to tell you," he said. "It might make you mad all over again, but this time hear me out before beating me up, okay?"

She flushed. "I'm not an evil-tempered witch, but okay, I'll listen first."

"Great." He leaned forward and rested his elbows on his knees. "I went and spoke with Gary Warner's parents."

There was a moment of silence. He didn't risk glancing at her. Instead, he waited.

"Why?" she asked at last.

"Two reasons. I went because I was concerned about what had happened with Blake. The kid hit him when Blake wasn't looking. That's not right. I've known his folks for a while and they're good people. I thought there might be trouble at home, and they should be aware of what was happening in their son's life. The second reason I went was because if Gary's already acting like this when he's ten, by the time he's thirteen, he could be stealing or causing other kinds of trouble. As a deputy in this town, I want to prevent that. So are you mad or what?"

"Or what," she said softly.

He glanced at her. She was smiling. He liked the way her lips curved up and the faint crinkles by her eyes. He liked the way she leaned toward him. The sweet scent of her perfume drifted to him. He inhaled the fragrance knowing other women could wear the scent and it would never be the same.

"I meant I'm not mad," she said. "I appreciate your taking the initiative. What happened when you went to see them?"

He straightened and angled toward her. He rested his left foot on the opposite knee and stretched his arm out along the back of the bench. "They were very nice about the whole thing. They're getting a divorce and fighting over who gets full custody of Gary. According to his mother, he's been acting up for a while, but they didn't know it was so bad. They're going to talk to him and make sure he gets some counseling. Then I spoke with Robby's parents." He glanced at her. "Did Blake mention him?"

"Yes, he said he liked him a lot and wanted to know if he could play with him again."

"Robby's a good kid. I talked to his dad. He's going to sign his son up for a martial arts class. He thinks it'll give him some confidence." He opened his mouth to tell Sandy she should think about the same thing for Blake, then reminded himself it wasn't his business.

"Maybe I should do that, too," she said.

"Gee, that's what I was thinking."

"I know. I could read your expression. But you were afraid to say something." She bit her lower lip. "I was horrible yesterday, Kyle. I really am sorry."

"I know. It's okay."

"It's not." Her green eyes darkened with regret. "Some of my anger wasn't even about you. Thomas used to take Lindsay with him on his trips now and then. They always had a good time. It made me feel left out. I think that's how I felt yesterday. You'd been there for Blake, and I was jealous." She stared at her hands. "Pretty shallow of me."

"Actually, it makes perfect sense." He studied the top of her head. He'd never thought of Sandy as being insecure, but maybe she was. "Why didn't you ever go with Lindsay and Thomas?" he asked.

"I couldn't. I had two other smaller children to look after." She glanced at him and sighed. "I know what you're thinking. Maybe I was using them as an excuse. Maybe I said I couldn't go, hoping Thomas would insist and prove it was important to him that I come along. Maybe I wanted him to think I was still fun to be around."

He was so startled by her confession he didn't know what to say. "Sandy, I—"

"No." She shook her head. "It's true. I can be a little grim. But it's hard to be spontaneous *and* responsible. I don't want my kids growing up the way I did. Always afraid. Wondering if there's enough food for dinner."

She sniffed and he realized she was close to tears. He'd never seen her cry. "I think you're a fine mother," he said. "I admire you."

Her smile was a little shaky at the corners. "Really?"

"Yeah." He touched her cheek. "Really."

"Thanks. You're not so bad yourself." She stared at his face, then dropped her gaze lower, to his chest. "I haven't seen you in uniform before. It sort of shocked me when I came in."

"Most women like it," he said.

"Mmm, I can see why."

Instantly her eyes widened and a bright spot of color flared on each cheek. The sight of Sensible Sandy reduced to embarrassed silence went a long way to restoring his ego. He knew enough about women to know she wasn't immune to him, but he wasn't sure attraction was enough. Of course, he wasn't sure what he wanted yet, either. He just knew he didn't want to have to think of being without her. He was going to risk trying. Just this once. If she walked all over him, then he would have to figure out a way to recover. If she was interested in a relationship, he was going to have to learn to face his fears.

"I'm sorry we missed our barbecue," he said. "Maybe we could try rescheduling."

She glanced at him, then away. "Sure. The kids really missed you last night. I got an earful from all three of them."

"Did you miss me?"

She swallowed. "Um, yes." Her voice was a whisper.

He placed his hand on top of hers, stilling her nervous movements. She hadn't put her wedding ring back on. He was pleased. "Maybe we could try being friends as well as neighbors. I'm willing to admit I'm too charming if you'll admit you're a little too responsible."

She glared at him, but didn't pull her hands away. "Oh, sure. You get to admit to a fun thing. I'm supposed to admit to being a stick-in-the-mud. That's not fair."

"I like that you're responsible. Being Sensible Sandy is one of your best qualities."

"Don't call me that." She wasn't mad. The tone of her voice was low, soft and sultry. The look in her eyes was anything but annoyed.

The air around them thickened with tension. It wasn't just about sex and it should have scared him away, but it didn't. It made him want to lean closer. Not necessarily to kiss her, although he wouldn't mind that. But to be with her, a part of her life. It was different from desire—it terrified him, yet he wanted more.

"I like everything about you," he admitted. "Except that you've forgotten how to have fun. I could teach you. It's something I'm good at."

"I'll bet." She started to pull away.

He grasped her hands more closely. "The world won't end if you let go of your control for an hour or two."

"I know. But—"

He leaned closer. Close enough to feel the heat of her body. Close enough that kissing was only a temptation away. "Trust me."

Her lips parted. "I shouldn't."

He moved that last inch and brushed his mouth against hers. The quick contact left them both breathing hard. "You're right, you shouldn't trust me, but you do."

She smiled. "I guess I do."

"But I don't want to," Lindsay said, glaring at her mother.

Sandy took a deep breath and prayed for patience. "Honey, it'll be fun for you. I feel badly that you haven't had a chance to make any friends your own age." She glanced around at the large park. Children from five through fifteen milled around. The summer park program had started its last session, and Sandy had enrolled all three kids.

"I don't want to be friends with anyone dorky enough to do this," Lindsay complained. "Look how weird-looking they are."

She pointed at a pale, dark-haired boy wearing thick glasses and orthodontic headgear. Sandy bit back a smile. "You be nice to that boy," she said. "He might be a nerd now, but in a few years, he might be the president of some fast-growing high-tech company. He'll be rich."

Lindsay looked doubtful.

Sandy gave her a hug. "Come on. Just give it a try. One afternoon. If you hate it, I won't make you come back."

"Promise?"

Sandy nodded. She gave Lindsay a little push toward the row of tables set up by the parking lot. The posted signs told children to register by age group. "I swear I won't force you to do it again. But you have to try. No sitting in the corner and sulking."

Lindsay rolled her eyes. "Mom, it's a park. There aren't any corners."

"You know what I mean. Now, Robby's mom is going to give you a ride home. I'm going to the grocery store this afternoon. If I'm not back before you guys, you know what to do."

"Stay inside with the door locked. Watch TV and avoid snacks that require heating. We've been over this a hundred times. I'm twelve. Lots of girls my age are baby-sitting."

"I know. I can't help worrying. Do you have your house key?"

Lindsay pulled a chain up from behind her yellow T-shirt. The house key dangled on the end.

Sandy bent down and gave her a quick kiss on the cheek. "See you later."

"Bye." Lindsay turned and walked toward the registration tables. A cute boy who looked about fourteen smiled at her. Lindsay tossed her head and suddenly looked incredibly grown-up. They were changing fast, Sandy thought as she returned to her car.

She paused before getting in and scanned the park. Children played everywhere. The younger kids were on the far side, so she couldn't see Nichole, but Blake and his new best friend, Robby, had already joined a softball game in progress. Her son was laughing as he waited his turn at bat.

She slipped into the driver's seat and started the engine. Blake was going to be all right. For a long time, she'd worried about her only son. No matter what she'd said to Thomas, she couldn't convince her husband that his son needed him. Thomas had neglected the boy shamefully. It didn't help that she knew why. Blake was too much like Thomas—the red hair, the glasses, the slight build. After all her years of marriage, she'd finally realized that Thomas liked his dangerous sports because they proved his masculinity. He'd been ridiculed as a child for being small and skinny. She thought that might have made him more compassionate with Blake, but it hadn't. Instead, he'd turned his back on his son, and Blake had been the one to suffer.

That was changing, Sandy reminded herself as she drove down the quiet streets of Glenwood. They were all starting to fit in. Sandy and Robby's mother, Alice, had become friendly. They were sharing car-pool responsibilities for the summer camp. Nichole and Mandy had become best friends. Blake had Robby. Only Lindsay hadn't met someone her own age. Hopefully, the camp would change that.

She turned onto her street. Overhead, tall, leafy trees touched over the center of the road creating a tunnel of shade. She liked the older houses with the wide porches and big windows. She liked that she knew her neighbors, that they waved when they saw her and that she could let her children play outside without worrying about them.

She was a long way from Los Angeles, but she didn't miss the city at all.

She turned down her driveway—and hit the brake. Kyle was waiting for her in front of her house. He sat on the porch stairs and next to him was his large, black motorcycle. Nestled together on the seat were two safety helmets.

He'd promised to teach her how to have fun. Did this mean the lessons began today?

She eased the car forward. Self-consciously, she touched her hair. She hadn't done anything but slip on a headband. Her red shorts and white T-shirt were clean, but not especially stylish. She wasn't ready for this.

She'd seen Kyle a few times since she'd gone to apologize to him, but he hadn't said anything about having fun together. She'd thought maybe he'd forgotten or had just been kidding. In the deepest, most secret part of her heart, she'd been disappointed. Apparently, he hadn't forgotten, he'd simply been biding his time.

She stopped the car and got out. "Hi."

"Hi." He stood up. Six feet two inches of lean, sexy male. Worn button-fly jeans hugged his hips and thighs. His tank shirt exposed tanned, muscled shoulders. Aviator sunglasses hid his eyes, but his mouth was smiling. Did he know what he did to her? Did he sense that her stomach clenched every time she saw him or that her heart pounded harder and faster? Did he know he made her palms damp and her knees tremble? She kept waiting for her nervous reaction to him to go away, but it didn't. She wondered if it ever would.

"I thought we'd go for a ride," he said, walking over to the bike.

"I've never been on a motorcycle before."

He raised his eyebrows. "Then it's time. Go put your purse inside."

She ran upstairs and unlocked the front door. After dropping her purse on the floor of the coat closet, she tucked her keys into her shorts' pocket, stepped back outside and locked the door behind her.

Kyle had already put on his helmet and straddled the bike. He looked dangerous and exciting. He tempted her and she didn't know how to resist. She told herself she should. He would only bring her pain and heartache. But she didn't want to listen to that voice today. She didn't want to hear dire warnings about what might happen in the future. She wanted to live for the moment.

"Come on," he said, holding out the extra helmet.

She walked down the stairs and took it from him. When she'd settled it on her head, he adjusted the chin strap. "How does that feel?" he asked. "Shake your head and see how loose it is."

She quickly turned her head from side to side. "It's fine." The fit was perfect. Too perfect. "So, how many women have you taken out on this thing?" she asked, motioning to the bike.

He laughed. "Not many. Don't worry. It's not part of my seduction routine. I don't need props. Slide on behind me."

Of course he didn't. She was walking, breathing *quivering* proof of that. His raw sexuality was enough to seduce anyone.

She glanced at the house. She'd planned to spend her afternoon lining her dresser drawers and relaxing. She glanced back at Kyle. The drawers could wait. After all, how often did a woman like her get to spend an afternoon with a man like him? She might as well experience the

Haynes charm full on. Besides, she'd always wanted to ride a motorcycle.

She rested her hand on his shoulder for balance, then slipped her leg over the seat. When she was settled, he showed her where to put her feet.

"Hang on," he said, grabbing her hands and pulling them around to hug his midsection. "I'm about to change your life."

Chapter Eleven

Kyle had thought the motorcycle ride would be fun for Sandy. He hadn't given any thought to what it would mean to him. As he headed down the driveway toward the street, he felt her shifting on the seat, trying to get comfortable. He grinned. The ride was going to be pure torture, and he couldn't think of anything he wanted more.

From breasts to knees, her body pressed against him. He could feel the heat of her. Slender thighs cradled his rear, her hands gripped his midsection. The neighbor's dog came running out to bark at them. Sandy laughed and he felt the vibration through his back.

At the bottom of the driveway, he paused. "Lean into the turns," he said. "That'll help me steer. I'm not going to go fast, or get on the highway, so don't be scared."

"I'm not," she said into his ear. "I like it already."

He liked it, too. "Hold on," he called and hit the gas.

They turned onto the narrow residential street. At the stop sign, he turned left, then left again at the first light.

They headed toward the west side of town, which was less populated. Sandy clung to him. He moved with the speed of traffic. It was a warm summer afternoon. Mothers and their children walked along the wide shady sidewalks in front of the stores in the shopping section. To their left was the park where Sandy had taken her kids for the summer program.

"Do you think they can see us?" she asked as they drove past the children.

"I don't think so. They won't recognize you with your helmet."

He thought she said "good" but he wasn't sure. At the next signal, he put his feet on the asphalt and steadied the bike with his legs. "You're squeezing the stuffing out of me," he called over his shoulder.

"Oh." She glanced over his shoulder at her hands clutching together in front of his belly. "Sorry. What should I do?"

He was making it worse, he told himself. He was a fool for taunting himself with what he couldn't have. At least not today. But he wanted to feel her touching him, and he wasn't above using devious means to make that happen.

"Try keeping your hands flat. That way, you won't be able to squeeze so tight."

She had been holding on pretty hard, but it hadn't bothered him. When she did as he asked and opened her hands so her palms pressed against him, he had to hold back a groan. Her touch was sweeter than he'd thought it would be. He reacted instantly and predictably. Good thing they were on a public street, otherwise he would be tempted to push her hands lower, to the hardness pressing against the button-fly of his jeans.

The light turned green and he maneuvered them through the traffic. As they continued to drive through town, they passed fewer and fewer cars. At the turnoff for the highway, he went in the opposite direction, circling around the industrial park and coming out on a two-lane road that narrowed quickly. About three miles up the way was a park. Hardly anyone used it, even in the summer. He thought it would be quiet there and they could spend some time getting to know each other.

He'd planned the outing specifically for a time when her kids were gone, but he knew himself. If he and Sandy stayed someplace private, like his house or hers, the temptation to make love would be too strong. He wasn't worried about her rejecting him. He was more concerned about her saying yes and then having second thoughts. Better for them not to do it, than for her to live with regrets.

But he didn't want to think about that now. Not with the soft summer-afternoon breeze blowing in his face and Sandy plastering herself against him.

She laughed again. "Everything looks different from the back of the bike," she called. "It's as if I'm seeing Glenwood for the first time."

"Do you like it?"

"I love it! Don't turn, okay?"

Before he could answer or ask why, she released him and raised her arms in the air.

"Look at me!" she called.

"Damn it, Sandy, hang on. You could hurt yourself."

"I'm fine."

"I mean it," he growled. He didn't dare turn around and look at her. He didn't want to jiggle the bike at all and upset her balance.

"You're a stick-in-the-mud," she said, leaning close to him again and wrapping her arms around his waist.

"And you're crazy."

"Maybe." She rested her chin on his shoulder. "I like this a lot. I might get a bike."

"Sure. It's real practical with three kids."

She chuckled. "Now you sound like me."

Up ahead he saw the park. At one end were several brick barbecues and rest rooms. He drove past those to the small duck pond surrounded by grass and trees. Several picnic tables had been put in place. He slowed the bike, then stopped it. After standing up, he moved forward on the seat.

"You can slide off now," he told her.

"Okay." Sandy grabbed his shoulder as she swung her leg over the seat, then she stepped away. While he set the kickstand, she pulled off her helmet.

Her cheeks were flushed, her eyes bright with excitement. "That was terrific. I can't wait to do it again. Can I drive home?"

He looked at her. This was not the Sensible Sandy he remembered, but he liked this adventurous woman. "No. It's not as easy as it looks."

"Kyle." She actually pouted at him. She stuck out her lower lip and tilted her head to the side. "Are you sure?"

He fought against the need to pull her hard against him and kiss her into forgetfulness. "I'll teach you to ride the bike, but not here. The parking lot is too small and it wouldn't be safe."

"But you will teach me."

"Yes, I said so."

"Good."

While he took off his helmet, she walked toward the small pond. A family of ducks were taking their nap on the grassy slope. She walked close to them, stopping only when one of the large birds opened its eyes and glared at her.

"I won't hurt you," she promised, bending toward the ducks. "It's okay."

Her red shorts pulled tight across her derriere. As Kyle walked toward her, his palms itched to cup those curves and pull her against his arousal. He was so hard, it hurt. He welcomed the pain. He liked that Sandy turned him on. In a strange way, he liked knowing they couldn't make love today. The anticipation would make the consummation sweeter.

He placed his hand on the small of her back. She straightened and smiled at him. A headband held her light brown hair off her face. It had grown in the last few weeks and now fell about an inch below her shoulders. He liked the way her hair moved easily and caught the light. Hell, he liked everything about her.

He gazed into her eyes. "You're very beautiful," he said quietly.

"Kyle, I thought we agreed no lines."

"It's not a line."

He continued to stare at her, memorizing her features, grateful she hadn't changed much in the time she'd been gone. For a moment, he thought about confessing his sixteen-year-old crush, but he decided against it. He didn't want her to think this was only about the adolescent desires of a fourteen-year-old boy.

Slowly, so she could pull away at any time, he slipped his hand down her back, over the curve of her derriere to her hip, where he captured her fingers in his. Her gaze never left his. She didn't move at all, except to tremble slightly and catch her breath.

"Come on," he said, tugging her hand.

They walked over to the picnic tables and straddled them, facing each other. With his legs spread apart, it was impossible to hide his physical reaction to her closeness and his own erotic thoughts. He wasn't sure if he wanted her to notice or not. He liked the idea of her knowing she turned him on, but only if it didn't embarrass her too much. He wanted to get to know the adult Sandy and that wouldn't happen if he scared her away.

She raised her chin slightly and stared at the trees above them. "It's lovely here. I'm surprised the park is empty."

He motioned to the open field across the road and the wooded area behind the pond. "There isn't anything around here, and most people don't want to make the drive. At night we have to patrol the area though. Teenagers come here to park.''

"Oh? I never did.'' She raised her eyebrows. "But I'm sure you were a regular.''

"Every weekend.'' He grinned at the memories. "I had my first encounter with paradise right here in the back of a '68 Ford Mustang.'' He rubbed his lower back. "There wasn't a lot of room to maneuver. Of course, I was pretty inexperienced, but very enthusiastic. The first time.''

"How many times were there?''

"That night? About five. I was just getting the hang of it when it was time to go home.''

She leaned one elbow on the tabletop. "There is something to be said for the enthusiasm of youth.''

"I prefer the skill of experience.''

She straightened and folded her hands in her lap. "Yes, there is that, too. Well, now that we're here, what do you want to talk about? Is there a specific type of conversation when one is having fun?''

Why had she changed the subject? If he didn't know better, he would think she was suddenly nervous. But at what? It couldn't be the fact that they were alone. Maybe he shouldn't talk about his sexual past. It was probably not the smartest thing to do. Although he doubted she'd been threatened by his romantic escapades at the age of seventeen.

"We don't have to talk about anything if you don't want to,'' he said. "The point was to break out of the regular routine. I see you convinced Lindsay to go to camp.''

Sandy wrinkled her nose. "She agreed to try it for a day. If it's horrible, I promised she doesn't have to go back. I realized the other day that she hasn't had a chance to make any friends since we moved. Nichole has Mandy, and Blake is hanging out with Robby. Lindsay is pretty much stuck around the house.''

"Or haunting me," he said grimly.

"Oh, Kyle, she's just a little girl."

"She's a barracuda. The only good thing about your being mad at me was that I didn't have to worry about an ambush every time I left the house. She was always waiting for me, wanting to do things."

"Do you want me to tell her to leave you alone?"

"No." He scooted forward until their knees were touching, then he stretched back on the bench and rested his head on his hands. "That would mean explaining why I'd like her to lay off and I still want to avoid hurting her feelings if I can."

"You're being very nice about this."

"Never tell a man he's nice. It doesn't do a thing for our egos. Look, that cloud looks like a dragon."

He stared at the sky because looking at Sandy was driving him crazy. Her breasts seemed to thrust forward in invitation and he couldn't stop wishing her nipples would get hard. He was horny and disgusting, but mentally beating himself up wasn't doing anything about reducing his state of arousal. Maybe if he stared at something other than her, he could calm down.

"It's not a dragon, it's a teapot."

"No way. That part sticking out at the back is the tail," he told her.

"It's the handle. See." She leaned forward and pressed her right hand on his thigh. With her left hand, she pointed up. He swallowed hard. Her nipples were getting hard, dammit. He could see the faint outline of them through her T-shirt. And she was burning him, the heat of her fingers searing through his jeans to his skin. If she moved her hand a little higher and touched him, he would explode.

He had to change the subject and fast. Talk about something nonsexual, he told himself. Something that would make her stop touching him.

"I never knew your mother was an alcoholic," he said.

His statement got the desired result. Sandy pulled back and straightened. "I didn't talk about it much."

"Do you want to now?"

"There isn't anything to say."

He continued to stare at the sky and let the silence of the peaceful afternoon surround them. "That one looks like a race car," he said, pointing. He glanced at Sandy. She stared at the picnic tabletop.

"I don't remember much about her," she said, tracing initials that someone had carved in the wood. "I suppose I've blocked it all out. I was pretty young when I figured out something was wrong. Sometimes she would be fine, but other times she would be asleep and I couldn't wake her up. I remember one time, crying for her to cook dinner. I must have been about five. She had passed out on the sofa. Finally, I made myself a peanut-butter sandwich. The next morning, she was sorry and promised it would never happen again. It did, of course. It never stopped."

Kyle sat up. Sandy turned toward the tabletop, swinging her outside leg over the bench and pressing her knees together.

"She dried out a few times. At first, I kept hoping it would work, but after a while I didn't expect anything to change. While she was gone, I stayed with friends. I spent the summer here, once, with my aunt, before I moved in with her permanently. I suppose that's where the control thing started. I remember being so afraid all the time. I couldn't count on her to take care of me, so I had to take care of myself. I know that's why I need to be in control now."

"You never saw your dad?"

"He didn't care about us." She looked at him, then away. "At least that's what my mom told me. I'm not sure I believe that anymore, but I never wanted to look for him or anything. There wasn't any point."

Kyle wanted to pull her close and comfort her. Not the adult Sandy. That woman didn't want to admit weakness. Instead, he ached for the child who had been left alone and abandoned by an alcoholic mother. He wanted to comfort the five-year-old who didn't have any dinner, and the second-grader who would have wanted someone to see her in the school play, but who probably hadn't told her mother about the event in case she showed up drunk.

"And then Thomas let you down," he said.

"I don't blame him for disappointing me," she said. "I'm beginning to see I was the one with the illusions. I wanted more than he could give. It's not his fault he wasn't responsible and together."

"But it is his fault he hurt his son."

She glanced at him. "How much did Blake tell you?"

"Enough for me to put the pieces together. Remember, I had a jerk for a father, too. I know what it's like."

"I worry about Blake. He seems to be doing better here, though. I'm glad he's friends with Robby. And I'm glad you've been there for him."

The praise made him proud and uncomfortable all at the same time. "Yeah, well, he's a good kid. They all are."

"Even Lindsay?" she teased.

"It's not that I don't like her."

"I know," she said. She angled toward him. "She's confused. I'm sure this is a phase that will pass. Right now, she's caught between being a child and being a teenager. She doesn't fit in either world. She's terrified of moving forward, but she's too grown-up to return to the past. Plus, Lindsay misses her dad a lot."

"She mentioned they did a lot of stuff together."

Sandy smiled sadly. "Lindsay always had spirit. Thomas admired that. I probably shouldn't have let him favor her, but I didn't know how to stop it. Nichole was the baby and had me, so she didn't really notice, but I know it bothered Blake."

She rested her left arm on the tabletop. He placed his hand on top of hers. "If your marriage was so unhappy, why did you stay?"

"I used to ask myself the same question. I still don't have an answer. Partly it was for the children. I remembered what it was like having only one parent, and not a very good one at that. I wanted more for them. Maybe it was also that I didn't want to admit failure." She sighed. "I guess the truth is, I was afraid. If I left, I would be on my own. I didn't want to risk it."

"You're alone now," he said. "I think you're doing a hell of a good job."

"Thanks. Some days I think it's going to be fine. Other days I don't think I can make it. Then I remember I don't get a choice. They're depending on me. I have to make it."

He brushed his thumb against the back of her hand. Her skin was soft and smooth. He turned her hand over and rested his fingertips on her palm.

"You could get married again," he said, staring at the shape of her wrist and the clasp of her watchband. "It's not as if you're mourning the love of your life."

"I've already made one mistake. I don't want to make another one."

"What makes you think it would be a mistake?"

"The odds are not in my favor."

He glanced at her. Her eyes were wide and flickering with emotion. He thought he might have seen a spark of desire there, as well, but he wasn't sure. Or maybe he was sure, but he wasn't ready to act.

"What's the worst that could happen?" he asked.

"I'd end up with another child. And I'm not talking about an infant. Actually, I wouldn't mind another baby." Her expression became dreamy. "I like babies."

"Me, too."

She blinked and looked away. "I wouldn't want another Thomas. Someone who only pretended to be grown-up. If I ever get involved again, it's going to be with someone responsible, who understands life is serious business and we don't always get to have our way. I want a partner, not a playmate.''

He chose not to take offense at her words, mostly because he knew she wasn't directing them specifically at him. She'd recited her list of requirements as if she'd spoken them before. They were, he realized, a talisman to keep away all that she was afraid of.

"You're putting up barriers to keep people from getting close to you," he said, "and calling those barriers 'responsibility.' I suspect that if you found a responsible man who was everything you wanted him to be, you'd get so scared, you'd take off running in the opposite direction.''

"That's not true at all."

She tried to pull her hand free, but he wouldn't let her. "I also think that you'd come up with another list of excuses to keep from getting close. You don't trust what you can't control, and you can't control love. Or passion. You blame your failed marriage on Thomas, but how much of it was your fault?''

"Mine? He's the one who was always gone."

"You let him go. It takes two to fight, Sandy. You let him leave because you were afraid."

"You don't know what you're talking about."

"Don't I? You're still afraid. Look at me and tell me the thought of making love with me doesn't make you tremble with fear."

She stared at him, then, and he saw her confusion. "I'm not afraid," she whispered.

"Then why are you shaking?"

Because she always reacted that way when she was close to him, Sandy thought. Because he made her think of things she wanted to forget. She didn't want her problems

with Thomas to be her fault. She'd been a good wife. He
was the one who—

She shook off the memories. She didn't want to remember any of this now. "I thought we were supposed to
be having fun," she said.

His dark eyes flared with the fire of arousal. "Be careful what you ask for," he warned.

She looked at him and allowed the flames to burn away
her doubts. She swayed closer to him. She could feel
tremors racing up her legs and arms, and the fluttering of
her heart, the sharp cadence of her breathing. She could
lose herself in him, in the passion.

He swore under his breath and moved close to her. Before she could react or say anything, he gathered her in his
arms and kissed her.

His mouth was hot and firm, the taste of his lips wonderfully familiar. She clung to him, angling her body toward him, trying to get closer and closer still, as if she
could dissolve into him. He moved one arm to her shoulders, supporting her upper body, then scooted her nearer,
so her hip nestled between his thighs. His free hand rested
on her belly.

Even as she parted her lips to urge him inside, she willed
his hand to move higher. Since she'd ridden on the back of
his motorcycle, she'd been in a state of arousal. He'd been
hard and unyielding to her curves, steady to her shaking.
All male, designed with the sole purpose of making her
forget herself. And around him, she did forget. Her responsibilities and sensibilities disappeared, until there was
nothing but sensation— a world of heat and desire, where
she at last understood the true beauty in the differences
between male and female.

His mouth angled over hers as his tongue plunged inside. He swept around and over, searching out her secrets,
making her tingle and gasp, making her clutch at him and
no longer need to breathe.

She raised her hands to his head, tracing the shape of his ears, burying her fingers in his short hair. She wiggled her butt slightly and felt the hardness of him surge against her hip. In her mind's eye, she saw him popping open the buttons of his fly one by one. She saw him springing free, then imagined herself touching his silky length. Her fingers curled toward her palm in anticipation and she whimpered.

His free hand slipped up her midsection. *Yes,* her mind screamed. She arched forward, thrusting her chest toward him. His palm moved over her breasts, circling against her nipples. Electricity raced to her female place. She tightened her thighs together, but it did nothing to alleviate the tension there.

Around and around he moved, teasing her through the layers of clothing. She wanted more. She wanted to touch flesh.

She moved her hand down his shoulder toward his waistband. Without stopping to think or let herself get scared, she tugged his T-shirt free of his jeans, then pressed her hand against his bare belly. His muscles jumped at the contact. Curly hair tickled her palm.

He raised his head and stared down at her. Passion had darkened his eyes to the color of midnight. "Sandy? What are you doing?"

"I would have thought it was obvious." She slipped her hand higher. He clenched his jaw and swallowed. "You feel great. Hot and hard." She realized what she'd said and flushed.

He grimaced. "I could show you hot and hard, but I won't. We're in a public park."

She'd forgotten. She glanced around. There was no one else there but a duck family and none of them looked very interested in what was going on. There wasn't any traffic on the road.

She pulled his shirt higher until she could see as well as touch. "There's no one here."

"That doesn't mean there might not be."

"I don't care."

That was the amazing part. She didn't care. With him, there was no controlling the passion. She wanted it all. She wanted to feel everything, do everything with him. She didn't care about convention or practicalities. Her body was on fire and she was learning to enjoy the heat of the flames.

"Then I have to care for both of us," he told her.

"I know you want this," she whispered.

"Of course I do, but not here. Not like this."

She reached up and nipped his chin. "Exactly like this. Wild." She kissed him from his lower lip down to the neck of his T-shirt. He tasted salty and sweet. She could dine on him.

"Sandy—"

"No," she said, cutting him off. "Stop thinking. If I think, I'll have to be responsible. I'll get all embarrassed and we'll have to stop. Don't you see? Don't let me think."

She continued to stare at him, willing him to understand. She'd spoken the truth. Her reaction to his touch was as foreign to her as riding the motorcycle had been. But she didn't question it. She loved how he made her feel. She loved being able to forget. For once in her life, she was being swept away.

He glanced over his shoulder as if to make sure they were still alone, then he lowered his mouth to hers. This time, his kiss was impassioned, as if he was determined to have her be consumed by desire. They clung to each other— hungry, inflamed. Then, as she prepared to give herself up to him, he straightened.

"We can't do this here," he said regretfully.

"But, I—"

He placed his index finger on her mouth. "You know we can't. Not only are we in a public place, but I'm not convinced it's what you want."

She stared at him uncomprehendingly. "Do I look like I'm not interested in this?"

"Let's just say I want to wait until we can make love slowly. I don't want you getting lost in the moment. I don't want you having regrets." His expression was determined.

"I can't believe you're stopping this now," she grumbled.

He stood up and winced. "Parts of me can't believe it, either."

As she rose to her feet, she pressed on the picnic table. "It would have worked fine."

"What about the audience?" he asked.

She looked at the ducks. "They aren't impressed."

"They weren't the audience I meant," he said, pointing to the road. At that moment, a car drove by.

She thought about the state they'd been in a moment before. What had happened to her? She didn't usually lose control like that. Was it him, the passion, or was it her? She wasn't sure she wanted to know.

Kyle walked to the bike. "We'd better head back."

She stepped closer, then paused. "Are you mad at me?"

He touched her face. His eyes were serious, the flames of passion banked, but not extinguished. "No. Never." He handed her a helmet.

A minute later, they were speeding back toward the house. Sandy clung to him, savoring the feel of his body pressed so close to hers. The sensations Kyle aroused in her intrigued and frightened her. She didn't know what they meant, or if they had to mean anything. She refused to consider the idea that they were more than a sexual response, though. They couldn't be an indication of deeper feelings. Not for him. She was determined to avoid making the same mistake twice. When she got involved with a man, he was going to be different from Thomas—not a charming womanizer, which would be even worse.

He turned into the driveway and stopped in front of her house. Sandy sat on the bike for a minute, not wanting to get off and have the adventure end. "I had a good time," she said as she unfastened the helmet.

"So your first lesson in having fun was a success?"

She stepped off the bike and smiled. "It was near-perfect." Her gaze settled on his mouth. "I can't wait for the next one."

"Sandy," he growled.

"Don't worry. You're safe from me." She glanced at her watch. "My kids will be home any second."

He grabbed her hand and squeezed. "I'll see you soon."

She leaned forward to kiss him. In the back of her mind, she registered the front door opening. She tried to pull back but it was too late to stop her forward momentum. As her lips touched his, she heard, "Mom?"

Lindsay! Sandy straightened and turned toward her daughter. Lindsay stared down at the two of them. The girl's face paled. "Mom?" she repeated, louder this time. "You said you were going to be at the grocery store, but you were with Kyle, weren't you?" Her voice rose to a shriek. "I hate you. I'll hate you forever." She turned and ran back inside; the front door slammed shut behind her.

Chapter Twelve

"Lindsay," Sandy called. She threw down her helmet and raced after her daughter.

"Wait," Kyle yelled. He secured the kickstand and jerked off his helmet, then took off after her. He caught her on the stairs. "I want to talk to her, too," he said.

"This isn't your problem."

"I'm the one she has a crush on."

"I'm her mother."

They paused by the front door. Kyle waited. He didn't want to walk away from this. Lindsay was important to him. He knew how she was feeling; he'd been there himself. "I'm not leaving," he said.

Sandy sighed. "Suit yourself, but I'm warning you, it could get ugly. Lindsay has never been shy about saying what she's thinking."

She opened the front door and started across the foyer. Nichole saw them from the family room and got up. "Mommy, I had the best time at camp today. I want to go back tomorrow and the next day." Her green eyes sparkled with excitement. "I even made you something." She glanced past her mother toward him. "Hi, Kyle."

"Hey, kitten."

She dimpled.

Sandy looked at her daughter. "Honey, Lindsay's really upset and we have to go talk to her right now. But as soon as we're done, I want you to tell me everything about your day, okay?"

"Sure." Nichole plopped down on the sofa. "I'll wait."

Kyle was surprised. He'd expected her to get upset at being ignored. "You've got some great kids," he said as they started up the stairs.

"They all know I'll keep my promise to listen. They don't like waiting, but they're old enough to stop making a fuss about it." She winced. As they neared the second-floor landing, they could hear Lindsay's harsh sobs.

Kyle swore. "The kid sounds like her heart is breaking."

"It is."

He grimaced. It wasn't fair. Growing up was tough on everyone. He had a fleeting thought that this wasn't his problem, that he could bolt and no one would blame him. Instead, he forced himself to keep climbing the stairs. Lindsay needed him, and whether she knew it or not, so did Sandy.

Lindsay's door was closed. Sandy knocked.

"Lindsay, Kyle and I want to come in."

"No! Go away." Her voice was thick with tears. Kyle felt a sharp pain in his gut. The kid was really suffering.

Sandy opened the door and stepped inside. Lindsay lay on her bed, curled up and facing the window. Her long brown hair streamed over the pillow.

"Lindsay, we never meant to hurt you," Sandy said.

The preteen didn't move.

Sandy looked at Kyle helplessly. He held up his hands, indicating he didn't know what to say, either. This was way out of his league.

Sandy moved closer and sat on the edge of the bed. Before she could touch her daughter, Lindsay rolled toward her. "No," she said loudly. "Don't sit down, don't say anything. I don't want to hear it." He face was flushed, her eyes red from crying.

Sandy stood up slowly. "Lindsay."

"No. I saw you, Mom. How could you? It was disgusting." Her mouth twisted. Her gaze shifted to Kyle. "You don't really like her, do you? You don't think she's pretty. She's old and never does anything but yell at us to do our chores and be responsible. You're not like that. You're fun, Kyle. You don't like her. You can't."

Tears flowed from her eyes. Her voice caught. "I'll never forgive you. Never."

Kyle moved closer to the bed. Lindsay stared at him for a moment. The raw pain in her gaze made him flinch. "Lindsay, you've got to understand."

"No, I don't," she said, turning her back on him. "I hate you, too. Go away."

"I can't." He sat on the edge of the bed and placed his hands on her shoulders. She jerked away. He tried again and this time she let him touch her. After a few minutes, he drew her close, turning her so she was pressed against him, her head leaning against his chest.

She continued to cry. He could feel the moisture of her tears as they dampened his T-shirt, and the sobs shaking her slight body. Sandy stood beside the bed with her hands balled into fists. She was hurting, too. He didn't know how to comfort them both.

"I know how you feel," he said to Lindsay.

"No, you don't."

"Yeah, I do. I had a crush on someone once." He stared at the top of her head, then rested his hand on her hair. "I was fourteen. She never knew I was alive."

Lindsay sniffed and looked up at him. "Really?"

He nodded. "She was an older woman and dating one of my brothers."

"What happened?"

He cupped her chin and brushed the tears from her face. "I tried to tell her how I felt, but she didn't listen. She was polite and friendly, but she wasn't interested in me. Basically, she shut me down big time."

Brown eyes widened with curiosity. "Did it hurt?"

"Like someone had reached inside and ripped my heart out. It hurt bad."

Lindsay nodded and stared at the bedspread. "I know," she whispered. "What happened after that?"

He shrugged. "She left for college and I eventually got over it." He smoothed her hair away from her face. "You will, too. Because you don't really want me for a boyfriend, Lindsay. For one thing, I'm way too old. For another..." He paused.

Sandy had stood silently beside the bed listening as he talked. He didn't want to look at her and find out what she was thinking. After all, she was the one he'd had that crush on sixteen years ago. He figured he could easily go another sixteen years without her finding out the truth. He wondered what she would say if she knew. He wondered how mad she was going to be with what he was about to tell her daughter.

"What?" Lindsay asked.

"You want me to help fill the hole your dad's death has left in your life." When she would have turned away, he held her close. "Listen to me, Lindsay. If you think about it, you'll know I'm right. You were always doing things with him. You and he had a very special relationship. It's only natural that you would miss that. Then you met me.

I remind you a little of your dad. I'm fun to be with, I don't take things as seriously as your mom. But you felt guilty and disloyal. You think the only person who can be a father figure in your life is your father. You didn't know what to think, so it was easier to pretend you had a crush on me."

Her mouth opened, but she didn't speak. "It's okay," he told her. "You can have more than one adult male in your life acting like a dad. You'll always love your father the most, and that's how it should be. That doesn't mean I can't give you a little advice from time to time." He scowled. "Especially when you start dating. I plan to look those young men over very carefully, Lindsay Walker, so don't expect to bring home any biker types."

Her eyes filled with tears, but this time she was smiling. She flung herself at him and squeezed hard. He hugged her back.

"Are we gonna be all right?" he asked.

She nodded, but didn't let go. He risked a glance at Sandy. She was staring at him as if she'd never seen him before.

"How'd you know all that?" Sandy asked.

"It just sort of came to me."

Lindsay raised her head. "Mom?"

"Oh, honey." Sandy walked toward them. Kyle shifted on the bed and stretched out his left arm toward her. She moved close and hugged them both.

"I love you, baby," she said.

"I love you, too, Mom."

Kyle swallowed against the sudden tightening in his throat. He wasn't sure where he'd gotten the words. When he'd needed them, they'd just sort of been there. He was grateful that they'd been the right thing to say.

Now, holding Sandy and Lindsay close, he felt something he hadn't felt for years, if ever. He felt as if he belonged. As if all the years of playing daddy with his brother's kids, or the neighbor kids, had finally paid off. He felt strong enough to carry all the troubles of the world on his shoulders, and weak enough to fight the burning at the back of his eyes.

When Lindsay wiggled free, he didn't want to let her go. He didn't want the perfect moment to end. Because when they all stood up and looked at one another, he would be the one on the outside. He wasn't part of the family. He wasn't likely to be. Sandy might be interested in sleeping with him, but she'd made it clear that he wasn't the sort of man she wanted in her life permanently.

Lindsay scrambled off the bed and walked over to the window. She stared outside. "I guess I made a fool of myself, huh?"

"Not with me," he said. "I'm not sure what you've been doing with the other men in the neighborhood, though."

She looked at him and rolled her eyes. "Kyle!"

"Lindsay!"

She grinned.

"Your secret is safe with me, kid," he said.

"I can still come over and make fresh lemonade if you want," she said.

"I'd like that."

"Tomorrow."

"I'll be waiting."

He started toward the door. Sandy followed. When they reached the staircase, she paused.

"You did really good in there," she said.

"Thanks. I was nervous."

"It didn't show." She looked up at him. "Thanks, Kyle. It could have gotten ugly, but you were great."

He liked the hero worship shining from her green eyes. He liked that he'd impressed her. But he hadn't done it for her; he'd only been thinking of Lindsay. "I'm glad it worked out."

"Me, too." She put her hand on the railing, but didn't step down. "So what's the real story about this crush of yours? I don't remember any of the Haynes brothers ever being without a date."

"I was only fourteen at the time. A little young for dating."

"And she really didn't notice you?"

"You sound surprised. I was a kid. She wasn't. It's no big deal, Sandy. It happens all the time."

"But not to you." She smiled. "I guess I can't imagine who it would be. One of the cheerleaders? Oh, you said someone one of your brothers dated. Which brother? Travis? He always had the prettiest girls."

"Why is this so important to you?"

"I'm just a little curious."

He could tell her. What would she do with the information? Would it make a difference? He watched as her mouth curled in a smile. Her nose was a little red, as if she'd been in the sun too long on their bike ride. Instantly, images of what had happened on that picnic-table bench flashed into his mind. He had to fight the need to bend over and kiss her. Just once. Instead, he started down the stairs.

"You're not going to tell me?" she asked.

"No."

"But, Kyle, I want to know."

At the bottom of the stairs, he turned toward her. She was grinning. "Just one little name. What will it hurt?"

She was right. It couldn't hurt anything. It had been a long time ago. If he was going to risk it with Sandy, he might as well risk it all. Then, if it didn't work out, he could tell himself he'd done his best. It would be small comfort if she left him, but he would need all the help he could get.

He walked to the front door, then paused. "It was you, Sandy. Always you. I'm surprised you didn't figure it out." Then he stepped outside and closed the door behind him.

"Mom, when can I learn how to drive?" Lindsay asked.

Fortunately, Sandy was already at a stop sign, so she didn't accidentally hit the brakes and risk being rear-ended. She glanced at her twelve-year-old daughter. "Where did that question come from?"

Lindsay shrugged. "I just asked. Sheesh, you always make such a big deal out of everything."

"You'll learn to drive when you're fifteen and a half and get your learner's permit. Not before."

"Figures." Lindsay slumped back in her seat.

It was her turn to ride in front. The children rotated weekly. Blake sat directly behind her, playing a hand-held video game, and Nichole was having a quiet conversation with her doll. All in all, life had settled into a routine. The children went to camp every day, she had finished unpacking and was planning her lessons for the coming semester. She'd figured out where everything was in the grocery store and she'd managed to reduce the time she spent thinking about Kyle from all of her day to about three-quarters of it. Not bad considering she couldn't get his confession out of her mind.

It was you, Sandy. Always you. I'm surprised you didn't figure it out.

How could he have said that to her and then just left? She'd been too shocked to do more than stare at him as he'd walked out of her house, and then it had been too late to go after him. Nichole had claimed her attention. Next, she'd had to deal with making dinner. Suddenly, it had been the next day and she'd been too embarrassed to seek Kyle out and ask him what he'd really meant.

He'd had a crush on her? It didn't make sense. She barely remembered him as a fourteen-year-old. Of course, if she couldn't remember him, she probably had ignored him, but why would he have had a crush on her? She wasn't a cheerleader. She was just ordinary. Sensible Sandy, as he called her. She wasn't the type to inspire that kind of affection. She certainly hadn't in Thomas.

Maybe she would ask him today. They were all getting together at Travis and Elizabeth's house for a cookout. All the brothers would be there, along with their dates, kids and possibly dogs. It would be a madhouse, but she might be able to steal a quiet moment alone with Kyle. There hadn't been an opportunity in the last couple of weeks. One of the deputies had been on vacation and Kyle had been working extra hours.

Nichole leaned as far forward as her seat belt would let her. "Mandy's mom said they were going to buy a blow-up pool and that we could go swimming."

"Sounds like fun, honey," she answered.

"Blake can come, too, if he wants," Nichole said graciously. She and her brother always got along well. Sandy often wondered if it was because Lindsay had been singled out by their father, that the two younger ones banded together.

Lindsay sighed loudly and muttered something about children. She was upset because her friends hadn't been able to come to the cookout, so she wasn't going to have anyone to hang out with. Since Kyle had talked to her, she'd seemed a little more like a twelve-year-old and a little less like a seductress in a training bra.

Sandy turned onto the tree-lined street where Travis and Elizabeth lived. Her children were doing well, she thought happily. They were adjusting to their new lives, thanks in great part to Kyle. He was always there for them. Even though she hadn't seen him much in the last couple of weeks, and never alone, he'd made sure he was available to her children.

She started down the long driveway, and parked behind an expensive German sedan. Austin, his wife, Rebecca, and their two children were already here. Her kids scrambled out of the station wagon as soon as she turned off the engine, but she was slower to exit. There was a part of her that was shy about facing all these people. Not because she didn't belong, but because she didn't know where she stood with Kyle.

It was ridiculous, she told herself as she got out of the car. The man was her neighbor, nothing more. Yet, that wasn't completely true. He was also a good friend, and a good surrogate father to her children. He'd been there for her, and his touch made her forget herself. She blushed as she remembered how willing she'd been to make love with him in a public park. She hadn't cared about anyone driving by and seeing them. She hadn't cared about anything but getting close to him, kissing him, stepping into the fire they generated and giving up her soul to the flames.

They weren't dating, but they'd almost become lovers. She didn't want a man like him in her life, but she couldn't stop thinking about him. She wanted it to be real, yet she knew in her heart that Kyle was everything she wanted to avoid in a man. She walked to the rear of the vehicle and opened the back door. So why couldn't she turn her back on him and forget about it? Why was she having trouble sleeping and eating, and why did her heart still pound so hard every time she saw him?

She had to make her body, or her hormones, or whatever was causing the reaction stop. She couldn't go on like this. What would happen if things got tough? She wanted a man who would make the difficult decisions no matter what they cost him personally. She wanted someone she could depend on.

"You're looking serious about something."

She jumped and turned toward the sound. "Kyle," she said, pressing her hand on her chest. "You startled me."

"I was on the porch," he said, pointing toward the house, "but you didn't notice me waving."

"Sorry. I was thinking."

"About what?"

His brown eyes studied her face, his firm mouth smiled easily. The sheer male beauty of his features took her breath away. He wore black shorts and a T-shirt that advertised a local deli. Everywhere she looked, she saw hard muscles and tanned skin. It was enough to make a woman swoon. Her palms dampened, her mouth got dry and she couldn't think of an intelligent thing to say. If she were eighteen, or even twenty, she would swear she was in love. But she was thirty-two, and she knew better.

"Nothing important."

He reached up and cupped her chin. "I haven't seen you in a while. Everything okay?"

"Couldn't be better."

"Vacations are over for now, so my schedule is going to be normal again, starting Monday. Maybe we could take another bike ride."

Her thighs began to tremble. "I think that would be a mistake—"

He bent down and kissed her, cutting off her words. There was nothing seductive about the pressure of his mouth on hers. It was soft and sweet. Still, she felt her body begin to hum as need and desire flashed through her.

He straightened. "What were you saying?"

Had she been saying something? She leaned toward him hoping he would kiss her again, but he just gave her that cat-who-ate-the-canary grin of his. "Huh? Ah, nothing. Why?"

"I could have sworn you were going to tell me another bike ride wouldn't be a good idea."

She reached into the station wagon and picked up a covered casserole dish. She handed it to Kyle, then reached for the covered cake plate. He slammed the car door shut, then fell into step beside her as they started for the house.

"Why would I say a foolish thing like that?" she asked.

"That's what I was thinking."

When they reached the stairs leading to the porch, she paused and stared at him. Sunlight caught his short dark hair. He was tall and broad, strong. In the last few weeks, she'd come to think of him as dependable, which is a word she never would have associated with one of the Haynes brothers. Yet, they'd all changed. They'd grown up. For a brief moment, she wanted it to be enough.

"Is it true?" she asked. "Did you really have a crush on me?"

He looked past her toward a grove of trees next to the house. "It's the only time I hated my brother. The first time Jordan brought you home, I wanted to kill him and steal you away for myself."

"Really? Why?"

"I'm not going to answer that."

"When did you get over your crush?"

His gaze settled on her. "Don't ask questions unless you're sure you want the answers."

Her breath caught in her throat. What was he saying? That it had been over so quickly that she would be insulted if she knew, or something else? That he'd never gotten over it. But he had to have. He couldn't still have those feelings for her, could he? He was right, she wasn't sure she wanted to know.

"Why didn't you say anything?"

He laughed. "Sorry, that's as much of my confession as you're going to get."

"But Kyle—"

"But nothing." He raised the dish in his hands. "What did you bring?"

"Potato salad and chocolate cake."

"Sounds great. I brought yams."

She giggled. "Is it true? That's the only thing you can make?"

He looked insulted. "It is not. I just like yams."

"Okay, me, too. I thought they were great."

He bent toward her. For a second, she thought he was going to kiss her again. She wanted him to. She wanted him to hold her and touch her and take her to that magic place they disappeared to when they were together. She wanted to make love and talk about the past and the future. She wanted to hear about his crush, then whisper that she couldn't keep her heartbeat under control when he was around.

Then the front door opened and he straightened.

"We need less interruptions and more privacy," he murmured.

She glanced up and saw the third oldest Haynes brother standing in the doorway. "Jordan!" she called and started up toward him.

"Hey, Sandy." Jordan wasn't as tall as Kyle, or as good-looking, but there was something soulful in his eyes. He'd always been the moody one, the brooder. While Craig had been the athletic star and Travis had collected ladies based on his charm, Jordan had been the James Dean of the county. Even Sensible Sandy hadn't been immune.

He met her at the top of the stairs and wrapped an arm around her shoulders. "I heard you were back in town. How's it going?"

"Really well."

"I met your kids," he said, then gave her a kiss on the cheek. "The littlest one has your smile. She's going to be a heartbreaker."

She was pleased at the compliment. "Thanks. Nichole is a sweetie."

She looked at her old boyfriend. Time had been kind to him. The new lines around his eyes only made him more good-looking. The Haynes family had an incredible gene pool, she thought, then realized she was standing right next to Jordan, talking to him, staring at his smile and feeling absolutely nothing. Not a twinge of attraction, not a flicker of a faster heartbeat. It was as if he were her brother.

"Before you get too charming," Kyle said, coming up and elbowing his brother out of the way, "the lady's with me."

Jordan's dark eyes met hers. "So that's how it is?"

Sandy glanced up at Kyle. Her heart kicked into high gear and her stomach dived for her toes. Maybe it was just the flu, or an allergy. "That's exactly how it is," she whispered.

Fifteen children, eight adults and an assortment of pets could go through enough food to feed an army and still have room to argue about who got the largest slice of cake. Sandy looked sadly at the few crumbs that were all that was left of her three-layer masterpiece.

"At least they enjoyed it," Elizabeth said, coming up and taking the dirty side plates. "This family sure can eat."

"I'll say. I think that lone pickle floating in the jar is about it for leftovers."

Elizabeth grinned. "Less work for us."

"That's true." Sandy gathered up a handful of flatware and set it on the cake dish, then carried everything into the kitchen. Rebecca and Christina, a petite blonde who was dating Kyle's oldest brother, Craig, were already washing dishes.

"More work," Elizabeth called. "No rest for the wicked."

Rebecca glanced at her over her shoulder. "We're not the wicked ones. It's those men who should be in here cleaning."

"I heard that," Kyle said, walking in with an armful of plastic glasses. "I'm helping."

Elizabeth picked up a dish towel and tossed it to Sandy, then grabbed another one for herself. "Kyle, would you please bring in the rest of the dishes. Sandy and I will dry."

"No problem." He left the kitchen.

Rebecca grinned. "You notice how well behaved he is all of a sudden. As if he's trying to impress a certain someone."

"I thought that same thing, myself," Elizabeth said. "Now, who could he be strutting around for? Is he dating anyone?"

"Not that I know of." Rebecca looked at Sandy. "You wouldn't know anything about this, would you?"

Sandy could feel herself blushing. "Gee, I haven't seen anyone at his house."

"Except for yourself, of course," Rebecca teased.

"I'm just there to collect the children."

The two women exchanged knowing glances. Kyle returned with more dishes and conversation became more general. Sandy enjoyed her time with the women. She liked their friendly manner.

"Only two more weeks until camp," Elizabeth said. "I can't wait. With Mandy gone, we're hiring a sitter every night for the baby, and Travis and I are going to be alone. I feel like it's been years since our honeymoon."

"It has been," Rebecca reminded her. "Austin and I are doing the same thing. Paying a sitter to mind the baby is a small price to pay for romantic time with my husband. David is so excited about going to camp. I adore him, but I sure look forward to the peace and quiet."

"What camp?" Sandy asked.

Elizabeth dried a plate and set it in the cupboard. "Glenwood sponsors a three-night camp for all the children in town. They have to be five or older. It's great. All the parents get some time off and the kids are supervised. The best part is, because they go as a group, they're with people they know, so they don't usually get homesick."

She sighed. "Three whole nights and four days. I can't wait."

Rebecca looked at her. "Are your three going?"

"I didn't know about it." Although now that she thought about it, she did remember hearing Lindsay and Blake talking about a camp, but she'd thought it was the park's program they were already in.

"These are the last of them," Kyle said as he walked in carrying several serving dishes.

"Sandy didn't know about the camp," Elizabeth said, then raised her eyebrows. "I'm shocked that *you* haven't already mentioned it."

He surprised Sandy by clearing his throat and shuffling his feet. "The kids know about it and want to go," he said. "We were, um, discussing the best way to bring it up. Lindsay didn't think you'd want them to go."

"Why would she think that?" Sandy asked.

"She said you hadn't let her go to camp two years ago."

"But that was right after her father had died. I thought she was trying to run away from his death and I was afraid of what would happen to her. She'd never been away from home before on her own."

"Oh." He looked up and smiled. "They'd like to go."

"I don't have a problem with that."

"Good." His brown eyes darkened to the color of a midnight sky. The air between them seemed charged with electricity and she was having trouble breathing.

"Is it hot in here, or is it me?" Elizabeth asked.

But her voice seemed to come from a long way off. Sandy knew what Kyle was thinking. If the children were gone for three nights, then they wouldn't have any interruptions or excuses. There would be nothing to stop them from taking the next natural step in their relationship.

She bit down hard on her lip. Relationship? She and Kyle didn't have a relationship. They were neighbors. Friends. Nothing else.

But as she stared at him and listened to the other women chuckling at their expense, she knew it was already too late. She and Kyle were involved. There was nothing she could do except wait it out and see what happened. It wasn't as if he was the love of her life. She was far too sensible to fall for a guy like him. It was just about attraction and sex.

She could always recover from a broken heart. What she couldn't recover from was regretting something she hadn't done.

''I'll make the arrangements tomorrow,'' she said.

Chapter Thirteen

She wanted to ask him to pull the car over because she was about to lose her lunch. Not that she had eaten any-thing. She couldn't. Sandy closed her eyes and leaned back against the passenger seat of her station wagon. While her three kids had inhaled burgers and fries, she'd picked at a small salad. Even Kyle had gotten his lunch down with no trouble at all. Damn him!

She opened one eye and glanced at him. He was driving through the streets of Glenwood, heading back to her house. He looked calm, unconcerned. He was even hum-ming with the radio! Didn't he know what was going to happen? Did he realize what they'd just done? Her three children were on a bus heading to the Glenwood city camp where they would spend the next four days and three *nights*. Nights he had implied the two of them would be spending together. Alone. Making love.

So why wasn't *he* nervous? Were his palms sweating and his stomach heaving and his body alternately hot and cold?

No, not Kyle. He was calm and relaxed. As if he had nothing to worry about. As if they weren't going to do *it*.

Her eyes shot open and she sat up straight in the seat. Maybe that was it, she thought grimly. He'd changed his mind. He didn't want to do "it" with her anymore. Or he'd never wanted to. She'd misunderstood everything. He'd kissed her before because . . . because . . .

"Stop fidgeting," Kyle said. "We've got plenty of time."

She stopped breathing. "Time?" she squeaked.

At the next stoplight, he glanced at her. Something warm and sexy glowed in his dark brown eyes. He grinned at her. "I was going to give you until tonight to let you have your way with me, then I figured why waste a perfectly good afternoon. So don't worry, darlin', we've got four days for loving."

She sucked in a breath and coughed. "Great."

So much for being Sensible Sandy. So much for being in control and acting dignified and sophisticated. She felt as prepared as a virgin facing a sacrificial altar. Maybe she could tell him she'd changed her mind. Maybe she should tell him that she wasn't his type. After all, she was just a mom with three kids. Hardly the sultry vixen he must be used to. She clutched her belly as it rolled one more time.

He turned into the driveway. She thought about jumping out of the car, but she figured she would only maim herself, and the thought of trying to make love with skinned knees was just too depressing.

Instead of continuing toward her place, Kyle turned the station wagon into his driveway and parked in front of the garage. He turned off the engine, then got out of the car and walked around to her side. It was her moment to bolt. She didn't. Sandy sat there like a rabbit caught in the hypnotic stare of a snake. She could do nothing to escape. It was inevitable. She might as well make the best of the situation.

He opened her door and held out his hand. She hesitated before placing her palm on his. Their gazes locked. Instantly, something hot and alive crackled between them. The rolling of her stomach quieted as anticipation took its place. Her body still trembled, but this time from need, not nerves.

"Stop thinking about it," he told her. "It'll be fine." He pulled her to her feet and slammed the car door shut behind her, then tugged her along to his back door.

"I'm not nervous," she lied.

But once she was standing in his living room and he released her hand, all her doubts crashed in on her. It was as if Kyle's touch kept her insecurities at bay, but as soon as she was by herself, she began to question everything.

"You want some champagne?" he asked as he headed for the kitchen.

Champagne? In the middle of the afternoon? "Ah, sure." Oh, God, she was out of her element. She should have known. She should have never agreed to this.

She crossed the room toward the stone fireplace. There were several photos on the mantel. Kyle with his brothers, Travis and his family, Craig and his kids. Happy pictures. No women who weren't related. That was something.

There was a slight popping sound as the cork was released. Sandy flinched. She continued to stare at the photos as if her life depended on memorizing them.

She sensed the moment he entered the room. He didn't make any noise, or say anything, but she knew he was there. Behind her. Waiting.

"There's something you should know," she said, touching her finger to one of the wooden frames. She smiled at the picture of Kyle graduating from the police academy. How handsome and strong he looked in his uniform. "I've only ever done it, you know, the boring way."

"Okay."

"I mean, there was this one guy in college, but it was only a couple of times, and frankly I didn't like it very much. It was better with Thomas. At least I figured out what all the fuss was about. Sort of." She could feel herself blushing, but she had to get it out. It was only fair. Otherwise, he would be disappointed. She wanted him to know up front. So if he didn't want to anymore, she would know why.

"I know that you've been with lots of women," she continued. "I'm not sure I could, um, keep up. Or do anything strange. I'm not very adventurous. And I've had three children. I've got stretch marks." She thought about telling him that her breasts were a little saggy, too, but didn't think he would want to know that in advance. Maybe he wouldn't notice. If she was on her back when she took off her bra, it would be hard to tell, wouldn't it?

She cleared her throat. "So I'm sure you're thinking this is a bad idea. I wouldn't blame you. Really."

She heard a clinking sound. She thought he might be putting the champagne glasses on the coffee table, but she didn't want to turn around and see.

"I thought you were beautiful the first time I saw you and I still think that," Kyle murmured.

From the sound of his voice and faint puff of breath on her cheek, she knew he was standing right behind her. "But I'm not like them," she said, staring at the rocks that stretched to the ceiling. She touched their rough surface.

"Like who?"

"Those other women that you've been with. I don't know what you expect of me."

He put a hand on her shoulder and forced her to turn. She wanted to close her eyes, but she knew that was too cowardly. She would just have to face him and get it over with. She swallowed hard, then looked at him.

His face was taut with an emotion she could only describe as need. The corners of his mouth tilted up slightly, but his eyes burned with fire. He was close enough to touch, close enough for her to see the smooth line of his jaw, close enough for her to wonder if he'd shaved just before leaving with her to drop the kids off for camp. The thought pleased her.

He kept his hand on her shoulder. "What do you expect of me?" he asked.

"Huh? I don't expect anything." Well, except maybe that it was going to be wonderful between them.

He reached up and pulled the headband from her hair, then slipped his fingers through the loose strands. "I don't have any secret tricks. I won't do anything you haven't done before. There aren't going to be any surprises."

Ha, she thought grimly. He hadn't seen her naked.

He startled her by frowning. "No doubts, Sandy. They're not allowed. I've been waiting a long time for this moment."

She searched his eyes. "This isn't just about your crush, is it?"

"Of course it is. It's also about how I feel about you now, today, with both of us adults. I can't forget the past, but that's not all it's about." He smiled slightly. "Why can't you believe you turn me on?"

She felt the color flaring again on her cheeks. "I'm not the type who inspires grand passion."

He grabbed her hand and brought it to the fly of his jeans. She could feel the hard length pressing against her. "Who do you think inspired this?" he asked.

She squeezed him gently. Maybe it *was* real, she thought to herself. Maybe he did think she was attractive and maybe he really did want to make love with her. Maybe it was going to be all right. He certainly wasn't lying about his desire. It was hard to fake that large an arousal.

She rubbed her palm up and down the length of him. She swayed toward him, suddenly eager to find out how he would feel inside of her.

He groaned, then pulled her hand away. "I have two things to say."

She could feel the desire lapping at her body. It was faint at first, the slightest of tugs, but as she stood in front of him, staring at his perfect body, it grew until it was a riptide threatening to pull her under.

"Are you listening to me?" he asked.

"Uh-huh." Why was he talking so much?

"First, I haven't been with lots of women. Some. A few. In this day and age, it would be crazy to be indiscriminate. Second, I'm using protection."

She blinked. The desire faded in the reality of his pragmatic statement. "Protection?" Oh, God, she'd forgotten. After Nichole had been born, Thomas had taken care of birth control permanently. She hadn't had to think about it anymore. But Kyle wasn't Thomas and this was the nineties. "Protection?"

"You just said that."

She turned from him and started for the door. "I can't do this."

She got all the way to the entrance to the kitchen before she realized he wasn't going to stop her. She paused and glanced back at him. He was still standing where she'd left him, in front of the fireplace. Her gaze lowered to his bare feet. While he'd been pouring the champagne, he must have also taken off his cowboy boots. She'd never thought of a man's feet as sexy before, but she liked Kyle's. They were broad and strong. Like him.

On the coffee table, bubbles floated to the surface of the tulip-shaped glasses. She looked at him. He was waiting. Patiently. It was her decision.

"You'd let me walk out?" she asked.

"If that's what you want. No being swept away this time, Sandy. No excuses. If you want to make love with me, stay. If you're not sure, you should go." With that, he

picked up the two glasses and carried them into the bedroom.

At least she assumed it was the bedroom. She'd never
explored his house before. She stood there in silence,
wondering when she'd become such a wimp. This wasn't a
difficult decision. Of course she wanted Kyle. All that was
holding her back were her own insecurities. And a faint
voice that whispered she would be in big trouble if she was
foolish enough to fall for him.

She was a grown woman. In all her thirty-two years,
she'd never reacted to a man the way she reacted to him.
No one had ever left her breathless before. She'd spent her
whole life playing it safe, doing the right thing, the expected thing. For once, she'd promised herself to walk on
the wild side. She raised her chin slightly and started after
him.

There was a short hallway. On one side was an open
door leading to a bathroom. On the other, a second door
stood open. From where she was standing, she could see a
dresser and the foot of a brass bed. Light filtered in
through open-weave drapes of blue and rust. She stepped
into the room.

It was a man's room. Large pieces of wooden furniture
lined the wall. A dresser, a highboy and two nightstands.
An overstuffed blue chair filled one corner. A rust-colored
comforter had been pulled back, exposing cream-colored
sheets. Kyle sat on one side of the king-size bed. He'd removed his shirt. Sunlight caught the smooth skin of his
bare shoulders and highlighted the hair on his chest. Sandy's fingers curled into her palms.

He reached for the two glasses he'd left on the nightstand and handed her one. She crossed the room and took
it from him. He didn't want her swept away. He wanted
her aware of everything that was going on. Her breath
caught in her throat. That wasn't going to be difficult. No
way she could think about anything else.

She took a sip of the cool liquid. Bubbles tickled her nose and the back of her throat. She'd forgotten how much she liked champagne. He drank also. She watched his throat as he swallowed. The air in the room heated, as if someone had turned on the furnace. Or maybe it was just being so close to him.

Her gaze traveled over his bare chest. She wanted to touch him, taste him. She wanted to feel him next to her without the encumbrances of clothing, or worrying about privacy or interruptions. Her breathing increased.

Kyle took the glass from her and set it down next to his. Before she could figure out what he was going to do, he'd already reached for the hem of her T-shirt and was gently tugging the garment over her head. Thank goodness she'd had the foresight to put on her best underwear. Her bra and panties matched, probably for the first time in her life. They were both a pale pink with a print of roses woven into the fabric. The bra gave her a little extra support and made her looked chesty. She hoped Kyle appreciated her silhouette. She hadn't had dessert since she'd decided to send the children to camp and then indulge with Kyle. She'd been doing sit-ups, but doubted two weeks of diligence made up for years of neglect.

With practiced ease, without even turning her around or glancing behind her, he reached for the button and zipper of her denim skirt and unfastened them. A quick tug had that garment pooling around her feet.

"You've done this before," she said without thinking.

He grinned at her. "Once or twice."

Then he reached for her bra. She wanted to stop him. Her breasts weren't as perky as they had been when he'd fantasized about them sixteen years ago. If he even had fantasized about them. Instinctively, she crossed her arms over her chest.

"Wouldn't you rather I was lying down?" she asked.

He raised his eyebrows.

She realized what she'd said and wanted to die. Right now. If the floor would just open up and swallow her. But it didn't. "What I meant was..."

He waited, watching her, grinning that damn knowing smile of his.

"Fine," she said through gritted teeth and reached for the back fastener. "I'll just take it off. But don't say I didn't warn you." She unhooked the bra, slid it off her arms, and glared at him. Then she bent over and jerked her panties down to her ankles, then stepped out of them.

"Are you happy?" she asked. "Look." She brushed her palm against her belly. There were faint lines from her pregnancies. "I'm marked, wrinkled—" She pointed to her breasts. "Definitely past perky. I could probably stand to lose ten pounds."

This was awful. The most embarrassing moment of her life. "I'm going home now," she said and started for the door.

"Naked?" Kyle asked.

She reached the doorway and stopped. "You're supposed to stop me. You're supposed to lie and say all those things don't matter, that I'm really the most beautiful woman you've ever seen."

As if her humiliation wasn't complete, she could feel tears burning in her eyes. She *never* cried. She refused to start now. About this.

"Are you done?" he asked.

She sniffed. "I think so."

"Good."

She shrieked as he came up behind her and lifted her in his arms. She supposed most women reacted well to being carried, however she didn't like the feeling of being up in the air. She clung to Kyle's neck until she was probably choking the poor man, and kicked her feet as if that would help propel them the short distance to the bed.

He knelt on the mattress and lowered her. When her head touched the pillow, he stretched out beside her. "What happened to Sensible Sandy?" he asked.

"I think she got packed with the kids' stuff by accident."

"I like this Sandy, too."

"Really?" Her mouth twisted. "You're just saying that because you're afraid I'm going to cry."

"Are you?"

His dark eyes promised her the world, yet she was afraid. "Maybe."

"Only tears of joy," he said quietly and reached for the champagne.

She expected him to take a sip, or offer her one. Instead, he held the glass over her midsection and tipped it until a stream of bubbly liquid poured onto her belly. The shock of cold made her jump.

"What are you doing?" she asked. "It's wet."

He grinned.

Kyle rose to his knees, then bent over her. He licked at the champagne. She stared at him in disbelief, then collapsed back on the pillows. It was a contrast of temperatures and textures. The bubbles tickled, his mouth was smooth. The champagne cooled her skin, his tongue heated her to melting. He drank the liquid from her belly, licking the last drops from around her hipbones, then he moved between her knees and stared down at her.

"You still doubt," he said, then held out his hands. She glanced at his fingers, then looked closer. They trembled.

"Why?" she asked.

"Because it's you. It's always been you."

The beauty of his face made her heart beat faster. He was male to her female, experienced to her awkwardness, and she wanted him more than she wanted to draw her next breath. For some reason she would never understand, he also wanted her. He thought she was special. Perhaps it was the past, or some combination of chemistry. Perhaps it was just dumb luck. Whatever the reason, she, an ordinary woman with nothing special to set her apart from the thousands of other ordinary women in this world, had worked magic on him. She made him tremble. Saggy breasts and stretch marks, three kids and a slight need to organize the world. She was done trying to explain it away. If he wanted her that much, far be it from her to deny him.

She opened her arms and spoke his name.

She was all he'd dreamed she would be, Kyle thought as he lowered himself to kiss her. She tasted of champagne and promises. She was hot and willing, tentative and bold, all things. She was his world.

He angled his mouth and sought entrance to hers. She parted for him. When his tongue touched hers, he felt the jolt clear down to his groin. His arousal surged painfully against the fly of his jeans. He would keep them on until the very end. He'd been ready since the moment she'd agreed to send her kids to camp. He'd been anticipating this moment since he'd woken up that morning. He had a bad feeling that if he took his jeans off, he would be compelled to plunge inside of her and explode like an adolescent. He wanted more than that for her. He wanted to be perfect.

To that end, he kissed her slowly. He touched her shoulders and her arms, rubbing his palms up and down on her smooth skin. She was softer than he'd imagined any woman could be. Her curves yielded to him.

He kissed her mouth, then her jaw and her ear. Her hands clutched at his back. He liked the way she held on to him as if she feared he would go away. If only she knew the truth. He had no other world save her.

After licking her earlobe and making her giggle and squirm beneath him, he trailed his mouth down her neck to her chest. Her breathing increased. Her body tightened in anticipation. He moved his hands from her arms to her waist, then slipped them higher, up her rib cage to her breasts.

She arched into his touch. Her hips came up off the bed and her fingers dug into his back. He raised his head slightly so he could see what he was doing.

His long tanned fingers contrasted with her pale skin. Her nipples were dark pink and already hard. He cupped her breasts, learning their shape and texture. They moved in his hands, soft and supple. She writhed beneath him, her legs tangling with his, her hips rising to meet him and taunt him with a brief caress. Around and around, he circled, close to the taut peaks, but not touching. Then he released her and reached for the champagne.

Her eyes opened and she watched him take a sip. Her lips parted. He bent down and took her right nipple in his mouth. She gasped. The liquid had cooled his skin slightly. He suckled her, loving the taste of her. She was sweeter than the champagne, more intoxicating.

He repeated the procedure, this time filling his mouth with the liquid and then letting the bubbles explode against her nipples. She called his name. Her arms fell to her sides and she clawed at the sheet. He traced a trail of dampness to her belly button, then back to her breasts. He loved her there, over and over, until her breath came in pants and her hips were permanently plastered against him.

He taunted them both by moving back and forth against her center. Several times he had to stop because he was about to explode. He could feel the pressure building, so he backed off.

He bathed her thighs in champagne, then licked her clean. He dipped her fingers into the slender glass and suckled them. Her eyes glazed over, her head tossed from side to side. At last, when perspiration coated her body and she had drawn her knees back to expose her most secret place to him, he reached between them and touched her there.

Just once. Very lightly. The tip of his index finger found her center and rubbed it. Then again. She gasped. Her eyes opened, but she couldn't seem to focus.

"What are you doing?" she asked weakly.

"Trying to drive you crazy. How am I doing?"

She smiled. "Great. Except you lied to me."

"When?"

"You said it wasn't going to be different." She blinked and looked at him. "It is. It's wonderful. Why are you being so good to me?"

Because you mean everything to me. Only he didn't say that. Instead, he touched her again, in her most feminine place, and she forgot the question. He touched her over and over until she was begging him for release. He bent over her and kissed her breasts, even as his fingers moved faster and faster, even as her hips began to rotate in the age-old rhythm of desire.

He shifted until he was lying next to her, supporting his head with one hand. He stared at her face, at the way her breasts moved, at the faint lines on her belly. Every inch of her was precious to him.

His forearm was against her thigh and he could feel her muscles tensing as she neared her release. He moved faster.

Her lips parted. A flush started at her breasts and climbed toward her face. He glanced at the place he touched her. His fingers slipped back and forth, parting the light brown curls. Her knees drew back toward her chest and he could see all of her. His throat tightened as he stared at her beauty, at the tiny place that brought her pleasure, at the dampness that would soon welcome him home. He felt the moment when her muscles locked and heard her stop breathing. He continued his quick, light ministrations.

Then she exhaled his name. Beneath his forearm her legs trembled and jerked slightly. Her hands opened and closed against the sheets. He glanced at her face and watched her try to catch her breath. The flush had climbed to her hairline, her nipples were erect. Satisfaction poured through him, as if the pleasure had been solely his. He wished they could do it again and again until he learned everything about her. He wanted to make love to her until she was too weak to walk or even stand.

Instead, he drew her close to him. He held her tightly in his arms as she continued to shake. He released her long enough to brush away the tears that trickled down her temples and kiss the questions from her lips.

"It's never been like that," she said, staring up at him.

The gladness filling him made it impossible to speak.

After a few minutes, she pushed him away. "Take your clothes off," she demanded. "I want to see you."

He grinned and stood up. He was shaking so hard, he had trouble with the buttons on his fly, but he got them undone and pushed the jeans and his briefs down in one quick movement. Sandy knelt on the bed in front of him, staring at his arousal.

He wanted her to lie down or move back or something, but she just knelt there staring. It was going to be a problem in about two minutes, he thought. Already the pressure was uncomfortable. Soon it would be uncontrollable.

"Sandy, I can't wait much longer," he said. "I hate to be a jerk, but you've had me like this since the day you arrived and a cold shower can only do so much."

She raised her gaze to his. "Really? I turn you on that much?"

"You tell me."

"Can I touch you?" she asked, reaching toward him.

"No!" He stepped back. "That wouldn't be a good idea. Not unless you want me to ah—"

She raised her eyebrows. "As fast as that? Gee, I'm surprised. I would have thought you'd be more controlled." She scooted back on the bed.

"I have damn *good* control," he growled, bending down and pulling a condom out of his jeans' pocket. "You make me sound like some horny kid. It's not like that. It's just this situation has been difficult from the beginning."

"I understand," she said kindly. "You don't have to explain it to me."

"Dammit, woman."

She giggled. "I'm teasing. Come on, let's take care of your little problem."

"You said it was big," he grumbled as he opened the package and started to slide on the condom. He was still shaking, so it wasn't an elegant procedure, but when it was finally fitted in place, he moved to the bed.

Sandy was grinning up at him. She moved to the far side and relaxed back against the pillows. Her hair was loose around her face, her body naked to his gaze, her thighs parted in welcome.

"You're the most incredible woman I've ever known," he said, moving across the bed and kneeling between her legs. "I swear I'll make it up to you."

Her pupils dilated. "You already did. This is just for you."

She reached down and touched him. He about exploded right then and there, but managed to salvage a little control, just enough to press into her. Heat surrounded him as she stretched to accommodate him. She wiggled her hips and he almost lost it again.

"This is going to take about one second," he said, wishing he could do better.

"I don't mind." She touched his face, then his chest. "I wish I could make you understand how terrific it makes me feel to know that you're losing control with me." She tightened her muscles around him. "The faster, the better, as far as I'm concerned. Impress me later."

He took her at her word. He pressed in until she'd taken all of him and withdrew slowly. Her muscles clenched harder as if begging him to stay. He plunged in a second time, then a third. On the fourth time, she drew her knees back and grasped his buttocks. She pulled him closer until he was buried inside her, deeper than he'd thought possible. She did something incredible, tightening even more and he crashed into paradise.

The sudden explosion shocked him. His muscles turned rock-hard, then released. He tried to pull back and plunge in again, but he couldn't move. He could only feel. She caressed him from the inside, her body rippling around him, her hands holding him against her, her breasts brushing his chest. He thought he might have said her name, he was pretty sure he got loud, which was kind of embarrassing.

When the pleasure had faded to a memory and his body was limp with relief, he held her close and inhaled her scent. It had been better than he'd hoped for. Better than anything he'd done before. It wasn't just about passion, though. There was a tenderness, a sense of joining between them that scared him to death. Not because she might trap him into staying. Hell, he wanted to stay. What terrified him was the fear that as much as he wanted to be there for her, he didn't know if he had what it took to last through the long haul.

"I'm convinced," Sandy said as she struggled to catch her breath.

"You're sure?" he asked.

"Positive." She stretched her arms over her head and sighed with contentment.

"I could do more."

He thrust his hips forward. Despite their both having just found their release, the sensation of him moving inside of her sent a slight tingling through her body. Would she ever grow weary of being with him?

A faint light showed through the drapes at the window. The pleasantly tired aching of her body told her it was dawn. For the past four days, they'd done little but make love, eat and sleep.

Kyle had arranged for time off while the kids were at camp. Every afternoon, Sandy returned to her house to pick up the mail and water the plants. She was having her calls forwarded to his number, so if something happened with the children she would know. But there had only been blessed silence and the quiet isolation most enjoyed by new lovers.

"We've got to get some more sleep," she said, shifting to give him more room next to her.

"Why?" he asked as he settled on the pillow and drew her close. She rested her head on his shoulder.

"They'll be back this afternoon. We need to look rested."

"The fact that they're coming back is all the more reason not to waste time." He leered at her. "Besides, I have my reputation to think of."

She slipped her leg between his. His hand rested on her bare hip. She no longer thought about stretch marks or imperfect flesh. Kyle had seen it all, touched it all, tasted it all. He found pleasure in her body and that was enough for her.

"You've redeemed yourself a hundred times over," she reminded him. "It doesn't matter that you couldn't hold back the first time. Trust me, your control is amazing. I have the weak knees to prove it."

His control *was* amazing, as was his ability to discover exactly what pleasured her. In four days, he'd learned more about her body, her likes and dislikes, than Thomas had learned in thirteen years of marriage.

He brushed her hair out of her face. "You're good for me."

"I'm glad."

Contentment stole over her. Here in this bedroom, lying on sheets musky with the scent of their bodies, she felt as if everything would be all right between them. The world couldn't hurt them here. All things were possible.

But even as she sighed softly and smiled into his chest, worries stole over her. They couldn't stay in this room forever. In a few hours, she would go pick up her children, and life would return to normal. Then what? She didn't want to think about it, but she didn't know how to avoid the questions. What would happen then? Would they date? Continue as lovers? What did Kyle want of her? What did she want of him?

He exhaled. "I think you're right, kid. I need to sleep for a couple of hours. I'm not as young as I used to be."

She ran her fingers through the dark hair on his chest. "I don't see a single gray hair."

"They'll be there soon enough," he murmured. His body relaxed next to hers and his breathing deepened.

She listened to the rhythmic thudding of his heart. She wanted to hold on to him forever. Sometime in the last four days, she'd started to think of what life would be like with him there all the time and it frightened her. Not just because of who he was, but because of herself. She wasn't the kind of woman who inspired life-changing love in a man. She wasn't sure she was enough to keep Kyle happy. She hadn't been able to hold on to Thomas. No other woman had been able to get Kyle to commit to a long-term relationship. What made her think she could do any better?

Everything she knew about him told her he was wrong for her. Everything he did for her proved that he was the perfect man. Which was she supposed to believe? Which was right? Could she risk it again? What happened when things got rough? What happened when he had to make the hard choices? How could she trust him to think of herself and her children before he thought of himself? Did she even have the right to expect that?

She turned onto her back and stared at the ceiling. She wanted a partner, not a playmate. Was she wishing for the moon?

Kyle shifted toward her in his sleep, as if he missed her closeness.

"Sandy?" he mumbled, obviously not fully awake.

"I'm right here," she said, reaching over and touching his short dark hair. The individual strands felt like silk through her fingers.

"Love you," he whispered as his eyelashes fluttered against his cheek.

Her fingers froze. What had he said? That he loved her? She continued to stroke his head, all the while fighting back her tears. What a way for him to tell her. When she couldn't ask him to repeat it, or if he'd even meant it. She didn't know which would be worse. For the words to be true, or for them to be a lie.

Chapter Fourteen

Life was good, Kyle thought as he picked up the next report. He studied the name on the folder, then searched through the file cabinet until he found where it went and slid it in place. He continued to whistle tunelessly as he worked on the filing. He could feel the sun shining through the office window and onto his back. It was another beautiful day in Glenwood. The last bright moments of summer before—

"What the hell is wrong with you?" Travis grumbled as he came into the room. "You're whistling, for God's sake."

Kyle grinned at his older brother. "You look like hell."

"I feel like hell. Mandy ate something bad yesterday and I was up all night with her. What are you so cheerful about?"

Kyle closed the top drawer and pulled open the second one. "Just life, big brother."

"That's disgusting." Travis squinted at him. "You're doing the filing?"

"Dottie had a doctor's appointment."

"You hate the filing."

Kyle shrugged. "It's not so bad."

Travis stared at him for a second, then shook his head. "You're not a well man," he muttered as he left the main office.

Kyle didn't bother pointing out he'd never felt better. His life was perfect. He reached for the next report and chuckled. Okay, it could be a little more perfect if he and Sandy could find some privacy and make love. Since the kids had come home from camp the previous week, they'd all spent time together. He was crazy about her children, but there were times when he wanted school to start so they would go to bed early and leave Sandy and him with enough of the evening left to have some adult fun. Still, he wasn't complaining. Sandy hadn't shut him down and he'd thought she might.

He walked to the front window and stared out at the park across from the sheriff's department. All the way to the park to pick up the children from camp, he'd been terrified that she was going to tell him it was over. But she hadn't. After collecting the kids, they'd gone out to dinner and heard all about their time away. Everyone had had fun. Even Lindsay made a couple of friends. That night, he'd left Sandy and her children at their house and made the solitary walk back to his own place. For the first time in three nights, he'd slept alone in his bed. He'd used her pillow so he could smell her sweet scent and pretend she was with him.

He knew now that was what he wanted. He'd thought long and hard about it, and he'd decided to risk it all. He loved Sandy and he wanted to marry her. All he was waiting for was the right moment to tell her how he felt.

He wasn't sure if he was going to propose right off. She might need a little convincing. After all, on the surface, he was as bad or worse than Thomas. But he'd learned the truth about himself. He didn't just skate by on his good looks. There was more to him on the inside. He was willing to be there for Sandy and her children, no matter what it cost him personally. He returned to the file cabinet and started whistling again.

The phone rang. Not the main business line which would be picked up at the front of the station, but the private line businesses often used if there was a problem but it wasn't urgent.

"Glenwood Sheriff's Department," he said. "Deputy Haynes speaking."

"Kyle, it's Wilson Porter, from the Ragged Elephant. I've got a problem."

Kyle grimaced. The Ragged Elephant was a trendy boutique at the mall. Teenagers loved the exciting new fashions, but the store had more than its share of trouble. "Let me guess. Shoplifters checking out the new fall line."

"You got it. I'm holding the kids in my office. They're pretty young and scared, but I'm not going to let them off."

"I understand. I'll be right there."

He hung up, then reached for his cap. As he walked down the hallway, he called out to Travis. "Shoplifters at the Ragged Elephant. I'll radio you and let you know how many I'm bringing in."

Travis followed him into the hallway and nodded. "I really want school to start," he said. "The teenagers are getting restless."

Kyle pushed open the door and glanced back. "Ten more days."

"How would you know?"

Kyle grinned. "I've been counting 'em myself."

He didn't bother waiting for a reply. Instead, he walked to his patrol car and headed for the mall.

Twenty minutes later, he took the escalator to the second floor and turned toward the boutique. Several teenagers were standing in groups on the sides of the walkway. The young boys gave him challenging looks, but the girls smiled and said hello. He nodded at all of them. Today, nothing was going to interfere with his good mood. He loved Sandy—all was right with the world.

He entered the store. Wilson Porter hurried to greet him. "Kyle, I'm really glad you're here." The short overweight forty-year-old who managed the boutique motioned toward the back of the store. "They're crying. I hate it when they cry."

"They usually do," Kyle reminded him.

"I know." Wilson sighed. "Why can't they put things on layaway? But no. They have to try and steal them. Don't they know everything is tagged electronically? Do they think I'm stupid?"

"They don't think." Kyle pushed open a door marked Private and entered the back storage room. There was a short corridor to the left. He turned there and walked to Wilson's office. He waited while the manager unlocked the door. Kyle stepped inside.

Three girls sat around the small room. Two looked up at him. He didn't recognize them. They must be summer kids. Glenwood didn't get a lot of tourists, but there were a few families who came up from the city and rented houses in the woods. These girls were young, maybe thirteen. Two were blond, one with short straight hair, the other with long curly hair to her waist. Both had obviously been crying. The third, the one who hadn't looked at him yet, had brown hair.

"Who wants to tell me what happened?" he asked.

As he spoke, the third girl raised her head. Kyle stared at her in disbelief. "Lindsay?"

Her face was wet with tears, her eyes red. She flinched when he said her name. "Wh-what are you doing here?" she asked, her voice shaking.

"I got a call about some shoplifters."

The tears flowed faster. "I'm sorry," she whispered. "I didn't mean it. Please don't tell my mom."

"Your mom is the least of your problems," Kyle said, stunned by what he was seeing and hearing. "What were you thinking of? This isn't a game, Lindsay."

She seemed to fold in on herself. She pulled her knees up to her chest and dropped her forehead to her knees. "I'm sorry," she said again.

"You know this guy?" the short-haired blonde asked. Lindsay nodded miserably. "Cool." She looked at Kyle. "We didn't mean anything by this. Can't you talk to him and explain that?" She jerked her head toward Wilson.

Wilson glared at her. "Didn't mean anything? Honey, I've had my eye on you all summer. I know you took those dragon earrings a couple of weeks ago." He went into the hallway and returned with a shopping bag full of clothing. "This is what they were trying to steal. All this? Can you believe it? Not only do they think I'm stupid, they're greedy, too." He glared at the girls, then turned to Kyle. "I want to press charges. Against all of them."

"But it was an accident," Lindsay said for the third time. "I swear."

Kyle stared at the young girl in front of him. She was no longer the vamp in training who had trailed him the first month she'd been in Glenwood. She was a frightened child who didn't understand the consequences of what she'd done. But she was about to learn in a big way.

He leaned toward her. "You were the one carrying the bag, Lindsay. How was it an accident?"

"I didn't know they'd stolen the stuff," she said.

He waited. She fidgeted on the straight-backed chair he'd pulled up beside his desk. When the girls had realized he meant to bring them to the station, they'd all lost control. He'd had to hustle three hysterical crying preteens through the mall to the patrol car. The two blondes hadn't said much, but Lindsay kept apologizing. He'd called Travis with the details. As soon as they'd arrived at the station, he'd separated the girls. Travis and one of the other deputies were taking care of the two blondes, while Kyle had brought Lindsay with him.

He still didn't know what he was going to do with her. The part of him that cared about her, the part of him that understood how easy it was to get mixed up in trouble, wanted to ease her way. He thought about talking to Wilson. He could get the store manager to drop the charges. The other two girls were from out of town. They would be leaving soon and taking their trouble with them. Lindsay wasn't a bad kid. He could make Wilson understand.

But he wasn't going to. Not only because it was wrong to use his influence, but because it wouldn't help Lindsay. That was the hell of it. If she learned a hard lesson this early, she wouldn't make the same mistake again. If he let her off, then she would start to expect other people to always be cleaning up her messes. So he didn't speak to Wilson or tell Lindsay it was going to be okay. Instead, he glared at her, waiting for her to tell him the truth.

"Why are you doing this to me?" she asked, still crying. Her long brown hair hung limply over her shoulders. She pushed it away from her face. She was pale under her tan.

"Doing what?"

"Treating me this way? I didn't do anything."

"You carried a bag of stolen clothing out of a store. That's called shoplifting, and it's against the law."

"But I didn't kn-know. I thought they'd paid for it."

He didn't say anything.

She sobbed for several more minutes. He pushed a box of tissue close to the edge of the desk and then clutched the arms of his chair. He wanted to go to her and comfort her. He wanted to pull her into his arms and promise he would fix it all. He wanted to know that she would understand why he was doing this. That it was for her own good.

He hadn't thought doing the right thing would hurt so much. He hated watching Lindsay cry. Each tear, each sob was like a dagger in his heart. He'd come to care about Lindsay. He wanted to spare her the pain, but he knew doing that would only make it worse in the long run.

"Did you see either girl pay for the clothing?" he asked when she'd quieted some.

"No, but—" She looked at him. "I—I just didn't think they would have taken the things without paying for them. They gave me the bag and told me to start walking. What was I supposed to do? They're my friends. The first friends I've made here." She wiped her eyes. "I was sc-scared, and I didn't want to say anything. Then that buzzer went off and that little man came after us. He was screaming that we were thieves, then he grabbed me." She covered her face with her hands. "I was so humiliated. It was awful. I'm really sorry." She looked up at him. "I swear I'll never do anything like that again. Please don't tell my mom, Kyle. She'll kill me."

Lindsay wasn't the only one Sandy was going to want to kill. Her daughter's partners in crime had been girls she'd met at camp. The camp he'd encouraged the children to attend so that he could have some private time with their mother. Sandy was going to blame him for this whole damn thing. He didn't know how or why, but he could feel it in his bones. Things had been going too well between them. He wasn't looking forward to calling her.

"It's not just your mother, Lindsay. Mr. Porter is going to press charges. You're a juvenile and that will help. You have a clean record and people who will vouch for your character." He was willing to let her be charged, but he had every intention of speaking for her at the hearing.

She blanched. "I'm going to prison?" Her eyes filled with tears. "Kyle? That's not true, is it?"

"You won't have to go to a detention facility. You'll be released into your mother's custody."

"Custody? Like I'm a criminal? But I didn't do anything."

"You carried stolen clothing out of a store."

"But I didn't take it. It wasn't mine. I didn't even like the stuff they picked out." She sprang to her feet and started pacing the office. "Kyle, please, you've got to help me. I really didn't do anything. I didn't want to help them. I didn't even want to be there. I thought they were my friends. I haven't had any friends since we moved here. Everything is so horrible. I hate this." She stood in front of him and twisted her hands around and around. "Please help me. You've got to. Please?"

He couldn't resist her plea. He rose to his feet and hugged her. Her slender body was trembling. "I'm sorry, Lindsay," he said, smoothing her hair. "This is pretty ugly. Unfortunately, you're going to have to face the consequences of what happened. Your friends got you into trouble, and you're going to have to pay the price for that. You knew it was wrong to take the clothes, but you did it, anyway."

She pushed away from him. "You're not going to do anything, are you?" she asked, her voice getting loud. "Why?"

"Because you have to learn. I know this is hard. It's damn hard for me, too."

"I don't care about you," she said. "You're not the one in trouble." He tried to touch her shoulder, but she jerked away from him. "Get away from me." She sank into the chair. "Get away."

He stared at her for a long time, then left the room. Conflicting emotions swelled inside of him. All he wanted was to do the right thing. Nothing else mattered. His heart told him to talk to Wilson and get the charges dropped. His head told him that was a mistake. With a flash of insight, he realized he was facing the double-edged sword of being a parent. Lindsay might not be his child, but he cared about her. The compassionate side of him wanted to make it easy for her. The logical side reminded him that she had to learn eventually and the lesson would be a lot less painful coming this early.

He walked into an empty office and stared at the phone. Putting Lindsay in custody was the second hardest thing he'd ever had to do. The hardest would be calling Sandy and telling her what had happened.

Sandy pushed open the glass doors and entered the sheriff's station. She was shaking—from concern and rage. How could Lindsay have gotten involved in something like this? How could she have shown such poor judgment? And how could she, as Lindsay's mother, have had no clue what was going on in her daughter's life?

She paused in the foyer and saw several people waiting. A couple, about her age, maybe a few years older, glanced up at her, then away. She wondered if they were one of the other girl's parents. Before she could go over and ask, a door opened and she saw Kyle. He motioned her to come with him.

"How are you holding up?" he asked when she got closer to him.

She tried to smile, then settled on a shrug. "Okay, I guess. I'm sorry it took me so long to get here. I had to drop Nichole and Blake at Elizabeth's." She followed Kyle down a long corridor to an empty office. When he'd shut the door behind them, she sank into the chair in front of the worn wooden desk.

"How did this happen?" she asked, then shook her head. "I'm sorry. You can't answer that, can you? I had no clue what she was up to. Are these the same girls she met at camp?"

Kyle hesitated before answering, then he nodded. "According to Lindsay, yes. She met them there, and apparently they've been hanging out together since they got back."

Sandy let her purse slip to the floor. "I blame myself. I shouldn't have sent her to camp. She didn't want to go. I thought—"

She clamped her mouth shut. She didn't want to say what she'd been thinking. That sending the kids away had been purely selfish. That she was the worst mother in the world. She could tell herself she'd sent the kids to camp so they could have some fun and make friends, but the truth was much uglier than that. She'd sent her kids to camp so she could have some private time with Kyle. She'd wanted to have sex, so she'd sacrificed her children's well-being. *She* should be the one arrested, not Lindsay.

"It's all my fault," she said.

"Bull." Kyle pulled the chair from behind the desk and moved it so it was in front of her. Then he sat down. "You didn't tell Lindsay to steal anything. She's a smart kid. She knows better. She got caught up in the moment. She didn't think, and now she has to face the consequences of what she did."

Sandy shook her head. "That's really easy for you to say. Lindsay isn't your child. Of course I know I didn't tell her to steal anything. That doesn't mean it's not my fault. Of course I had something to do with this. I just have to figure out what. Did I ignore her? Should I have investigated her friends better?"

"You're making yourself crazy over this. It's not that complicated."

"I met one of the girl's mothers," she said, more to herself than him. "I guess I should have met both mothers. Or not let Lindsay go with them. But I can't keep her locked up forever."

What had happened? Was it the move? Was this a late reaction to Thomas's death? She tried to fight off the ugly feeling that the root of the problem was her own selfishness. If she hadn't wanted to be with Kyle so much—

"You're not looking at this clearly," Kyle said. "Why does it have to be your fault? Why can't Lindsay have just made a mistake?"

"You wouldn't understand," she said impatiently.

"I might not be her father, but I've spent a hell of a lot of time with her this summer, and I think I've learned a few things. When I walked into that store and saw her sitting there, I felt like I—"

Sandy glared at him. "What did you say?" she asked, interrupting. She couldn't have heard him correctly. "When you went into the store? You were there?"

"I took the call."

She stood up. Kyle rose also. His expression hardened, then became unreadable, as if he sensed what was coming. Sandy felt her temper starting to rise. She tried to control it, but the rage pushed through.

"You arrested my daughter? How could you?"

"It's my job," he said coldly. All warmth disappeared from his brown eyes.

"Your job? Was it also your job to convince me to send her away so you could seduce me?" It wasn't a fair question, but she was past caring.

"One has nothing to do with the other. I arrested Lindsay because she'd broken the law, and also because I believe it's important for her to know that her actions have a price. You're the one who's so big on people being responsible. I would think you would be happy."

"Happy?" She curled her hands into fists and continued glaring at him. "Happy that you've destroyed her life? I know that you've hurt her and she may never get over this."

"Don't blame her actions on me. She'd old enough to know what she was doing."

"She's just a child."

"I agree she's not an adult. That's why I want to help her."

"You call this helping?" she asked scornfully. "We don't need your kind of help, Deputy Haynes." She turned away from him and walked over to the door. After pulling it open, she stared at the wall. "Please tell your superior that I want someone else assigned to the case. I don't want to have to deal with you anymore."

"Sandy, don't do this." He moved close and touched her arm. She pulled free of him. She wasn't going to listen to any more from him.

"Do I need to make the request in writing?" she asked.

"How much of this is about Lindsay and how much of it is you running scared?" he asked.

She didn't answer. Finally, he left the room and she was alone.

She had five minutes in which to try to pull herself together. It wasn't enough. When the door opened and Travis walked in, she thought she was going to start crying.

She could feel the blush climbing her cheeks. "Hi," she said, praying her voice would keep steady. "So this is the downside of living in a small town. Everybody knows everybody else's business."

Travis crossed the room and put his arm around her. "I know it's hard for you, but everything is going to be okay."

"If you knew how much I want to believe you." She blinked to hold back the tears. "Now that I'm going to have a convicted felon in the family, I hope we can all still be friends. I should probably warn you, I left Blake and Nichole with your wife."

Travis smiled. "Of course we're still friends. And shoplifting isn't a felony."

"Great." She allowed him to lead her to her chair. She sat down. "Now what happens?"

"Several things."

He took the seat Kyle had used. Sandy looked at him. Travis looked enough like his brother that if she squinted a little, she could pretend they were the same man. She wanted to apologize for what she'd said earlier and she suspected it would be easier to say the words to Travis. Of course, he wouldn't know what she was talking about.

"First," he said, "the other parents have already collected their children. Both girls are from out of town. The families will be leaving as soon as this is cleared up, so you don't have to worry about Lindsay hanging out with them anymore."

"That's a relief."

"We're going to keep this quiet, so Lindsay won't start school with a reputation."

"Okay."

He leaned back in his chair. "This was tough on Kyle. He really cares about your kids." And you.

He didn't say the last part, but she heard it. "I don't want to talk about him right now."

"All right. Let's talk about your daughter."

Sandy started to stand up. Travis grabbed her hand and pulled her back into the chair. "Hear me out," he said. "I've met a lot of kids. After a while, you start to get a feel for them. Lindsay's one of the good ones. She got a big scare today. It's going to stay with her a long time."

"What are you saying?"

"That it's probably not going to be a problem again. I don't usually tell parents not to punish their kids, but I'm going to make an exception. She's a frightened little girl, and you might want to consider just listening instead of acting."

Sandy shook her head. What was it with these men? Why were they always telling other people how to raise their kids? It seemed to her that their family wasn't anything to brag about. "I'll give it some thought," she said, standing. "Is she free to go?"

"Sure." He rose and walked to the door. "It's none of my business, but Kyle's hurting pretty bad. Maybe you could talk to him before you leave."

"You're right. It's none of your business." She started to walk past him into the hallway, then paused. "You can give him a message for me, though. Tell him I want him to stay away from me and away from my kids. And this time, I mean it."

"None of this is his fault," Travis told her.

"Then whose fault is it?"

"Why does it have to be anyone's? Sometimes these things just happen."

"Maybe," she said, knowing he was talking about the shoplifting and she was talking about a relationship that would never work. "But it's not going to happen again."

Chapter Fifteen

Despite the late hour, the lights were on in Sandy's house. Kyle paused at the edge of the porch and thought about waiting until morning to tell her what had happened. He was tired and defeated, and he didn't want to face her now. But he knew she would rest easier knowing what he had to say.

If only she would understand. If only she could see how damn hard it had been for him to take Lindsay into custody. He hadn't wanted to, but it had been the right thing to do.

He walked to the door and raised his hand to knock, then lowered it back to his side. What was the point of being right if it cost him Sandy?

Before he could change his mind, he rapped on the door once, and waited. He heard footsteps, then her voice quietly called, "Who is it?"

"Kyle."

She hesitated. At first, he thought she might not even let him in. He was right. She opened the door a crack and stared at him, but made no move to allow him into her home. "What do you want?" she asked.

Her face was pale and drawn, as if the trauma of the day had stolen away all her vitality. Her mouth trembled slightly and there were shadows under her green eyes. One strand of hair drifted across her cheek. She brushed it back impatiently in a familiar gesture that made his heart ache.

"That's it?" he asked. "After all that's happened between us, now I'm supposed to stand out here like I'm selling door-to-door and you're not even going to bother inviting me in?"

She ducked her head a bit and sighed. "It's late, Kyle. What do you want?"

"To talk to you. To make you understand. I think you owe me that, at least."

"I don't owe you anything."

He managed to stay upright and keep his features impassive, but it was as if she'd stabbed him in the gut. He could feel his life's blood oozing away. He thought about begging, but to what end? She didn't really want him, she never had. She was only interested in the fantasy. Reality had intruded on Sandy Walker's neat view of life in the form of their messy, imperfect relationship. She couldn't have that.

"Have it your way," he said. "I'm outta here. I just thought you'd want to know that Wilson Porter dropped all charges." He turned on his heel and started to leave. Behind him, the door creaked as Sandy opened it wide.

"What did you say?" she asked.

"You heard me." He kept on walking.

"Wait, Kyle. Maybe you'd better come inside."

He paused at the top of the stairs. It would be so easy to keep on going. Leaving was what he did best. He knew all the things to say, how to make it easier for everyone. He was good at saying goodbye. What he wasn't good at was staying or giving his heart. He wasn't good at taking emotional risks. So far, the one time he'd really tried, he'd managed to screw everything up. He hurt so bad, it was hard to breathe. He'd had to arrest Lindsay, and Sandy didn't want to see him. The pain of staying sure made leaving look good.

But he loved her. He hadn't wanted to, he'd thought he could avoid those feelings forever. But they'd crept up on him when his back was turned. Somehow, the adolescent crush had matured into something lasting. Something he would never get over. Walking away guaranteed it wouldn't work out. At least by staying, he was giving them both a chance. Didn't they deserve that?

He turned and crossed the porch in three long strides. Without looking at her, he entered the house and continued into the living room. Once there, he didn't know if he should sit down or not, so he walked to the open window and stared out at the darkness.

He heard her footsteps on the hardwood floor as she came in after him. "What happened?" she asked.

"You tell me," he said, still staring out the window. The nighttime beyond made the glass more like a mirror. He could see the reflection of the sofa against the wall, and the pictures above it. Sandy stood just inside the door. She'd folded her arms in front of her waist and was looking at him in confusion.

"When did it go bad?" he asked. "Was it wrong to want you to send the children to camp? Is that what you're punishing me for?" He shrugged, not waiting for an answer. "Maybe. I'll admit my feelings were selfish. I knew they would enjoy themselves, but my primary concern was being alone with you. I thought that's what we both wanted."

He waited for a moment, but she didn't say anything. He continued. "You told me a while ago that I didn't take

responsibility for my actions. That I was used to skating
through life on my looks and charm. I thought about it
and decided you might have a point. Not in terms of my
career. I'm good at what I do there, but in my personal
life." He drew in a breath. "I've always been afraid to
commit. So rather than risk being left, I would leave first."

"Kyle, this doesn't have anything to do with what happened today."

"No?" He looked at her reflection in the window. She
wasn't watching him anymore. She was staring at the
ground. Was it because she didn't want to listen to what he
had to say or was it because she feared the truth? "You
wanted me, too, Sandy, and don't say you didn't. You were
just as eager to become lovers as I was."

"I know," she said miserably. "Now I'm paying the
price for that. I was so caught up in myself, I didn't think
about my children."

"That's a crock and you know it."

Her head snapped up. "You're not a parent. How would
you know—"

"Having a child of your own doesn't give you instant
access to magical skills, so quit acting like it does," he interrupted. "I might not have raised kids, but I've been
around them my whole life. I see messed-up ones on the
job just about every day. You make it sound like you were
out with me while the house burned down. Chances are,
even if we'd never met, you still would have sent the kids
to camp. They wanted to go."

"Lindsay didn't."

"Lindsay's practically a teenager. She doesn't want to
do anything."

"That's beside the point. I sent her and look what happened. She met those two girls and she got involved in
shoplifting. If I hadn't sent her—"

"She might have met them here. At the mall or the park.
You can't protect her from everything. At some point,

Lindsay has to make her own choices. We both know that. She made a bad choice this time, but she learned a cheap lesson. With the charges being dropped, she won't even have to deal with the consequences."

Sandy planted her hands on her hips. "She spent the afternoon in the sheriff's station. She was taken away in a patrol car. Those are consequences."

"You sound like you're defending what she did."

"Of course not. I hate that she was a part of that. I can't even think about it." She moved over to the sofa and sank onto the middle cushion. "I don't know what's wrong with me. I'm not making any sense, am I?"

She rubbed her temples and sighed. "Maybe we should start over," she said. "Everything happened so fast. I got swept off my feet by you, and you couldn't resist the challenge. Maybe we've both learned our lesson, too. I can't be one of your women."

He turned to face her. "Is that what you think this is about?" he asked, keeping his voice low when he really wanted to shout at her. "You still think I keep a revolving door at my place. You think I've got fifty women at my beck and call and you were just some pit stop on the road of life. Don't you?" he demanded.

"Well, it's obvious that I'm not your type."

He stalked across the room until he was standing just across the coffee table from her. "What is my type?"

She blinked. "Well, someone young, I would imagine. And pretty. A blonde, maybe, or a redhead."

He jerked his head as if she'd slapped him. In a way, she had. "Is that what you think of me? That all I care about is how pretty she is and how her hips sway when she walks?"

Sandy flushed, but didn't look away. "Yes."

He clenched his teeth. He'd been eating himself up alive trying to figure out if he was worthy of her, if he was willing to take the risk, when she saw him as a male bimbo, interested in nothing but appearances. "And that's all this is," he said, motioning with his arm. "This whole damn thing was nothing but playtime for you. A chance to live out your fantasies. To get it on with one of the infamous Haynes brothers. You never cared about me at all."

Lord, he sounded like one of the many women he'd dumped. With a bitter flash of insight, he realized he was finally getting his. In a world of cosmic justice, his bill had just come due.

"Of course I care about you, Kyle. As a friend. But any other kind of relationship is unrealistic."

"Why?"

"Even if you claim I'm yours, you're not *my* type."

"Why?"

"Because you're not responsible."

He leaned toward her. "We've covered this ground before. But I think you're using it to hide behind. You're afraid, Sandy Walker. You're damn afraid. Not just of me, although I must leave you trembling in fear. Worse than that, you're afraid of yourself. You don't want to have to feel things. Emotions frighten you. You're afraid of being rejected, and of falling in love, of making another mistake, so you keep yourself safe from life. You hide the fact that you're a coward and you call it being a good parent."

She sprang to her feet. "I don't have to listen to this."

"Yes, you do, because I'm not leaving until I've said it all."

She glared at him, her chest heaving. He hated that he could smell her sweetness. It diverted him from his anger and purpose. He wanted to pull her close and kiss her until they both forgot what they were arguing about, but he couldn't. He knew this might be his last chance to get through to her. He had to give the moment everything he had. He had to be honest and avoid the cheap tricks and smoky mirrors.

"So say it and go," she told him.

"There's been something between us from the moment you came back to Glenwood," he said. "You can deny it all you want, but it's been there. Call it chemistry or kismet, I don't care."

"It's just sexual attraction," she said disdainfully. "So what?"

He wanted to remind her that the sexual attraction she wanted to dismiss had made her weep tears of ecstasy in his arms. That she'd moaned his name night after night, when they'd been together. He wanted to make her feel the heat again, bring her close to paradise, then demand that she discount all that her body told her was real. Instead, he decided to risk it all by going for the heart. That's what this was really about. Sandy didn't want to admit she believed in love.

"So it was there," he said. "And it was just the beginning. We both know there's something else. Something even more powerful."

"I don't know that."

"Then you're blind as well as a coward." When she stiffened and opened her mouth to speak, he held up his hand to silence her. "I'm not done. When I am, you'll get your turn. I'll admit it's always been easier for me to leave than stay. I didn't want to risk rejection, so I did it first."

"Admirable," she said sarcastically. "I'm so glad to have you as a role model for my children."

He ignored her. "It stopped being easier to leave when I met you. I didn't want to walk away because I couldn't imagine being without you and the children. I changed for you, Sandy. Even if this doesn't work out, I'm glad I did it. I like the man I am now better. I know I did the right things for the right reason."

She continued to stare at him, but her expression softened. Her arms relaxed and dropped to her sides.

"I thought we might try working it out as a family," he said, wishing it was going to be that easy. But it wasn't. He could feel it in his soul. Still, he had to say the words. He had to make the confession, all of it, not just the parts she would want to hear.

"All my life I've felt inadequate," he said. "My dad never taught any of us what it was like to be a good man. My brothers and I have fumbled with that, coming up with what felt right to us. We never knew what it was like to live in a stable home or have parents who cared more about us than they did about their latest conquest or how unhappy they were. All my life, people left. My mother left, my brothers left, the stepmothers left. Even you left."

"I went to college," she said, sitting back down on the sofa. "I didn't know how you felt about me."

"I'm not saying you should have stayed, I'm just pointing out the fact that everyone I've ever cared about has left me. So I decided I wasn't going to let that happen again. Next time, *I* was going to do the leaving. I did. Over and over again. Until it became a habit and I didn't remember how to do anything else. Until you."

She brushed her hair out of her face. "Kyle, I don't think I can deal with this now."

"That's too bad, because I'm going to say it. It would have been easier not to get involved with you and the kids. I knew what I was up against. But I couldn't resist. I didn't want to care, but I do. I didn't want to fall in love with you, but I have."

She stared at him as if she'd never seen him before.

"I had this fantasy that it would all work out," he said. "I wanted to ask you to marry me, but I know now you'll find an excuse to say no. You'll use that imaginary yardstick of yours to measure my intentions and find them lacking.

"You're never going to find anyone who loves you more," he told her, "but you might find someone who you think fits your picture of an ideal mate. I'd like to wish you well on your search, but right now it hurts too bad.

Frankly, I hope you never find him. I don't think you will because he doesn't exist. You don't want a man, Sandy. You want an excuse to ignore the fear. Loving someone means opening yourself up. You complain that you don't want all the responsibility, but you don't want to give anyone a chance to do it their way. You're so afraid of mistakes, you won't even try anymore.''

"You're wrong," she said, shaking her head. "I'm not like that."

He shoved his hands into his pockets so she couldn't see he was shaking from emotion. "Yes, you are. You're exactly like that. No one will ever love you more than I do. I know the worst about you and I still want to be with you. I want to be there for the kids. I want to watch them grow and pick them up when they fall. But it wouldn't work, because I would let them make their own mistakes, and you would want to make sure they never had the chance."

"What does that mean?" she asked.

"I didn't go to Wilson Potter and ask him to drop the charges, Travis did."

"What?" Her voice rose. "You wanted Lindsay to go to jail?"

"She wouldn't have gone anywhere, but yes, I thought she should learn from what she'd done. Travis thought she'd learned her lesson already." He shrugged. "Who knows, maybe Travis is right. I just thought you should know what really happened. I didn't want you thinking I'd gotten her off. I don't want you to be grateful to me."

"Well, good, because I'm not." She stood up and walked to the door.

He headed for the front door, then paused. "It could have been great between us," he said quietly. "I would have loved you forever. But all you can see is your own narrow version of the truth. I'll never be able to fit in that definition." He glanced at her one last time, memorizing her features, wondering what he could have done differently.

He stepped out into the night. He was glad it was dark. At least in the shadows, he could pretend to hide from the pain.

Sandy drew her knees to her chest and rocked back and forth. It was late, well past midnight, but she wasn't sleepy. Who could think of sleeping at a time like this? Her world was crumbling around her and she didn't know how to make it stop.

Questions, images and words filled her mind. She was torn between pain and rage. How dare Kyle say those things to her? How dare he tell her that Lindsay deserved the punishment she got? How dare he say she was afraid to love, that she used her high standards to keep the world at bay?

He'd asked her to marry him. Actually, he'd only taunted her with a proposal, mentioning it, then withdrawing it before she could refuse him. Marriage. She'd never thought about that. Well, that wasn't exactly true. Of course she'd thought about getting married. She'd fantasized about a civilized arrangement with someone much like herself. Someone who understood the importance of being responsible.

She could see them sharing the Sunday paper, then going over their schedules for the coming week. But when she tried to picture the man's face, she could only see Kyle and he would never allow her to organize much of anything. No doubt he would grab the part of the paper he wanted and go watch the game on TV. But when she walked in front of him, he would pull her onto his lap and kiss her into oblivion, making her forget her lists and schedules, everything but the joy of being with him.

She'd never thought about marrying Kyle. Why? Because what she'd said was true. That she'd always pictured him with young pretty girls, not a mature woman like herself. But was that about Kyle, or was that about her?

She shifted on the sofa, feeling uncomfortable at the thought of having to face her own inadequacies. It wasn't Kyle, she admitted in a painfully, honest confession. She didn't think he was that shallow. It was her. She was the one with the stretch marks and not-so-perky butt. She was the one who used her organized life-style to convince herself and the world that she wasn't lonely and didn't desperately want someone to share her heart with.

Had Kyle really said he loved her? A single tear slipped down her cheek. She brushed it away impatiently. What was she crying about? So he loved her? So what? It didn't mean anything. He wasn't the right one.

Who better?

The question came unexpectedly. She didn't have an answer. Who better, indeed. Who would love her more fully, more honestly? He hadn't had to tell her that Travis had been the one to approach the store manager about Lindsay. While she was here, alone, and there was no one to hear her confession, she was willing to admit she agreed with Kyle. It would have been better for Lindsay to face the full consequences of what she'd done. In the station she, Sandy, had reacted without thinking. She'd been scared and the fear had made her say ugly things. She'd wanted to blame someone other than herself and Kyle had been convenient.

She closed her eyes and remembered the first moment she'd seen him riding up on his motorcycle. He'd stolen her breath away. When he'd turned out to be kind, good to her kids and possibly interested in her, she hadn't known what to think. She hadn't had enough self-confidence to believe it was real, so she'd made sure it wasn't. She'd pushed him away at every chance because she'd been afraid he was playing with her. Ordinary women like her didn't get that lucky. They didn't attract the Kyle Hayneses of the world.

She hadn't wanted to believe he was different, so she'd convinced herself he was just like Thomas. Even when everything he did proved otherwise. She hadn't been willing to take a step of faith, so she'd lost her one chance at happiness.

A soft sound on the stairs caught her attention. She opened her eyes and turned toward the noise. Lindsay crept into the room.

With her long hair loose around her shoulders, and a sleeveless cotton nightgown falling to her calves, her oldest child looked closer to six than thirteen. Big brown eyes, Thomas's eyes, stared at her.

"What's wrong?" Sandy asked.

Lindsay hovered by the edge of the couch. She twisted her fingers together. "I couldn't sleep. Are you still mad at me?"

"No." Sandy held out her arms. "I'm not."

Lindsay dived onto the sofa and cuddled next to her. Her firstborn, the one who tried so hard to be grown-up and mature, buried her head in her mother's shoulder and sobbed.

"I'm s-sorry, Mommy," she said, her voice broken and contrite. "I didn't mean to do anything bad. I swear I didn't. I swear."

"I know." Sandy stroked her hair. "Hush, baby. It's going to be all right."

"It's not, but I'm going to do everything I can to fix it. I want to, Mommy."

Sandy knew she would go from "Mommy" back to "Mo-om" soon enough, but for the moment, she enjoyed the closeness.

"Tell me what happened," Sandy said. "I want to hear your side of the story."

Lindsay raised her head and stared at her. She brushed away her tears. "You never want to hear my side of anything," she said, obviously surprised.

"That's not true," Sandy said automatically, then wondered if it was. She knew she was pretty strict with her kids, but she didn't think she'd forgotten to listen to them. "Maybe it is true." She didn't want it to be. She made a vow it wouldn't be true anymore. "Tell me now, okay?"

"I will, but..." Lindsay picked at the hem of her nightgown.

"But what?"

"Could you please not ask me why. You ask that a lot and I don't always *know* why I do something. Sometimes I just do it and then it's done and I can't take it back."

She smiled at her daughter. "Believe me, I understand that more than you think. So what happened with those girls?"

Lindsay leaned against her mother's shoulder and talked about the two friends she'd made at camp. "I liked them a lot because they were, you know, older. There were a couple of other girls I met. They weren't as cool. I sort of liked them more, but I wanted to be popular." She grimaced. "Going to jail isn't going to make anyone like me."

"Don't worry, you're not going to jail."

Lindsay glanced up at her. "You'll get me a good lawyer? Like on TV?"

"You're not going to need one. Go on with your story."

Lindsay sighed. "When we got back from camp, there wasn't anything to do around here. I started hanging out with them. Millie wanted to go to the mall. She said there was a way to get clothes without having a lot of money. At first I thought she meant, like, you know, a sale or something. Then she said she wanted to steal them."

Lindsay sat up straight. "I knew it was wrong and I told her I didn't want to do it. So I walked away, but I was still looking at things in the store. Then Pam came and got me and we started walking out. Millie handed me the bag and told me to carry it." She looked at her mother. Her mouth trembled. "I didn't know the clothes were stolen." She grimaced. "I think I sorta knew, but I didn't want them to be. I didn't know what to do. I almost dropped them and ran out, but I got embarrassed, so I just carried them out." She lowered her head to her chest. "Then Mr. Porter came running after us. He grabbed us and called the police." She shuddered. "You know what happened after that."

"It's okay, baby," Sandy said, drawing her close again.

Lindsay came willingly. "I'll never forget the look on Kyle's face. He wasn't angry or anything, but he looked real disappointed. Like he'd expected more of me. At first, I thought he was going to let me go. I didn't want him to tell you because I knew you'd kill me. But he said he couldn't do that. He said I had to face what I'd done. I was crying and everything. I said some pretty mean things to him."

"Yeah, me too," Sandy said softly.

Lindsay had acted foolishly, but her heart had been in the right place. Blake was healing from his father's neglect, even little Nichole was more cheerful than ever. Sandy wanted to say the improvements were because of her, or their new environment, but she knew it was Kyle's influence that had changed their lives for the better.

"Have you decided what my punishment is?" Lindsay asked cautiously.

"You won't be able to see either of your friends again, but to make that easy, they're both going back home."

"What else?"

"Nothing."

Lindsay sat up straight. "Nothing? But aren't you mad? What about grounding me, or no TV or no dessert or something?"

Sandy shook her head. "Sorry. You're going to have to live without punishment this week, kid. I know you didn't set out to steal anything. You made a bad decision under pressure. I think you've learned a lot from the experience. If it ever happens again, then life as you know it will cease to exist." She smiled. "For now, though, you're off the hook."

"Wow! Mom, I'm impressed." Her happiness faded. "Unless I have to go to jail."

"I told you, no jail. Travis called the store manager, and the charges have been dropped."

"Really?" Lindsay flung herself at her mother and hugged her tight. "That's great." She scooted back, then grimaced. "Are you still mad at Kyle?"

"How did you know I was?" Sandy asked, wondering if any of the children had heard them tonight.

"I was in the room when you asked Travis to take Kyle off my case." Lindsay sighed. "It's not his fault he had to arrest me, Mom. He was just doing his job."

"How do you know that?"

Lindsay shrugged. "He told me it was hard for him to do it. I didn't want to believe him, but there was this look on his face. Like he was going to cry or something. Guys don't cry, do they?"

Sandy rose to her feet and crossed to the window. There was only one light on in the living room, so she could make out some shapes in the yard. Down the driveway was the faint outline of Kyle's house. It was dark. Was he sleeping tonight, or was he lying awake thinking of all that they'd said to each other?

"Sometimes they cry," Sandy said. "They get hurt feelings, just like women do."

"You could tell him you're sorry," Lindsay said. "Then he'd like you again."

"I don't think that's going to be enough." She wasn't sure there was anything she could do to make up for what had happened between them. He'd been right and she'd been desperately wrong. The worst part wasn't only that she'd hurt him. She knew he would understand she'd just lashed out and he would forgive her. Kyle was, if nothing else, fair-minded. The worst part was forgiving wouldn't be enough. She'd thrown his love back in his face and he likely wouldn't be willing to offer it to her again.

Chapter Sixteen

Sandy had hoped that by morning she would have come up with a brilliant plan, or at least found a way to accept the mess she'd made of her life. The sight of sunlight offered neither. She felt as if an entire herd of elephants had trampled over her heart and the thought of spending the rest of her life without Kyle was far too gloomy to even consider. She'd made a horribly hideous mistake and she didn't know how to fix it.

She sat up in the too-big bed and leaned against the headboard. Okay, Kyle was gone. She would never see him again. Now what? How did she go on? How did she survive knowing he was just at the end of her driveway? Maybe he would move and make things easier for all of them. But she didn't want him to leave. She liked knowing he was close.

She rolled onto her side and groaned in frustration. A shaft of light fell onto the nightstand. She stared at the photograph there. It had been taken the Christmas before Thomas died.

She picked up the picture and stared at the posed scene. She sat with Nichole next to her. Thomas was on her other side. Lindsay and Blake stood behind them. She remembered the inscription from the card: The Walker Family Wishes You Happy Holidays. But their family hadn't had a happy holiday. Thomas had taken off for a ski trip. His plane had left at three-thirty on Christmas Day. He hadn't even stayed long enough to carve the turkey. As the door had slammed shut behind him, she'd sworn there wouldn't be another Christmas like that. She'd been right. A few months later, as she was trying to decide on a divorce lawyer, he'd been killed while mountain climbing.

Sandy still remembered the numbness that had come over her when she'd received the phone call. She hadn't loved Thomas anymore, but she hadn't wished him dead. Still, the nightmare was over. Her life was her own again. She'd been determined to make a go of it, and to never fall into that trap again. She didn't want another man-child in her life, she wanted a partner.

She continued to study the photograph, looking at Thomas's face as if she'd never seen it before. Thomas would never have arrested Lindsay. He would have found a way to make it easier for her. Of course, Thomas wouldn't have wanted to be a cop in the first place. Way too much self-sacrifice in that profession for him. He wanted easy hours with lots of time to play.

She put down the picture and leaned back on her pillows. What had it cost Kyle to arrest Lindsay? She knew he genuinely cared for her kids. It had been wrong of her to accuse him of tricking her into sending them to camp. He wouldn't have suggested their going if he hadn't thought they would have a good time. Yes, it gave them time to be lovers, but what parent hadn't arranged for their children to go away in the hopes of some quiet, romantic time with their spouse? It's not as if he'd wanted to lock them in the closet or something.

He was a good man. A kind man. He made her blood boil and her palms sweat. He'd told her he loved her and she'd let him walk away. Sandy closed her eyes and groaned. She'd been a fool. More than a fool, she'd been full of pride and stubbornness and determined to have it her way, even if that meant being unhappy for the rest of her life.

So where did she go from here? Did Kyle believe in second chances or had she blown it completely? Did she deserve a second chance? Could she risk trusting him with her children and herself? Could she risk giving up the control?

She got out of bed and pulled on her robe. She could already hear the kids downstairs. After washing her face and brushing her teeth, she started down toward the kitchen. As she passed the family room, she saw the scattered magazines and games. Somehow, in the last few weeks, her perfectly clean home had deteriorated into controlled chaos. But Blake was laughing more. And Lindsay picked up the dishes after dinner without being asked. Nichole was starting to make her own bed and asking how to help with the laundry. Her children might not be as tidy as they had been but they were happier and learning about growing up. Wasn't that worth a messy family room?

Kyle had had a hand in this. The kids looked up to him. They depended on him, and he was there for them. He'd taught Blake how to defend himself and how to throw a mean curveball. He'd built a dollhouse for Nichole and had often dropped everything to drive her over to her friend Mandy's house. He'd patiently listened to Lindsay's latest cassette, then later winced at the loud music he hated.

As she reached the bottom of the stairs, she realized she'd been searching for reasons to make Kyle like

Thomas. She'd wanted the two men to be alike so she wouldn't have to face her own fears. Kyle had been right that afternoon in the park. She hadn't wanted to face the truth, so she ignored it. But she couldn't any longer. The failure of her marriage hadn't all been Thomas's fault. Yes, he'd been like a child, always wanting to go and do, regardless of his commitments. But she'd always been the parent, scolding him, never taking time for fun. She could have gone skiing with him occasionally, or agreed to take the whole family camping. But she'd resisted. Maybe because she'd been so angry with Thomas for leaving her all the time.

As her mother had before him, Thomas had abandoned her. She'd punished him the only way she knew how—by withdrawing emotionally, retreating into her safe world of lists and schedules. The rules never let her down. But they did leave her lonely.

"I'm sorry, Thomas," she whispered, and in that moment saw all she could have done to meet her husband halfway. But it was too late. He was gone.

And here she was, repeating the same mistake again. She was about to lose another man. The man of her dreams. Her soul mate. She had to see him, to talk to him and explain. Except Kyle already knew her darkest secrets.

Sandy walked toward the kitchen. As she passed through the dining room, she remembered the last time Kyle had come over and they'd used this room. He'd sat at the head of the table and made the children laugh with his easy humor. It had felt right to be together, but even then, she'd been trying to find a way to destroy everything. She'd allowed her fear to control her heart.

She loved him, she thought as she walked into the kitchen. She loved him enough to try. But was it too late?

Her three children looked up at her. Their gazes were wary. Not because she might be angry, but because of what Lindsay would have told them about last night. That telling Kyle she was sorry might not be enough to get him back.

She pulled out a chair and sat down. Nichole set her spoon on the table. "You don't look happy, Mommy."

"I'm fine." She ruffled her daughter's bright curls. "We need to have a family meeting."

"What's that?" Blake asked. He was still in his space-fighter pajamas. His hair hadn't been combed and his glasses were sliding down his nose. But the shadows were gone from his eyes.

Lindsay rolled her eyes. "Don't you guys know anything? It's when we all sit around and talk about things. In some families, they even vote on things."

"Vote?" Blake asked. "You mean I get a vote."

Sandy wrinkled her nose. "Yes, we're going to have a vote, but first I have something to say." She cleared her throat. "It has come to my attention that I haven't been listening to you guys as much as I should. I want you to know I'm sorry for that. I love each of you very much. This move has been hard on all of us, but it's working out. I'm proud of how you're helping and I want you all to be happy. So from now on, we're going to have regular family meetings and discuss things. All right?"

They all nodded.

"Is there anything you'd like to say?" she asked. "Anything you want changed?"

"No more stars," Blake said. "I hate that dumb poster."

"Me too," Lindsay said. "I'm way too old to get stars, Mom."

"I like it." Nichole glared at her brother and sister. "I want to keep the stars. I like getting presents."

Sandy held up her hand. "Okay, Blake and Lindsay, you two will get a chore list but no stars. Nichole, honey, you can keep your stars and you'll still get your rewards when you've done what you're supposed to."

"Neat," Nichole said, then picked up her spoon and starting eating.

Sandy cleared her throat. The next part wasn't going to be so easy. "It has also come to my attention that each of us is very fond of Kyle. Is that true?"

"He's okay," Lindsay said, then grinned.

Nichole just nodded, but Blake stared at her. "You guys getting married?"

"I don't know," she answered. "We haven't exactly discussed it. In fact, he's not very happy with me right now."

"I told you, Mom, tell him you're sorry," Lindsay reminded her.

"It's not that simple. Between adults, things can get complicated." She didn't know what to tell them. That she'd completely messed up? "I'm going to go talk to him."

"When?" Blake asked.

"Later," she said firmly. "But if things do work out, I assume no one would object to his being a part of our family?"

"I like Kyle," Nichole said. "He tells me stories."

Blake and Lindsay nodded.

"Don't worry, Mom. Kyle thinks you're hot," her son told her.

She stared at him. "How do you know that?"

Blake blushed. "It's a guy thing, Mom. You're just gonna have to trust me on this."

Great. What other guy things had they been talking about? She shook her head and decided she didn't want to know.

She rose to her feet and tightened the belt of her robe. "So we're in agreement. Later today, I'll go talk to Kyle and explain things. I have to warn you, though, he might not want to get involved again. It wouldn't have anything to do with you children, though. It would be about me and Kyle. So no one should get upset with him. Okay?"

They nodded. She started out of the room. She heard whispering behind her, but when she turned to look at her children, they were staring at her. Smiling. She got a funny feeling in the pit of her stomach. Smiling, *whispering* children was not a good sign.

Kyle hosed off the Camaro. His car didn't really need washing, but he was tired of staying inside. He couldn't avoid Sandy forever. So what if she came by? He would smile and be neighborly. It was all she'd ever wanted from him. She'd made that clear from the beginning. He was the one who'd crossed the line.

He hadn't slept at all the previous night, but he wasn't tired. He wasn't anything except hurting bad. His chest tightened every few seconds to remind him his heart had been ripped out. As if he would forget. He'd hoped—

He shook his head. Hell, he'd been a fool. Yeah, he'd hoped Sandy would come running after him last night and tell him he was right. That she had been hiding and she was tired of it. That she was ready to admit she loved him and wanted to be with him always. But she hadn't. And all this morning, there had been nothing. She hadn't changed her mind. It wasn't going to happen. He supposed he only had himself to blame.

Maybe he should move. Waiting around hoping to catch a glimpse of her was a stupid way to spend his day off. He should go do something fun. The problem was, he couldn't think of anything. He had it bad if he would rather stand around missing her than be with someone else.

He heard the front door of her house close. He glanced up and saw Lindsay strolling toward him. He set the hose down and reached for the chamois.

"How's it going?" he asked as she got closer.

"Okay. I came to apologize," she said, shuffling her feet and looking embarrassed. "I was pretty stupid yesterday. I'm sorry you had to go through that with me."

He walked over and put his arm around her. "No harm done. Your mom told you the charges were dropped, right?"

"Yeah. She said you wanted me to go through everything. I wouldn't have wanted to, but I understand what you were trying to do. I got the message, Kyle. I'm not going to make that mistake again."

"Good." He tried to smile at her and failed miserably, then turned back to his car. Jeez, it even hurt to look at Lindsay. Mostly because she reminded him of Sandy. She might have her father's coloring, but certain of her actions—the way she pushed her hair off her face, or the way she walked—came from her mother.

Lindsay glanced over her shoulder at the house. "Um, my mom didn't sleep very good last night. Did you guys have a fight over me?"

"Not exactly. It started out being about you, but it was really about a lot of other things."

"Oh." She shoved her hands into her shorts' pockets. "I'm sorry, Kyle. I didn't mean to upset things."

"You didn't." He touched her cheek. "Your mom and I have had some problems from the start. You didn't have anything to do with them. We just have different ways of looking at things."

"But that doesn't mean you can't get along. Unless you don't really, you know, love her."

His gaze narrowed. "Why are you asking me that?"

She blushed. "I didn't mean to pry. I just thought if you cared, you could work it out."

Sound advice, only he wasn't the one with the problem. Sandy had thrown him out and said she didn't want to have him in her life. He'd been willing to marry her. That was the hell of it. He was *still* willing to marry her.

"Loving someone isn't always enough. I know that sounds strange, but it's true."

Lindsay brightened. "So you do love her?"

"Yeah, I do."

"Great!"

"Why all these questions?"

"Oh, no reason. No reason at all." But her smile was a little too wide and she couldn't hide the sparkle in her eye.

"What have you got planned, young lady?"

"Nothing." She raised herself on tiptoe and kissed his cheek. "You're the greatest, Kyle. I know you're not my dad, and I'll always miss him, but I'm sure glad you're around." She started to walk away, then glanced back at him. "Moms can make mistakes, too, you know. Sometimes they even figure it out, but then they have to apologize and they don't do that real well."

He froze in place. "What does that mean?"

"You'll have to wait and see." She took off running toward the house.

Kyle wanted to race after her and demand she tell him what was going on. But by the time his stunned brain got the message to his feet, she'd already disappeared inside.

Moms can make mistakes, too, you know. Did that mean what he thought it meant, or was this just another case of wishful thinking? Had Sandy realized he meant what he said? Did she believe that he loved her?

Before he could figure out the answer, Blake came walking around from the rear of his house. "I was at Robby's," the boy said. "I'm going to try out for pitcher next year."

"Great," Kyle said, still thinking about what Lindsay had told him.

"We had a family meeting today," Blake said. "We talked about you, but Lindsay says I'm not supposed to say anything."

"What?" Kyle stared at the boy. "What aren't you supposed to say?"

Blake shrugged, then grinned. "But I wouldn't mind if you married my mom."

Like his sister, he went running off. Kyle stared after him. Hope blossomed inside, like a dormant seed brought to life. He told himself he was a fool, and that he was heading for another fall. But he didn't care. If Sandy had called a family meeting and discussed him, then she couldn't want him completely out of their lives. Unless the meeting had been to tell the children that. But if that were the case, why would the kids seem so happy?

He tossed the chamois down and started toward her house. He was going to get some answers. When he got closer, he realized Nichole was playing with her doll on the porch, in the shade of a crepe myrtle tree.

"Hi, Kyle," she said as he approached.

"Hi, yourself. Where's your mom?"

"She's in the shower." Nichole giggled. "We painted our fingers. Look!" She held up her hand. The nails had been painted bright pink.

"They're very pretty," he said, trying to hide his impatience. If Sandy was in the shower, he couldn't just go barging in, although the thought of her naked and dripping wet was quite appealing. If nothing else, he wouldn't mind having the upper hand with her for once.

"Could you tell your mom that I—" That he what?

He thought about waiting until Sandy was finished, then remembered what Lindsay had said. That Sandy wanted to apologize, but that it might be difficult for her. He should give her the time she needed. Better for both of them if she came to him. Not only would he know for sure that she really wanted him, but his ego could use a little TLC after the way she'd run him off.

Nichole waited patiently.

"Don't tell her anything," he said. "I'll tell her myself, when I see her."

"Okay." Nichole returned her attention to her doll, then glanced up at him. "Lindsay says you're going to be our new daddy and I'm glad."

"She said that?"

"This morning. After our meeting. They're not going to do stars anymore, but I want to."

"Huh?"

He heard a sound from inside the house. Now more than ever he wanted to confront Sandy. Yet he knew it would be better if everything happened on her terms. He would have to practice patience.

"I gotta run, Nichole. See you soon."

"Bye."

He hurried back to his place and collected the bucket and chamois. After storing everything and coiling the hose neatly, he went inside and started pacing. How much longer?

By two that afternoon, he was ready to go crazy. What if the kids had been wrong? Was he wishing for a dream? Was Sandy only a fantasy, someone he would always want but never be in a relationship with? The waiting was getting to him. If he walked the living room one more time, he was going to wear a path through the rug.

"Enough of this," he growled, and grabbed his motorcycle helmet from the hall. A drive would clear his mind. He would leave a note on the door, in case Sandy came by.

He wrote it quickly, then crossed the kitchen floor and jerked open the back door. Sandy stood there, with her hand raised, ready to knock.

"Kyle," she said, surprised. "Hi."

He swallowed against a suddenly dry throat. God, she was beautiful. She'd put on a white gauzy dress with narrow straps and a full skirt. Her legs were bare, as were her arms. She wore makeup, which was unusual. So was the way her hands kept twisting together over and over again. Sandy was nervous.

In his gut, the pain he'd felt since she'd thrown him out last night faded. The band around his chest loosened and his heart rate increased.

"Were you going somewhere?" she asked, pointing at the helmet.

"What? Oh, no." He placed it on the counter, then stepped outside next to her. "I was thinking about taking a ride, but it can wait. What's up?"

He didn't want to hope, but he couldn't help himself. She was here. She'd obviously planned what to wear, maybe even what to say. The air around them grew still, as if even the plants and animals wanted to listen.

"I've been thinking," she said slowly. "First, I want to apologize for last night. I didn't want to listen to what you were saying, mostly because I knew you were right. I have been afraid emotionally, and I've been using my ideals of the perfect man to keep people from getting too close."

"People?" he asked.

"Men." She swallowed, then looked up at him. "You, specifically." Her eyes were wide and expressive. He could see her concern, her apprehension, and something else. Something wonderfully warm and welcoming. Something that, had he been less cautious, he might have labeled as love.

"You were right about Lindsay," she said. "About everything, really. All the children, me. I did have these preconceived ideas about your life and what you wanted in a woman. I couldn't believe you were interested in someone like me. I'm not special."

The hope inside grew until he couldn't deny it. He'd never been able to deny her anything. "You're perfect," he said, touching her cheek.

She turned her head into his caress and smiled. "Far from perfect, Kyle. You were right about Thomas—I could have done better in my marriage. I'm bossy and opinionated. I tend to jump to conclusions. My feelings scare me and I hide behind my specific ways of doing things. I make rules because I believe rules make my world safe. But they don't. They keep me from what is really important. I care about you."

She paused and drew in a breath. He dropped his hand back to his side. And waited.

"This is harder than I thought," she admitted. "You were much easier to talk to when I practiced in front of my bedroom mirror."

"It's not so bad," he said. "Just start at the beginning. Tell me that you love me."

She took a step toward him. Her skirt brushed against his jeans. He could hear the whisper of fabric. She reached for both his hands and held them tight. Their gazes locked.

"I love you," she whispered.

"Tell me you want to be with me always."

"I want to be with you." She smiled. "Forever."

Now it was his turn to get nervous. He brought her right hand to his mouth and kissed her palm. Her breathing increased slightly as she swayed toward him.

"Tell me—" He cleared his throat. "Tell me that you want to marry me."

"Will you marry me?" she asked.

"Yes." He swept her up in his arms. "Oh, Sandy, today, tomorrow, whenever you say."

She wrapped her arms around his neck. "Tomorrow sounds lovely."

"I love you," he said.

"I'll never get tired of hearing that," she told him. "Can you forgive me for being a fool?"

"Of course. I should have handled the situation with Lindsay better," he said. "You had every right to be mad at me."

"No, I didn't. You were the one who was right. I reacted like a fool. I was scared about how I felt about you. I wanted you to be irresponsible so I wouldn't have to love you, but you kept doing the right thing."

"I'm glad," he murmured, bending his head toward her. "I've waited over half my life for this."

"You don't have to wait any longer," she promised. "I'm here. For always."

"Is he *ever* gonna kiss her?" Blake asked.

"It doesn't look like it," Lindsay answered. "I didn't know grown-ups talked this much."

Kyle turned slightly and saw three faces peering up at them from the bushes next to his house.

Sandy giggled. "They must have followed me."

"Figures," he said. "We might as well give them what they want."

"Please," she said, reaching toward him.

As he brought his mouth to hers, he squeezed her tightly against him. Sandy felt right in his arms. As if she'd always belonged there.

"When can I tell them I want a baby sister?" Nichole asked.

"Not now," Lindsay said. "Hush. They're finally kissing. This is the good part."

*   *   *   *   *

Watch for Susan Mallery's next book
in early '96....

Silhouette®

SPECIAL EDITION™

COMING NEXT MONTH

#973 THE BRIDE PRICE—Ginna Gray
That Special Woman!
Wyatt Sommersby couldn't help but be attracted to the passionate Maggie Muldoon. When her free-spirited nature resisted Wyatt's tempting proposal of marriage, it left Wyatt wondering—what would be the price of this bride?

#974 NOBODY'S CHILD—Pat Warren
Man, Woman and Child
Feeling like nobody's child compelled Lisa Parker to search out her true parents. It brought her face-to-face with J. D. Kincaid, a man whose emotional past mirrored her own, and whose tough exterior hid a tender heart....

#975 SCARLET WOMAN—Barbara Faith
Years ago, Clint Van Arsdale watched as his brother eloped with Holly Moran, a girl from the wrong side of the tracks. Now Holly was a widow—yet despite the pain of a shared past, Clint could no longer escape their undeniable attraction.

#976 WHAT SHE DID ON HER SUMMER VACATION— Tracy Sinclair
Melanie Warren's vacation jaunt unexpectedly landed her in an English country manor. When the very proper and very sexy David Crandall invited her to become nanny to his adorable twins, she just couldn't turn him down....

#977 THE LAST CHANCE RANCH—Ruth Wind
Life's hard knocks forced Tanya Bishop to leave her son in the care of strong and sensible Ramon Quezada. Returning home to reclaim her lost child, she didn't count on falling under Ramon's seductive spell.

#978 A FAMILY OF HER OWN—Ellen Tanner Marsh
Jussy Waring's lonely heart longed for that special kind of family she'd only heard about. When Sam Baker came into her and her young niece's life, would she dare hope that her dream could finally come true?

Silhouette

SPECIAL EDITION

THE FAMILY ™ WAY

Gina Ferris Wilkins

Meet Celia Carson—and the rest of her family—in
the second book of THE FAMILY WAY series,
A MATCH FOR CELIA, by Gina Ferris Wilkins
(SE #967, July).

There were two things carefree Celia Carson wanted
from her vacation: excitement, and a man to match.
At first she thought Reed Hollander was like every
other man she'd ever met. Then she began to suspect
there was more to him than met the eye....

Don't miss the warm and wonderful FAMILY WAY
series! Only from Gina Ferris Wilkins,
and Silhouette Special Edition!

GFMINI-2

He's Too Hot To Handle...but she can take a little heat.

SILHOUETTE
Summer Sizzlers

This summer don't be left in the cold, join Silhouette for the hottest Summer Sizzlers collection. The perfect summer read, on the beach or while vacationing, Summer Sizzlers features sexy heroes who are "Too Hot To Handle." This collection of three new stories is written by bestselling authors Mary Lynn Baxter, Ann Major and Laura Parker.

Available this July wherever Silhouette books are sold.

SS95

FLYAWAY VACATION SWEEPSTAKES!

This month's destination:

Glamorous LAS VEGAS!

Are you the lucky person who will win a free trip to Las Vegas? Think how much fun it would be to visit world-famous casinos... to see star-studded shows...to enjoy round-the-clock action in the city that never sleeps!

The facing page contains two Official Entry Coupons, as does each of the other books you received this shipment. Complete and return all the entry coupons—**the more times you enter, the better your chances of winning!**

Then keep your fingers crossed, because you'll find out by August 15, 1995 if you're the winner! If you are, here's what you'll get:

- Round-trip airfare for two to exciting Las Vegas!
- 4 days/3 nights at a fabulous first-class hotel!
- $500.00 pocket money for meals and entertainment!

Remember: The more times you enter, the better your chances of winning!*

*NO PURCHASE OR OBLIGATION TO CONTINUE BEING A SUBSCRIBER NECESSARY TO ENTER. SEE REVERSE SIDE OF ANY ENTRY COUPON FOR ALTERNATIVE MEANS OF ENTRY.

VLV KAL

FLYAWAY VACATION
SWEEPSTAKES
OFFICIAL ENTRY COUPON

This entry must be received by: JULY 30, 1995
This month's winner will be notified by: AUGUST 15, 1995
Trip must be taken between: SEPTEMBER 30, 1995-SEPTEMBER 30, 1996

YES, I want to win a vacation for two in Las Vegas. I understand the prize includes round-trip airfare, first-class hotel and $500.00 spending money. Please let me know if I'm the winner!

Name_____

Address _____Apt. _____

City   State/Prov.   Zip/Postal Code

Account #_____

Return entry with invoice in reply envelope.

© 1995 HARLEQUIN ENTERPRISES LTD.   CLV KAL

FLYAWAY VACATION
SWEEPSTAKES
OFFICIAL ENTRY COUPON

This entry must be received by: JULY 30, 1995
This month's winner will be notified by: AUGUST 15, 1995
Trip must be taken between: SEPTEMBER 30, 1995-SEPTEMBER 30, 1996

YES, I want to win a vacation for two in Las Vegas. I understand the prize includes round-trip airfare, first-class hotel and $500.00 spending money. Please let me know if I'm the winner!

Name_____

Address _____Apt. _____

City   State/Prov.   Zip/Postal Code

Account #_____

Return entry with invoice in reply envelope.

© 1995 HARLEQUIN ENTERPRISES LTD.   CLV KAL

OFFICIAL RULES

FLYAWAY VACATION SWEEPSTAKES 3449

NO PURCHASE OR OBLIGATION NECESSARY

Three Harlequin Reader Service 1995 shipments will contain respectively, coupons for entry into three different prize drawings, one for a trip for two to San Francisco, another for a trip for two to Las Vegas and the third for a trip for two to Orlando, Florida. To enter any drawing using an Entry Coupon, simply complete and mail according to directions.

There is no obligation to continue using the Reader Service to enter and be eligible for any prize drawing. You may also enter any drawing by hand printing the words "Flyaway Vacation," your name and address on a 3"x5" card and the destination of the prize you wish that entry to be considered for (i.e., San Francisco trip, Las Vegas trip or Orlando trip). Send your 3"x5" entries via first-class mail (limit: one entry per envelope) to: Flyaway Vacation Sweepstakes 3449, c/o Prize Destination you wish that entry to be considered for, P.O. Box 1315, Buffalo, NY 14269-1315, USA or P.O. Box 610, Fort Erie, Ontario L2A 5X3, Canada.

To be eligible for the San Francisco trip, entries must be received by 5/30/95; for the Las Vegas trip, 7/30/95; and for the Orlando trip, 9/30/95.

Winners will be determined in random drawings conducted under the supervision of D.L. Blair, Inc., an independent judging organization whose decisions are final, from among all eligible entries received for that drawing. San Francisco trip prize includes round-trip airfare for two, 4-day/3-night weekend accommodations at a first-class hotel, and $500 in cash (trip must be taken between 7/30/95—7/30/96, approximate prize value—$3,500); Las Vegas trip includes round-trip airfare for two, 4-day/3-night weekend accommodations at a first-class hotel, and $500 in cash (trip must be taken between 9/30/95—9/30/96, approximate prize value—$3,500); Orlando trip includes round-trip airfare for two, 4-day/3-night weekend accommodations at a first-class hotel, and $500 in cash (trip must be taken between 11/30/95—11/30/96, approximate prize value—$3,500). All travelers must sign and return a Release of Liability prior to travel. Hotel accommodations and flights are subject to accommodation and schedule availability. Sweepstakes open to residents of the U.S. (except Puerto Rico) and Canada, 18 years of age or older. Employees and immediate family members of Harlequin Enterprises, Ltd., D.L. Blair, Inc., their affiliates, subsidiaries and all other agencies, entities and persons connected with the use, marketing or conduct of this sweepstakes are not eligible. Odds of winning a prize are dependent upon the number of eligible entries received for that drawing. Prize drawing and winner notification for each drawing will occur no later than 15 days after deadline for entry eligibility for that drawing. Limit: one prize to an individual, family or organization. All applicable laws and regulations apply. Sweepstakes offer void wherever prohibited by law. Any litigation within the province of Quebec respecting the conduct and awarding of the prizes in this sweepstakes must be submitted to the Regies des loteries et Courses du Quebec. In order to win a prize, residents of Canada will be required to correctly answer a time-limited arithmetical skill-testing question. Value of prizes are in U.S. currency.

Winners will be obligated to sign and return an Affidavit of Eligibility within 30 days of notification. In the event of noncompliance within this time period, prize may not be awarded. If any prize or prize notification is returned as undeliverable, that prize will not be awarded. By acceptance of a prize, winner consents to use of his/her name, photograph or other likeness for purposes of advertising, trade and promotion on behalf of Harlequin Enterprises, Ltd., without further compensation, unless prohibited by law.

For the names of prizewinners (available after 12/31/95), send a self-addressed, stamped envelope to: Flyaway Vacation Sweepstakes 3449 Winners, P.O. Box 4200, Blair, NE 68009.

RVC KAL